LOOKING FOR TANK MAN

ALSO BY HA JIN

Between Silences

Facing Shadows

Ocean of Words

Under the Red Flag

In the Pond

Waiting

The Bridegroom

Wreckage

The Crazed

War Trash

A Free Life

The Writer as Migrant

A Good Fall

Nanjing Requiem

A Map of Betrayal

The Boat Rocker

A Distant Center

The Banished Immortal

A Song Everlasting

The Woman Back from Moscow

LOOKING FOR
TANK MAN

HA JIN

Other Press | New York

Copyright © Ha Jin, 2025

Production editor: Yvonne E. Cárdenas
Text designer: Patrice Sheridan
This book was set in Adobe Garamond Pro by
Alpha Design & Composition of Pittsfield, NH

1 3 5 7 9 10 8 6 4 2

All rights reserved. No part of this publication may be reproduced or
transmitted in any form or by any means, electronic or mechanical, including
photocopying, recording, or by any information storage and retrieval system,
without written permission from Other Press LLC, except in the case of brief
quotations in reviews for inclusion in a magazine, newspaper, or broadcast.
Printed in the United States of America on acid-free paper. For information
write to Other Press LLC, 267 Fifth Avenue, 6th Floor, New York, NY 10016.
Or visit our Web site: www.otherpress.com

Library of Congress Cataloging-in-Publication Data
Names: Jin, Ha, 1956- author.
Title: Looking for Tank Man / Ha Jin.
Description: New York : Other Press, 2025.
Identifiers: LCCN 2025002249 (print) | LCCN 2025002250 (ebook) |
ISBN 9781635423839 (paperback) | ISBN 9781635423846 (ebook)
Subjects: LCSH: Political activists—Fiction. | China—History—Tiananmen
Square Incident, 1989—Fiction. | LCGFT: Novels.
Classification: LCC PS3560.I6 L66 2025 (print) | LCC PS3560.I6 (ebook) |
DDC 813/.54—dc23/eng/20250224
LC record available at https://lccn.loc.gov/2025002249
LC ebook record available at https://lccn.loc.gov/2025002250

Publisher's Note: This is a work of fiction. Names, characters, places, and incidents
either are the product of the author's imagination or are used fictitiously.

FOR LISHA

1

IN THE FALL of 2008, my sophomore year at Harvard, China's premier came to visit and gave a speech. Urged by the officials of the Chinese embassy in D.C., we gathered in the central quad of campus to welcome the delegation. We were each holding a tiny red flag printed with five stars, provided by the Chinese Students and Scholars Association of our school. Most of us felt obligated to join the welcoming crowd, because the delegates, even though we disliked them as officials, were from our motherland.

There were more than four hundred of us, all dressed formally. Young men were in suits and ties and leather shoes, and women in colorful clothes, since the official instructions had urged us to treat the premier's visit as a festive occasion. I was wearing a long floral dress with a cloth belt cinched around my waist. Some in the crowd were from MIT, Boston University, Tufts, Brandeis, UMass, although for attending the premier's speech in the auditorium, one had to have a ticket, which was not given to regular students like me. But I wasn't that interested anyway, I had too much schoolwork to do.

A slender woman in a pageboy—she was in her early forties, and looked like a visiting scholar—stood away from us, alone. She raised a placard that declared: "We Won't Forget the Tiananmen Square Massacre!" The massacre, if there'd been one, had taken place almost two decades before, and I was amazed that the woman was still bent on making a protest about it today. As the solitary protester, she began walking around among us, but no police stopped her despite hundreds of them being around. Many of us were angry at her. What a drag! What a crazy woman! Some called her an idiot. One man yelled that she was a professional China-basher.

A few of us tried to intervene. My friend Rachel, wearing a polka-dot dress, stepped out and said to the bespectacled protester, "I grew up in China and never heard of such a massacre. Why help Americans demonize our country like this?"

The skinny woman said with a Hong Kong accent, "You're too young to know the truth, it has been erased from the public memory by the Chinese government."

Joe Ma, Rachel's boyfriend, pitched in: "You'd better knock it off, all right? You're a pathetic liar, and nobody believes you. I lived in Beijing for many years and never heard of the Tiananmen Square Massacre. Look around, see who believes you and your nonsense."

"I won't just forget what happened and I want to tell the truth. I was there and saw the killings with my own eyes. I was stained with the blood from a young boy who was killed in Tiananmen Square. My nose still can smell his blood, and my ears still hear him crying."

LOOKING FOR TANK MAN

"Shut your trap!" Joe bellowed, flinging up his hand. "There were no random killings at all. Even if the insurrection was squashed with force, it was the right choice, and it later earned an economic boom for China. See how strong and prosperous our country is today."

"But the Chinese people are still living under tyranny and oppression. They deserve freedom and human rights."

"Get out of here!" Joe cried. "The top priority of human rights is to let people have a decent livelihood, which our country has managed to provide for our people."

"No, the Communist regime oppresses our people, treating them like dumb animals in a corral. Besides, people earn their livelihood, which isn't something given by the state."

"Bitch, go away!" a female voice cried.

"Fuck your mother!" a man barked at the protester.

"Stupid cunt!" came a female voice.

"What a loser!"

The middle-aged protester said calmly, "You're all college students here and ought to be more civilized. Haven't you learned more words than those obscenities?" I was also surprised by their using our mother tongue this way, lapsing so suddenly into such vulgarity.

My pulse was beating as I watched them, and I pushed the butterfly hair clip I was wearing for the occasion up above my ear. I worried they might manhandle her, but two officers came up and stopped the squabble. It couldn't go on anyway, as the premier's retinue was already appearing at the front gate. The quarrel quieted down, and a few in the crowd turned their phones vertical to snap photos. The solitary protester raised her placard higher and waved it while we were fluttering our little flags and crying "Welcome!"

The smiling premier raised his hand and waved at us as he passed by, his legs slightly bandy. He was escorted by his aides and bodyguards. Behind him was a petite young woman in a navy suit and black pumps who must have been his interpreter.

Later I came to learn more about the solitary protester. Her name was Liu Lan. Some students dug around online for more information on her, which they shared with us. She worked at a Hong Kong media company and was currently a visiting fellow in the Nieman program for journalism at our university. People in my social circle called her a traitor and a diehard Chinabasher. But deep down, I was fascinated by her. She was bold and headstrong, to say the least.

I looked more into Liu Lan online and found some video clips of her. In the photos of her youthful days, she looked elegant and was kind of a beauty, with bright eyes, smooth skin, slender limbs, and a soft voice. She looked like a typical college student, mild and maybe even frail. But she had been an activist of sorts even then and given a speech at every memorial meeting held in Hong Kong's Victoria Park on the anniversary of the Tiananmen tragedy. In one interview she broke down, sobbing wretchedly. Then she collected herself and went on to tell her experience in Beijing on the night of June 3, 1989:

LOOKING FOR TANK MAN

"We were sitting on the eastern side of Tiananmen Square and meant to block the army from advancing to harm the students. There were more than one thousand people in the crowd, most of us sitting on the ground. The soldiers, all wearing helmets and carrying assault rifles, were facing us. Both sides stood confronting each other. Then some workers appeared, all toting wooden clubs. One of them shouted at us, 'Hey, get up and run. Those bastard troops have started killing civilians. Don't stay here waiting for death.' I was a media major at Hong Kong Baptist University and had been assigned to lead the students from Hong Kong to join the demonstrators in Tiananmen Square. But we were caught in the violent clashes and had no idea what to do or where to go. We just joined the local citizens who had come out on the streets to stop the army. We sat among them on the ground.

"A few moments later I rose to my feet and went up to a young commander of the troops in front of us. I grasped his hand and begged, 'We're students from Hong Kong. Believe me, officer, those in the square are not counterrevolutionaries. They are the brightest youths of our country, and they're peaceful and just demonstrating for a more liberal and fair society. They are doing this for all of us. Please don't harm them, don't open fire on them!' I couldn't hold myself any longer and dropped to my knees in front of the officer, who looked at me with watery eyes but said nothing.

"When I rejoined my fellow students, a boy in his early teens turned up, bawling and telling people that

5

the army had just shot his elder brother. He kept crying, 'Brother, brother, where are you?' I can never forget his hoarse voice, which sounded like an old man's in spite of his young age. Some people in the crowd were sobbing with him and calling the soldiers fascists. Then the boy grabbed a club from a man and broke out running after an army truck while yelling 'Brother, Brother!' He meant to avenge his brother. We tried to stop him but couldn't.

"Two hours later, after we had been dispersed by the soldiers, I ran into the boy in Tiananmen Square again. He was bleeding from several gunshot wounds and had been carried over by two workers. I helped them load him into an ambulance; my shirt was stained with his blood. I was so overwhelmed that I blacked out. So they put me in the ambulance too. On arrival at a Red Cross emergency clinic, I came around and saw two wounded soldiers lying nearby. A nurse went over to check their injuries and treat them, but some people stopped her, shouting that they were murderers and didn't deserve any medical attention. Then a doctor, a middle-aged man, said loudly, 'Stop interfering with our work. Even though they're soldiers, they're still human beings. Our job is to save lives.' That shut everyone up.

"The makeshift clinic could only treat the wounded preliminarily, and most of the victims had to be transferred to hospitals nearby. When an ambulance came, a female doctor ordered the medics to put me into it together with three wounded people, I said I was not injured and was fine now. But the doctor just told them,

'Take her with you too.' I kept protesting but was interrupted by the doctor, who said in English, 'Child, we need you to get away and tell the world what has been happening here. Otherwise, people in other places cannot know the truth.' Obviously, she spoke English because of fear. She was afraid that those around us could know her intention and might stop me and even inform on her. I promised her that I would spread the truth."

Liu Lan sobbed again. A moment later, calming down some, she added, "In Benevolent Hospital, some armed soldiers turned up to arrest the wounded counterrevolutionaries. The doctors stopped them, saying the real counterrevolutionaries were all in the bicycle shed, which was being used as a stopgap morgue and was already crowded with dead bodies. I sneaked away. Ever since that day, I haven't stopped telling the world about the massacre. If they had put another wounded person instead of me into the ambulance, that person would likely have survived. In other words, my life must have been saved at the cost of another life, so as long as I can breathe, I won't stop acting as a voice speaking for those victims!"

That explained why she had shown up in the central quad of our campus to protest alone the other day. I half believed her—her truth might just be another version of what had happened. I emailed the link to her interview to Rachel and Joe, curious to see how they would take it. Joe wrote back, saying Liu Lan was just a crazy woman who couldn't see any positive side to our country. Rachel also said Liu Lan might be a liar. I tended to agree with them. I had grown up in Beijing and often passed Tiananmen Square. I had never heard about the massacre either, though in history class we were once told that there'd been a rebellious mob who intended to overthrow the government, but who were subdued mostly by peaceful means.

2

A FEW DAYS later, at dinner, I chatted with Rachel Guo and Joe Ma about the odd journalist, the lone protester. They both dismissed her as a crazy woman, someone who had only been able to survive in the West by becoming a democracy activist. There were many of them like that, self-styled exiles and dissidents who couldn't stop striving for the limelight by bashing China. I felt my friends were too opinionated, though I tended to share their conviction that even if there had been a bloody crackdown on students in June 1989, that had been almost two decades ago—history moved on and life continued, and it was silly to get bogged down in the mire of the past.

Rachel's family was wealthy. Her father was the general manager of Baobao, an internet retailing conglomerate headquartered in Nanjing. It was believed that her parents had given Harvard six million dollars for an endowed chair, and that was why she had been admitted. But I don't think that was the reason she had gotten in. She was an excellent student, smart and perceptive, and she would have been qualified for any top college in the States, though she could be willful, less tolerant of people who didn't have her kind of privileges. Perhaps her parents had made the donation just to ensure that she would be accepted by Harvard, her number one choice. I suspected that Joe was running after her with an eye on her family's clout and wealth, but to be fair, she was attractive in her own way, tall, with an open face and glossy skin. In my opinion, Joe was a bad influence on her, because he was actively involved in the politics of the Chinese Students and Scholars Association, which was sponsored and controlled by China's consulate in New York and the embassy in D.C. Such involvement made him a little red flag waver, and this must have affected Rachel's political attitudes.

Soon I forgot about Liu Lan, the only protester. The coursework at Harvard was overwhelming. I had been an exceptional student back in Beijing, but here I felt out of my element, especially in my freshman year. I had to struggle to survive. Last semester I had received two Cs, and that had never happened in my life. At the beginning of my sophomore year, I declared my major—history. It felt like a mistake. Back in China, the humanities and social sciences are viewed as easy fields, mostly for inferior minds that cannot survive the rigors studying the sciences. But here, history is one of the hardest majors. On average, I had to read three books a week. This was killing me. In China, for a history class, you usually read one book a semester, a standard college textbook. Worse yet, for each course here we had to write two or three papers, and they had to present original views. This was something alien to students of my background, who had been good at regurgitating what our teachers had fed to us. We were excellent back home mainly because we were skilled in taking exams.

Due to the heavy coursework, I hardly had any social life. Rachel, Joe, and others in our circle went on outings quite often, skiing in Vermont and visiting Martha's Vineyard and Newport in Rhode Island. I hardly ever went with them. I was on a scholarship and had to earn decent grades to have it renewed. To me, studying hard was like a matter of life and death.

My diligence helped stabilize my life, which was confined to the library, the dorm, the cafeteria, and the classroom buildings. The hard work paid off—at the end of my freshman year, my average grades were B+, which wasn't great, but good enough for me to retain my scholarship. Gradually I realized that courses had different amounts of reading assignments. Some were extremely heavy, while some were quite light. For example, if you took a film course, there wasn't a large amount of reading materials, whereas a seminar on the Civil War meant you had a pile of books to read, besides the research papers you had to write.

We often talked about the amounts of coursework in various classes. So in my sophomore year, I took some lighter courses, most of them related to China, partly because I could do the readings in Chinese if the original works were written in my mother tongue. By now, I felt confident that I could survive academically here. This year, the Spring Festival, the Chinese New Year, fell on February 15. Many Chinese students flew back to join their families for the holiday, as long as their parents could afford the plane fare. I didn't go, because the flights were too expensive for me—flying round trip would have cost my mother two months' salary. My father urged me to go back, saying he'd pay for my plane tickets, but I didn't listen to him, nor would I take any extra money from him. As he had agreed with my mother, he gave me a monthly allowance. They were divorced, living in different cities now. He had abandoned her for another woman many years before.

Contrary to expectations, two weeks before the spring recess, my mother informed me that her father was gravely ill, and that I should go back to see him in case he didn't make it this time. So in early March I flew back to Beijing. My mother didn't want me to miss too many classes, and urged me to go to Harbin the next morning, where my grandparents were living. I took the high-speed train, on which I spent most of the hours reading *God's Chinese Son*, by the Yale professor Jonathan D. Spence. It's a book about the Taiping Rebellion, and we had to read it for the seminar Christianity in China. I enjoyed it very much. Spence wrote history like a novel. The book, on the leader of the rebellious kingdom, was a long narrative told in the present tense, giving immediacy to the drama and events. History was no longer just long-dead occurrences, and instead it quickened with life and human experiences. If I became a historian, I hoped I'd be able to write like this.

It was freezing in Harbin, the icy clouds hardly mobile in the sky. My grandfather was seriously ill, but he wasn't in the hospital. In the past decade, he had had many problems with his heart, kidneys, and lungs, and he had had to retire early, before reaching the age of sixty, the standard retirement age for male employees in China. In recent years, his brain seemed to have been gouged by a kind of dementia, his memory disordered and nebulous, and he had grown senile.

My grandmother wasn't in good health either, so she had hired a maid to help her with chores and with caring for my grandfather. That meant my mother had to send them more money every month.

Grandma was happy to see me back and took me to Grandpa's bedside. "My old man," she said, "look who is here." She stepped aside to let me get closer to him. I took hold of his hand, which was waxy and cold. The windowpanes of his bedroom were frosted over, displaying various patterns of vegetation, and in spite of broad daylight, the room was dusky, as if it were twilight.

Grandpa looked wizened, like a mummy, his face sallow and emaciated. He breathed flutteringly, as if unable to inhale enough air. Something may have been blocking his windpipe.

I asked, "How're you doing, Grandpa?"

He looked blank, not recognizing me at all. He grunted, "I'm still alive." He then turned to Grandma. "Who's this girl? Our neighbor's daughter, Little Lambkin?"

"I'm Lulu, your granddaughter," I said. "I came back from America to see you."

"From where? America? Where's that?" He still couldn't make any connection.

"On the other side of the world, Grandpa."

"You came a long way and must have calluses on your feet now."

"I flew to Beijing first, then hopped on the high-speed train to Harbin."

"I wouldn't do that if I were you." He was batting his bleary eyes and looked befuddled.

I bent over him and looked into his face, wondering what to say. My grandmother tugged on my arm and said, "His mind comes and goes. He must be tired. Let him rest for now, so we can have dinner together."

I followed her to the dining table in the other room, where we ate the shrimp wontons the maid, Auntie Liu, had cooked for us. As we were eating, my grandmother said that Grandpa's mind might be clear again the next morning. Usually he got his head back after a good night's sleep.

Sure enough, he recognized me when I went in to see him the next day. But he kept giggling to himself. This was out of character and made him look like an idiot. "Why are you chuckling like that, Grandpa?" I asked.

"Oh Lulu, I remembered your mom. She was a stupid girl and should never have fallen for that scoundrel, your dad."

"What do remember about my mom?"

"She joined some hunger strikers in Tiananmen Square, and I'd told her to avoid that kind of crazy activity from the very beginning, but she wouldn't listen to me."

LOOKING FOR TANK MAN

"When was that, Grandpa?"

"In the spring of 1989."

"So there was a massacre then?"

"You bet. Thanks to me, your mom escaped the crackdown without a scratch. Thank heaven she didn't get hurt, not a scratch."

"What did you do to her?"

"I had heard on the radio that lots of students at Beijing University had started a hunger strike in Tiananmen Square. They demanded that the government recant an announcement that said the student movement was a reactionary scheme supported by foreign powers. I knew your mother was a little hothead and might join them, so I went to Beijing to drag her home."

"Did you find her?"

"I searched for her everywhere. There were so many cops and troops that on the way they stopped me time and again. Toward the evening I found her among thousands of hunger strikers sitting in the square. I dragged her back."

"Back to where?"

"Home. We returned to her college first, and on the same day we took the train back to Harbin. We kept her here for three months, until it was safe for her to start working in Beijing."

"So she didn't go back to her campus again?"

"She couldn't, because the day after we had come back, troops began to move into Tiananmen Square. They killed a lot of people, by the thousands."

I was shocked. "Are you sure they killed civilians?"

"Positive. Your mom listened to American and British radio every day, so we knew what was going on in Beijing."

"Was my dad her boyfriend at the time?"

"That was why I had to go to Beijing. That man was no good and was just going to bring her more trouble and put her in danger."

"So you didn't approve of their relationship?"

"Of course not."

"Then how come they got married?"

"Because your mom was too pigheaded to consider any of the young fellows we found for her. Your dad was a sweet talker and put her under a spell. But to be fair, he wasn't my concern. By going to Beijing, I just wanted to keep your mom out of harm's way. We never liked your dad."

I asked him more questions, but he couldn't answer them coherently. He seemed stuck with that single episode—his dragging my mother away from Tiananmen Square, and therefore saving her from the bloodshed unleashed in the following days. He didn't remember that I had gone to college in America. His mind was vacant, except for the most prescient trip he ever made in his lifetime. I couldn't help but wonder why my mother had never told me about her involvement with the student movement. In fact, she had never breathed a word about the government's violent crackdown on students in June 1989 either. She must have hidden many things from me.

My grandfather once again lapsed into oblivion, unable to speak clearly. Afterward, we couldn't talk again, his mind wandering in too many directions. Even when I said goodbye, he drew a blank, not knowing what to make of my leave.

He passed away a month later, but it was so close to the end of the semester that I couldn't go back for his funeral. I had finals to cram for and term papers to finish.

3

BEFORE RETURNING TO Boston, I asked my mother about her involvement with the student movement. She dodged most of my questions, saying there was no need for me to know, but I kept asking. She wouldn't give me a definite answer. At most, she admitted that she, an anthropology major at Beijing University at the time, had been silly and taken part in some demonstrations without knowing their true intentions or the consequences of her participation. I got impatient and demanded, "Didn't you take part in the hunger strike?"

"Yes, I was with them briefly. Then your grandpa came and dragged me away."

"Did you believe in freedom and equality and democracy?"

"Of course I did, but what the students demanded was infeasible at the time. We were too idealistic. In hindsight, the whole thing was more like a puppet play. Lulu, please don't bother looking into this. Concentrate on your schoolwork. It's not easy for your father and me to scrape together the money for your college education. You must cherish the opportunity of studying abroad."

LOOKING FOR TANK MAN

My mother had aged considerably since the previous year, her eyes dimmer and her lips puckered when she smiled, and there was more gray in her bangs. Seeing her worried face, I told her I wouldn't take the trouble to look into the student demonstrations and would focus on my studies. It was true that in China a diploma from Harvard signified success. In many people's eyes I was already a success, so my mother believed I ought to live up to the respect they had for me.

Before heading back to school, I phoned my father. He was in his studio, working on his sculptures. His medium was clay. Besides teaching at an art school, he sculpted statues of dragons and Buddha in his spare time and sold them to international art dealers. He made good money and often said to me that it was those clay sculptures that funded my education in America. In fact, my mother also contributed to my living expenses at college (my tuition was covered by a scholarship), so I didn't feel that grateful to him.

On the phone I told him about my visit to my grandfather, saying the old man had lost his memory and the only thing he could recall was his trip to Beijing two decades ago to drag my mother from Tiananmen Square back to her university, and then to Harbin. My father said in his smoky voice, "Don't believe everything the old codger told you. But I have to say he was really something. He could see danger in advance."

"Grandpa said he saved my mother."

"That's right, or she might have landed in jail or gotten hurt."

19

"You mean she was super active in the student moment."

"I wouldn't say that. She was small fry, but she took part in the hunger strike."

"How about you?"

He seemed stumped, then continued, "Why do you want to know so much about this? Your mom and I agreed long ago that we'd do our best to protect you. We both believe it will be safe for you not to know about the Tiananmen event, so don't stick your nose into this, all right?"

"I'm just curious."

"Lulu, you must focus on your schoolwork. You don't know how proud we are of you. Don't let us down."

Realizing he wouldn't tell me any more, I said I was flying back to Boston the next day. I was never attached to him, though I continued to accept him as my father, as long as he treated my mother with basic decency, letting her keep the apartment owned by both of them and sharing the costs of my college education with her.

Unlike me, Rachel never had money problems, always having a considerable amount at her disposal. Most of us students sublet our apartments when we went home for the summer, but she'd leave hers vacant. I offered to house-sit for her, and she was glad to let me use her apartment for free from early May to late August. She didn't even let me pay for the utilities. Her place was just off Massachusetts Avenue, with a high ceiling and oakwood

LOOKING FOR TANK MAN

paneling. Because I had just spent so much for the trip back to see my grandfather and wouldn't have to pay rent for the summer, I decided not to go home to join my mother. I found a part-time job at a laundromat in Allston. It was owned by Becky, a Russian woman who spoke rudimentary English. She was pleased to hire me, though I made clear that I could work for her only in the summer. She used foreign students constantly, assuming we all could work legally. Or maybe we were just cheap labor to her. I didn't tell her that I had an F-1 visa, meaning I wasn't allowed to work off campus, but many international students did anyway, and to my knowledge nobody had ever been caught. Becky paid me cash, seven dollars an hour, a dollar below the minimum wage. That was all right with me. She didn't bother to ask for my Social Security number, so I didn't have to pay taxes.

My job was simple, receiving customers at the counter. For the regular kind of laundry, I did the wash and drying and the folding. Once in a while, a customer tipped me a few dollars, so I tried my best to be pleasant. Becky preferred to work behind the scenes. She did dry cleaning exclusively, because she had to use a chemical powder, perc, that could ruin clothes if not handled properly. She said she had once had to pay five hundred dollars for a suit she had messed up. The owner of the clothes had threatened to sue her when she at first refused to pay. So Becky didn't let me do any dry cleaning.

My job also included cleaning the place. In the evening, Becky left before eight o'clock, so I continued minding the laundromat until ten thirty. Before

21

closing, I mopped the floor, cleaned the bathroom, and wiped down the tables and windows. I enjoyed it when Becky was gone. I could read a bit if no one showed up. Every once in a while, a fellow student came and looked amazed that I was working here, but I just pretended that this was nothing unusual. Indeed, it was only a summer job. We all have to find a way to get by. This was a pragmatic mindset I had acquired in America, and it was also part of my education, a positive aspect, I believe. Several times men asked me for my phone number, and I pretended I didn't understand their intentions. Once a man in his thirties named Eliot said, his brown eyes pulling me close to him, "I want to take you out. Can we have dinner together?"

I replied, "Can my fiancé come too?"

"Oh my, you're already engaged?" he asked, his whiskers quivering a little.

"Yes, my fiancé is going to Harvard Law School."

"Then he must be a cheapskate," Eliot grunted.

"Why do you say that?"

"If the guy can afford law school, he shouldn't let a pretty girl like you work here."

"I'm independent and don't take money from him."

Eliot left a ten-dollar tip before leaving with the trash bag containing the laundry I had washed and folded for him. He must have thought it easy to sway an Asian woman to go on a date with him, but I wasn't worried about his irritation. He was good-natured, harmless.

In fact, I had no boyfriend at the time, though I was drawn to some schoolmates. I was still rather overwhelmed with schoolwork. Even during the summer, I read books at night. I also watched a lot of TV to practice my English, which I couldn't speak naturally yet. I liked working and studying alone, just following the promptings of my interest without a fixed schedule. It was a leisurely life, immersed in solitude.

Becky had a granddaughter, Lala, a tall redhead attending Bentley University. Becky was proud of the girl and often bragged to me about her, saying Lala was majoring in finance and had a bright future. She once told me that Lala had just gone to New Hampshire with a group of her male and female friends, where they shared a large hotel room. I was surprised and asked if they had shared the beds as well. Becky said, "Probably, they sleep together too. Sex can be fun for young people, you know."

I knew Lala had spent her childhood in a Siberian city called Novosibirsk. So I asked Becky whether they would have done that if they had been in Russia.

"Depends on what time period," Becky said. "Now you can do anything there. But back in the Soviet time, if you had group sex, they put you in jail and maybe even shot you. The commies controlled everything—your soul and your body."

"Also your sex life?"

"Of course, people must hate each other, not love each other."

She hated the Soviet regime with a passion, and she blamed their harsh rule for the fact that her parents had died before they reached old age. Still, the way she indulged her granddaughter amazed me. Becky loved everything American, including fast food and Coca-Cola—she drank at least two liter bottles a day. Small wonder she was so pudgy, her midsection wider than her shoulders. If she continued to drink Coke like that, she would probably grow heavier and rounder and develop a heart problem.

Across the street there was a hair salon that also manicured nails. Its owner was a middle-aged white woman, Jane. Jane often came to the laundromat and was fond of chatting with me. Her husband, Alec, was Greek and didn't speak much at all. His reticence made me wonder if he even spoke English, but Jane said his English was good and that he used to work at high-end hotels. The man looked a lot younger than she was, at least by a decade; he was also strapping, with amber eyes. Jane seemed obsessed with him, talking about him a lot. She would say that he used to attract plenty of women. She even said to me that once in a hotel, he had been summoned by an older lady to her room, because both she and her daughter wanted to have sex with him. They were going to pay him as a gigolo. I was surprised, and asked Jane if he had gone through with it. "Of course he did. Alec was paid to do it," she said matter-of-factly. "It was part of his job."

"You mean the hotel hired him for providing sex?"

"It was not spelled out, but the employees understood that."

I nodded, but it was hard for me to think of that as part of a job. Wouldn't it be too degrading to be summoned for sex, even though Alec had been paid well, I wondered. If a woman was ugly and repulsive, could he still manage to have sex with her? I knew men and women differ in this matter. A man can hardly get an erection if he isn't turned on. Alec must have had a tough job. If he couldn't make a disgusting woman happy and satisfied, he might have gotten into trouble. I thought of asking Jane about the details, but held back. Maybe she didn't know how Alec had managed either. Still, I wondered why Jane had revealed so much about her husband. Probably there was trouble in their marriage. She seemed anxious to keep her hold on Alec.

One afternoon, Jane came by again and stayed a long while. When the laundry room was empty of customers, she leaned in over the counter and asked, "Do you like babies, Lulu?"

"Of course, especially if they are my own," I said. "I want to get married someday and raise a family."

"Then how about having a baby for me?"

"What do you mean?"

She explained that Alec and she couldn't have their own baby. It was her problem, and they'd love to have a baby by other means. She also said they could offer me fifty grand for being a surrogate mother.

I was shocked and asked, "Why...why pick me for this?"

"Because you're smart and pretty, and healthy. Alec saw you, and we both admire you and would love to have your help with having a baby. Think about this, okay? It would take you two or three years to make that kind of money by working full-time at this place. That much money could give you a good start in life, don't you think?"

I shook my head and said, "I can't help you that way, Jane. I'm a student and have to finish college first. If I did what you're asking, my mother would disown me for sure."

"Why? You're already out of your teens and have rights as an adult."

My twentieth birthday had been a month before, and I had told her that without knowing she had been gathering information on me. It was all right that she had planned this, but I didn't want to be involved. Jane even said that if I was unwilling to become a surrogate mother, I could sell her and Alec my eggs. This did pique my interest, but it would involve a lot of tests and hospital visits, so I dismissed the idea. Deep down, in spite of never being rich, I believed I would always have enough money for my needs as long as I worked. Above anything else, I didn't want my baby to grow up without me in its life. So I turned down Jane's offer flat. She grimaced but said it was all right, and that her offer remained open.

After that she didn't come to the laundromat as often as she used to. In America, everything boils down to dollars—that was a lesson I learned that summer.

Rachel was amazed to find me slightly different when she came back. "My, you looked so mature now," she half teased, "like a serious young lady, with lots of gravitas."

"Come on, I've always been serious," I said. "But maybe I'm more independent now."

"Apparently so." Her big eyes kept flickering. She still couldn't contain the excitement of our reunion.

I thanked her for allowing me to house-sit for her. It had made my summer peaceful and enjoyable. In the past three months I had read more than a dozen of the books that every history major was supposed to know.

4

I PICKED LESS-DIFFICULT classes for the fall semester. Among my choices was a seminar taught by Loana Hong, a Canadian postdoc: Memory and Amnesia: The Tiananmen Suppression and Its Consequences. I went over the course description and saw that a good portion of the reading assignments were in both English and Chinese. This was encouraging and might suit me better than other classes. I thought I was relatively familiar with the context of the subject and would be able to read the assigned books and papers rapidly, especially those in Chinese. So I signed up for the class before it was full.

Rachel was taking the course too, for the same reason. In the back of our minds lingered an unstated motivation—since the teacher was of Chinese descent, she might be lenient on us when it came to grades. It had occurred to me that Hong could also be a Korean last name, because few Chinese women had "Loana" as a first name, but Rachel had met her and was positive she was Chinese, probably Canadian-born. Rachel said she'd greeted Loana in Korean—*jal jinaesseoyo?* (How are you?)—but the professor didn't know how to answer.

Then she switched to Chinese—*ni hao*—to which Loana responded right away.

Unlike us, Joe didn't bother with such classes, believing it was lightweight and a waste of time. He was a science whiz, and had once been on a team that competed at the Chinese Chemistry Olympiad during high school. Though only a junior, he had already participated in one of his professor's research projects, and he worked in the lab at night and on weekends, being paid a small stipend.

Loana Hong's seminar was a 500-level course and attended mostly by seniors and graduate students. There were only four juniors enrolled, including Rachel and me. But we were not intimidated by the older students and felt confident that we could manage, since the subject matter was on our own turf, in a way. During the first class, Loana asked us to introduce ourselves briefly and tell each other why we were taking her class. This was unusual, and most of us only said something perfunctory. Some claimed they wanted to know more about China. Sarah, a rosy-cheeked English senior from Nebraska, said she had been to Beijing, where a tourist guide had told the visitors to avoid talking about three T's: Taiwan, Tibet, and Tiananmen, so she wanted to take this class to learn about one of the taboo topics. Gary, with flaxen hair and an aquiline nose, said he felt like he was possessed by the Tiananmen suppression, particularly by Tank Man, who embodied the fearless spirit of the individual against the oppressive state. I had only a vague idea whom he was referring to. Derek, skinny and curly-haired, said back in Jamaica he had heard of the Tiananmen crackdown, but he didn't have any concrete idea what it was about, so this was his chance to learn more. Rachel was quite straightforward, saying she was curious about this course, having recently heard about the Tiananmen Square Massacre in the American media, but she wasn't sure if there had been such killings, so she wanted to know what had really happened. When my turn came, I said, "I believe this course might be less hard for me than others. I am familiar with China and can do the readings faster in Chinese." That made the class laugh.

Loana Hong smiled with her white teeth gleaming and nodded, apparently appreciating my candor. She went on to introduce herself in a low-pitched voice, saying she had written her dissertation on this subject and had a book, *The Tiananmen Ramifications*, which was coming out from a university press. We were impressed. She also told us not to worry about the reading assignments, because there'd be a lot of visual materials—films, videos, slides, photos—to watch and examine. She explained that although the course would be centered around the Tiananmen tragedy, we would also look into historical events and movements that occurred before the suppression, as well as its aftermath. She emphasized that this wasn't just a regular history seminar, and that we were going to study various areas related to the Tiananmen democracy movement: the social structure, economy, literature, ideological discourses, popular arts. We would also have some visitors who had participated in the student movement. In short, it was a comprehensive course.

LOOKING FOR TANK MAN

The class turned out to be harder than I had expected. I mean that it was hard for us to take emotionally. After a week, we could clearly see that the tragedy had taken place, since Loana showed us some footage of the Tiananmen demonstration and lots of photos. I accepted the veracity of the event, but I was not sure if the students had really just staged a peaceful protest against official corruption and for political reform and more freedom. We didn't need the teacher to offer us a conclusion. Loana didn't try to disabuse us of our views, either—she just assigned reading and visual materials for us to go through before class. In the basement of the Harvard-Yenching Library there were twenty-eight boxes of items gathered from Tiananmen Square. Loana led us down there to look at some of them: pamphlets, pants and skirts drilled with bullet holes and stained with blood, banners, some student leaders' notes on meetings, headbands inscribed with slogans and also blotched with blood. As the class continued, it began to take a heavy emotional toll on us. Often someone would break down in class, sobbing wretchedly.

Samantha Su, a public health senior, started to cry one afternoon after a video had just been played. She said, "I grew up in Beijing and passed Tiananmen Square every day on my way to school. But why did nobody ever mention the bloodshed and the violent killings twenty years ago! We were made to live in a big lie." She was sobbing bitterly.

I also felt miserable, anger and grief swirling in my chest. But compared to the other women in the class, I was shy and quiet. I didn't volunteer to speak much. I didn't reveal that I had heard the tragedy described as a counterrevolutionary uprising. Nor did I mention that my mother had taken part in the hunger strike. I tried to remain clearheaded so as to make my own assessment and judgment. That was also what Loana wanted us to do.

She made us listen to songs that the students had sung in their demonstrations, particularly "The Internationale," which was kind of an ironic choice, since it was the de facto anthem of the global proletariat, the supreme Communist march. Loana also played some popular music for us, like Cui Jian's "I Have Nothing to My Name." Cui was an iconic singer at the time, and his band performed in Tiananmen Square. Loana was a huge fan of Cui Jian, the rock star who seemed to possess her generation, but to my taste, "I Have Nothing to My Name" was too loud and lacked deep resonance and nuance. I preferred songs by the Taiwanese composer Lo Ta-yu, which were also sung by students at the time, after their movement had been quelled. Lo Ta-yu's songs usually had delicacy and subtleties, and they resonated with deep grief and political awareness, particularly "The Orphan of Asia" ("The orphan of Asia is crying in the wind / The yellow face smeared with red mud / The black eyes full of white fear..."). The music and lyrics gripped your heart, and they suited my generation better. Rachel agreed with me, saying Cui's songs had no poetry, though we didn't share our opinion with Loana and the rest of the class. I also felt that Cui Jian's songs tended to be too folksy and too blunt, often over-macho,

LOOKING FOR TANK MAN

without universal appeal, making them particularly hard for women of my generation to embrace.

We also read some poetry, which I didn't like that much either. Rachel also felt that the poems were too nebulous and mushy and lacked intelligence. She called them "juvenile" and "unnecessarily fuzzy." We both liked poems that spoke to one's heart and shone with wisdom. I guessed that our sensibility might have been shaped by the literature in English we had read over the years. Rachel was harsher in her literary judgment because she was an English major and had learned many great poems by heart.

In class, I didn't want to just follow the views established by the media in the West and by the overseas Chinese and by student leaders who had fled China. So I began to study all the materials I could get my hands on. There were a lot. For weeks, I devoted myself to reading books and watching documentary films and examining photos. I wanted to figure out whether this had truly been an insurrection against the government, totalitarian though it was. My conclusion was that it wasn't, and I shared my view with the class.

I offered three pieces of evidence to support my argument that the students were peaceful and hadn't staged an uprising at all. First, on April 22, 1989, three students, representing more than a hundred thousand others in Tiananmen Square, knelt on the stone steps at the east side of the Great Hall of the People with a petition raised over their heads, requesting that Premier Li Peng come out to accept it and talk with the demonstrators.

Just two days before, many students had been beaten by the police when they gathered in the square to mourn the death of Hu Yaobang, the liberal-minded former general secretary of the CCP. The three young men stayed on their knees for twenty minutes, but no official came out to accept the petition. I believed that if the students had meant to fight against the government with force, they wouldn't have bothered to beg the national leaders that way.

My second piece of evidence showed how the students reacted to others. On the afternoon of May 23, two days after martial law had been declared, three young men from Hunan Province went to Tiananmen Tower and threw eggs mixed with paint on the giant Mao portrait there. Students in the square immediately apprehended the three culprits and handed them over to the police; one was given a life sentence, another twenty years in prison, and the youngest one got sixteen years. Though in the course of time many student leaders regretted having handed over the three men to the police, this very act indicated that the students were law-abiding and that they didn't tolerate any acts against the government.

My third piece of evidence was conclusive. On the early morning of June 4, an armored personnel carrier, No. 003, which belonged to the Thirty-Eighth Army, ran amok, charging into the square and crushing several people. Local residents hit it with stones and wooden clubs to no avail, but then someone thrust rebars into its caterpillar tread and stopped it. The outraged people climbed up on it and smashed all the devices that were on the outside, and then they threw some quilts over it. They then doused the quilts with gasoline and lit them on fire. The flames heated up the vehicle, and in no time the soldiers had to climb out to avoid being burned alive. People began to beat them up. However, some students rushed over and saved the three soldiers, taking them away to an emergency clinic while they were being followed by a mob chasing them with clubs and bricks. The students' intervention in the midst of the violent suppression showed that they were peaceful and self-restrained and wouldn't do anything unlawful. All the class agreed about my conclusion, since the evidence I had presented was well documented and familiar to them.

The issue of casualties arose in our discussion. There was no definite number for the number of people killed. The Red Cross estimated that the number of deaths had reached 2,700, but many people argued that the number must be over 10,000. I said it was not that meaningful to be fixated on the number, which had already become a riddle. What was essential was to identify as many victims as possible so they could be given a name or a bio or even a face. I was enlightened by an old woman who had found her son's body in a shed behind a hospital building. She saw a pile of trash bags containing decaying bodies that were not identified and were about to be trucked away to be disposed of. In comparison with others, she said, she was lucky to be able to bring her son's body back and be able to set up a memorial tablet at home so as to offer him a good meal and burn joss money for him. I argued that for many families who had lost members, the wounds couldn't begin to heal until the lost ones were located, so it was much more of a priority to identify the dead. That was exactly what Tiananmen Mothers had been doing. To date, they had identified 202 people killed by the army, their names and ages and occupations all listed. Loana showed us a map made by those brave old women. On it every spot where a victim had fallen was marked by a purple dot. Their map of Beijing swarmed with purple dots that made the landscape almost unrecognizable. Loana had been a high schooler in 1989, so she hadn't gone to Beijing to demonstrate, but in her hometown of Nanjing tens of thousands of students gathered and marched before the city hall in protest against the violent crackdown in the capital. The national tragedy had shattered her belief in the government and made her decide to go to Canada for college. To study this tragedy and its consequences and to keep it in the public memory had become her calling. We admired her for that.

Loana was well connected with the exile communities in North America. Every other week she invited a former student leader over to talk with us. In late September Wang Dan came. At the time he was teaching at a university in Taipei, but he would often come back to Boston, since he had earned his PhD at Harvard and had many friends in the area. He was happy to be back in a classroom here, he told us. He had been number one on the wanted list issued by the Chinese government after the Tiananmen crackdown and was arrested in Beijing in July 1989. Together with several other students

LOOKING FOR TANK MAN

and local demonstrators, he was put in the notorious Qincheng Prison, which the Soviets had helped the Chinese government build in the late 1950s. Located to the west of Beijing, it was primarily a destination for senior officials defeated by their political enemies within the party. Wang Dan was an elegant man, like a scholar in the traditional manner, with delicate sensibilities and lofty aspirations.

I had noticed that the best of his generation tended to possess an altruistic worldview, carrying the weight of the nation on their shoulders, because they believed they were the elite of the country and that it was their duty to save it from totalitarian tyranny. They were educated that way—taking "all under heaven" as their responsibility. Unsurprisingly, Wang Dan said that the imprisonment hadn't frightened him that much. In fact, when he was leading the demonstrations and the hunger strike in Tiananmen Square, he had felt vaguely that if the movement failed, he might land in jail. At the time he even had a romantic view of imprisonment, assuming he would have more time to study and read in there, as Vladimir Lenin had done in the czar's prison. It turned out to be true. He read about a thousand books in prison and also worked on his English. "Many inmates were studying foreign languages in jail. It was an efficient way to kill time," he said to us. "Once a middle-aged warder told me he had learned Japanese when he was imprisoned in the same place a decade before." Wang Dan seemed romantic as well as brave. I was convinced that he was sincere when he said he wasn't that afraid of death. He quoted from Zhou Guoping, a popular contemporary philosopher: "The worth of one's life lies in its density, not in its length." That enlightened me.

Rachel asked him, "Didn't you fear anything at all in prison? You must have had some fear, didn't you?"

"Of course." Wang Dan smiled. "I was young and quite innocent. I was afraid my health might get ruined, because the food was so bad. Mildewed cornmeal buns and salty vegetables at every meal. Still, I forced myself to eat as much as I could. I feared I wouldn't last many years if the government viewed me as a chief criminal. They might do something covert to damage me physically and mentally."

He was twenty when he was arrested and imprisoned, but the wanted list stated that he was twenty-four, because the government didn't want to look ludicrous for having such a youngster as the number one criminal who had organized and led the so-called rebellious insurrection. Wang Dan also mentioned the mental suffering of solitary confinement. He could speak to no one and feared he might lose his speech. He was so desperate to chat with someone, anyone. To keep himself from losing his mind, he wrote a lot of poetry and recited ancient poems loudly.

I guessed that as a major student leader, he must have been used to addressing an audience. Now in jail, in a total vacuum, he didn't have any ears listening to him anymore. That must have felt like a plunge from his former life, like having his selfhood shattered.

Derek asked him what he remembered the most from his imprisonment. At that, Wang Dan's eyes dimmed,

LOOKING FOR TANK MAN

turning moist. "I was allowed to meet my parents only once during my first prison term," he said. "I was taken into a small room in which my parents were seated, waiting for me. I reminded myself of the rule I'd made: never cry in front of the guards. But I was shocked to see that more than half of my mother's hair was white now. Just a year ago she had had pitch-black hair. She also looked sick and had more wrinkles around her mouth and crow's-feet, her cheeks more hollowed. In the guards' presence, we couldn't say anything intimate and only exchanged greetings and some stock expressions. When they took my parents away, I saw that my mother could hardly walk. My father had to support her. I was biting my bottom lip to stop myself from sobbing. I bit it so hard that when I was back in my cell, I found my lip bleeding. Later, I discovered she had been imprisoned for nearly two months for my sake, and in jail she had developed a leg problem, unable to walk, her left leg somewhat withered, much thinner than her right leg."

Wang Dan's first prison term lasted three and a half years. Two years after that he was put in jail again. They gave him eleven years this time, because he had been taking correspondence courses with UC Berkeley. In 1998, he was let out on medical parole, right before President Clinton's state visit to China. That same year he came to Harvard to do graduate work in East Asian history. To date, he had not been allowed to go back to China, but even so, he viewed himself as a Chinese and wouldn't apply for U.S. citizenship. I guessed that a man like him had already become a political symbol in the public eye, so he couldn't just change his identity of his own free will.

Rachel developed a crush on Wang Dan, who we knew was gay. She confessed to me afterward, "Damn, if he weren't that way, I would chase him to the end of the world."

I said, "How about Joe?"

"Joe can wait," she said with a straight face.

Rachel liked smooth-faced men, the scholarly type. We often compared notes on our likes and dislikes. I preferred men who were a bit rugged, more energetic. I adored the John Wayne type of man's man. Rachel often made fun of me, saying I'd better hit up construction sites to find that kind of guy, with corded muscles and big pecs. I thought that my preference might have been due to my father's absence from home when I grew up. Probably deep inside, I longed to have a man who could love and protect me, like a strong father could. Of course, I didn't share my self-analyses with Rachel, who didn't know I'd been brought up alone by my mother.

Right after the fall break, we had another visitor, a pastor from Virginia named Zhang Boli. He had a nickname—Modern-day Robinson Crusoe, due to his long wanderings in flight through different lands. He understood English but didn't speak it well, so Loana acted as his interpreter. His weathered face and brushy hair showed he had gone through a great deal of hardship. He was also a former student leader, the deputy commander of the hunger strike, the editor in chief of

LOOKING FOR TANK MAN

the *News Herald* (the newspaper launched for the student movement), and the director of propaganda in Tiananmen Square—and he had even become the inaugural president of Tiananmen Democracy University, which existed for just a few days. Like Wang Dan, Zhang also landed on the wanted list. But he was older and more experienced than the other student leaders and managed to elude capture. He was not a regular college student and was attending Beijing University as a creative writer, somewhat like a graduate student in its writing program. As soon as the crackdown took place, he fled Beijing for Heilongjiang Province, where his parents lived in Wankui county, north of Harbin. But he didn't go to them, assuming that a posse of policemen must be waiting for him in his hometown. He headed farther north, pretending to be a farmhand and using a pseudonym. He tramped around as an itinerant laborer, working for peasants who needed help with their crops. He even wandered to inner Mongolia for some time, felling trees to earn his meals. For a brief period he returned to Harbin and stayed with his friend Hsien's family in secret, but the city was too dangerous, because his photos appeared on TV and in newspapers regularly. So he decided to flee the country. As a northeasterner, he assumed that the only feasible route was to slip into the Soviet Union, since many student leaders had been caught in the south when trying to flee to Hong Kong. Once in the Soviet Union, he could ask the Russians to let him go to the West for asylum. This was also because he'd heard from the BBC that Gorbachev felt deeply sorry about the Tiananmen suppression. But when Zhang reached the border with his friend Hsien in the cold winter, he couldn't cross the border and fell ill, afflicted with typhoid. His friend carried him to a village where he was able to be treated and stay with his friend's relatives. The family who took him in were Christians and cared for him, even though they knew he was an escapee at large. They fed him chicken soup every day in an attempt to nurture him back to health quickly. Everyone in the family was illiterate, but they had kept a gilt cross and hand-copied parts of the Bible, both wrapped in cloth and left behind by an underground clergyman. It was in that household where Zhang felt at home for the first time after fleeing Beijing. At the matron Sister Fen's request, Zhang often read aloud to her the tattered pages of the New Testament, mainly the Gospels of Luke and John. Once he started to read aloud, he got engrossed and moved to tears at the episode of Jesus's persecution. As a result, he often pored over the scriptures on his own under an oil lamp.

One day the village's head, a close friend of the family's, recognized Zhang and told them that the bulletin with his photos in it had just come in from the regional security bureau. The police believed that Zhang had arrived in this region. Clearly he couldn't stay here any longer, so he decided to leave at once. After midnight he and Hsien trudged to the Amur River, where they wept and hugged goodbye. He then struggled through the snow, some spots waist-deep, toward the other side, carrying his backpack. Four hours later, when he had finally crossed the river and set foot on foreign land, dawn broke, a huge sun was rising above the horizon. He walked eastward, in the direction of Khabarovsk. He dared not use any road and just followed the river so he wouldn't lose his bearings. Everywhere it was eerily quiet.

Soon he was caught in a blizzard, and he realized he might never be able to reach Khabarovsk. As he was plodding along, he often felt like he was floating in the air. It was turning dark, and he was exhausted, hungry, and cold, so he sneaked into an isolated barn in which were stacked large bundles of hay. He unpacked some bales and buried himself in the straw, fearing that he was going to be frozen to death or eaten by the wolves that were howling nearby. Even though he was not yet a Christian, he started to pray, begging God for protection. Soon he passed out.

Early the next morning some peasants came with a caravan of tractors to haul hay. They stumbled upon him in the straw, a rake having caught the leg of his pants. They gave him a lot of hot coffee to wake him up fully. They shouted "Tovarich! Tovarich!" (Comrade!) at him until he woke up. Then they argued among themselves what to do about him and decided to ship him to the Soviet Army's post nearby, since their village was far away from the border region, which was a restricted zone where they were not allowed to stay. At the army's post, soldiers cut off his boots and socks and massaged his frozen feet with pots of snow until his feet turned red and regained tingles of sensation. After giving him a big meal of tomato soup, beef, fish, and fried rice, they delivered him to the KGB, which shipped him to a prison in a big city. The men taking him there in a jeep wouldn't tell him its name. They interrogated him for many days. But two weeks later, on January 10, 1990, they took him back to the Amur. They left him at the riverside, miles away from the Chinese watchtower, so he could cross the ice back to China without being spotted. Apparently they were apprehensive about offending the Chinese government and also about potential condemnation by the West, so they felt that to release him in secret back to the other side of the Amur was their best option.

Zhang managed to return to Sister Fen's home a few days later. Again the matron of the household fed him chicken soup and nursed him back to health. A month later the village's head came again to tell him that the police had started an investigation in the village, though he wasn't sure if they were after him. So Sister Fen's husband took Zhang to a remote spot near Wide Deer River, which is a branch of the Amur. There was a deserted mud hut at the foot of a mountain. They fixed up the hut a bit, and it became Zhang's temporary shelter. He began to live there alone with a puppy. In the wilderness the most miserable part of his life was the loneliness. He was also afflicted with skin rashes caused by damp and tortured by lice, fleas, and bedbugs. In the spring the owner of the hut returned to farm his fields, so Zhang moved and built his own cottage deep in the thick woods, its front facing the river. He began scratching out a living by fishing and hunting. He also grew rice and soybeans and became known as Old Fourth Wang and was respected by the few locals, who really all lived far away. Once in a while he went to the county seat to sell fresh-caught fish, herbs, and mushrooms, and also wild animals he had trapped—hares, black game hens, even water deer. He sold the pelts of civet cats and water rats, and they brought good prices. From the town he bought things he needed: rice, dried noodles, wheat flour, cooking oil, salt, liquor, tobacco leaves, matches, batteries for his radio. Not until the next Spring Festival did he decide to flee again. In Harbin he learned from a friend that his wife had left him and declared the divorce in a newspaper. He felt bitter, but couldn't do a thing. His friend also told him that his wife had given away their four-year-old daughter and married another man. Down and out now, he became more determined to flee abroad. He went to Guangzhou, and with the help of an underground rescue group, Operation Yellowbird, succeeded in sneaking across to Hong Kong, where he applied for political asylum in the United States.

Soon after he landed in New Jersey, he was diagnosed with liver cancer. The doctor told him that he might have two years to live. Three years at most. Zhang became suicidal in the hospital, and he often thought about pulling out the tubes attached to him, but he was helped by people from his church. A Malaysian couple came and prayed for him. They calmed him down. He began to leave everything in God's hands, though the pain and fatigue caused by the chemotherapy nearly destroyed him. For months toxic fluid built up in him, more than fifty pounds of it; he was bloated all over, his face unrecognizable and even his scrotum swelling like a balloon. He didn't look at himself in a mirror, and he didn't take photos, and he was afraid to meet others. Miraculously his symptoms gradually subsided. A few months later his cancer was gone.

Everyone was thrilled, but soon the doctor found out that his kidneys were damaged. He had to be treated again. This time, through the help of his friends and the Taiwanese government, he went to Taipei for treatment, where he was admitted to the best hospital. He promised God that if he survived the new disease, he would dedicate his life to His service. Again, miraculously, he was cured. After recovery, he went to New York and became an editor at the dissident magazine *Beijing Spring*. Meanwhile, he enrolled in LOGOS Evangelical Seminary and earned a master's in Taoism. He also spent many years studying Christianity and eventually got baptized and became an ordained priest. He even authored a memoir, *Escape from China*, which was translated into several languages. Although now a full-time clergyman, he was also one of the most active dissidents in North America, having focused his attention on religious persecution in China. "In fact, I'm still working toward a PhD in theology for Singapore Bible College," he told us. He was done with all the coursework and had been writing his dissertation. One day, he believed, he'd go back to China to preach the Gospel.

I found Zhang Boli fascinating, probably because my mother's family lived in Heilongjiang Province. His northeastern accent, plus his vibrant baritone voice, sounded pleasant and endearing. Above all, the tremendous hardship he'd gone through hadn't diminished his good nature, his sweet smile coupled with twinkling intelligent eyes giving off warm, pleasant vibes. Rachel teased me at dinner, saying "If Zhang Boli were twenty years younger and Wang Dan were not gay, which one of them would you prefer as your boyfriend?"

Though embarrassed, I confessed, "I like Zhang better because he's more down-to-earth and is also a survivor."

"He reminded me of a northern peasant," Rachel said with a smile that was a little sidewise.

"That's the reason I like him. He's kind of charismatic, isn't he? He never had the kind of privileges Wang Dan had in the capital. Imagine, a country boy going all the way to Beijing University and then wandering through different lands. Most city men couldn't have survived all that hardship."

"It's too bad he has a new wife and a couple of kids now."

"Come on, I'm four years younger than his daughter from the first marriage. I'm just saying I like energetic men."

I didn't tell Rachel that my father was quite vigorous too. He was full of creative energy, producing sculptures constantly while teaching full-time. His young wife didn't work, and she drove a brand-new Audi. My dad had to make a lot of money to support his new family— a spoiled young wife and two small sons, who were both going to private schools in Tianjin, but he seemed to be doing fine these years. In some respects he was similar to Zhang Boli, headstrong and persistent in what he did.

Also a bit wild. Men like them seemed a little touched, somewhat possessed. But in my father's case, I could see that artistically he might not get anywhere, having spent too much time making money.

"Don't confuse a rustic man with a *rutting* man," said Rachel.

"What do you mean by 'a rutting man'?" I asked.

"A man with a lot of sexual drive and phallic power."

"You know, Rachel, you're a slut by nature," I joked.

"A slut at heart," she said.

We both cracked up. I went on, "Honestly, I'm more interested in what a man thinks."

"Then you should prefer a man like Wang Dan, shouldn't you?"

I was stumped. Indeed, Wang Dan seemed more thoughtful than Zhang Boli, but I wasn't at all attracted to him as Rachel was. Why? I couldn't answer at the time. Later I figured out some grounds for my preference: Wang Dan seemed book smart, whereas Zhang must be a man of the world—life smart. Compared to them, Rachel was merely school smart. I liked men who had actually lived.

Rachel and I usually spoke English together. She was better read and more fluent in it than I was. I admired her for studying literature, something that most people back home thought impractical and useless. She said she usually picked her courses just for fun. Because we were rarities among the Chinese students on campus and often took the same classes, we spent a lot of time together.

5

TOWARD THE END of the semester, we had another visitor, Fang Zheng, who had lost his legs to a tank. During the Tiananmen protests, he had been an athlete and a senior at Beijing Sport University—he still had a strong build. He talked to us in a deep, resonant voice while Loana interpreted for him. He was another kind of Tank Man, different from Wang Weilin, the iconic Tank Man.

He said, "On June 3, for a whole day we stayed in Tiananmen Square. From the evening to the early hours of the morning of June 4, we sat around the Monument to the People's Heroes, altogether about four thousand students. Around two in the morning, units of armed troops assembled around Tiananmen Square. Then, led by tanks and armored personnel carriers, they began charging into the square. All the students were outraged and scared, but most of us just huddled together. Around four o'clock we started to withdraw from the monument peacefully, moving toward the southeast corner of the square. I was at the end of the retreating procession. Once out of the square, we walked along West Front Gate Avenue, which was near Beijing Music Hall and led to West Chang'an Avenue. We continued slowly on West Chang'an Avenue. Around six a.m. the students became less organized, walking on the bicycle lanes and sidewalks, some mixing with the local residents who had been there to stop the army.

"When we reached Liubukou, poison gas bombs were suddenly pitched at us, dispersing the crowds in all directions. One bomb burst at my feet, and in a flash a cloud of gas, about eight or nine feet across, wrapped around me. A girl walking beside me was so frightened and so nauseated that she fainted and fell. I rushed over and picked her up and moved to the side of the street. At that moment I caught sight of a tank charging toward us at full speed, so I pushed the girl to the metal fence along the sidewalk. In a split second the tank reached the side of the street, its barrel pointing at me. It was impossible for me to step away, so I dropped to the ground and rolled aside. But it was too late, my upper body had gotten stuck to the front of the tank, between both caterpillar treads, and my legs were cut off. I saw my legs and my shoes and the rags of my pants entangled in the tank's tread. It dragged me for a distance until I used all my strength to pull myself off and roll into the side of the street. Then I blacked out. Later I learned that some locals and students had stanched my bleeding and sent me to Jishuitan Hospital, where they amputated parts of my legs. You see," he pointed at his left knee, "my leg below this is gone." Then he patted his right thigh, two-thirds of which was missing.

Gary, the blond kid, asked, "Did you see a lot of dead bodies at the hospital?"

LOOKING FOR TANK MAN

Fang Zheng answered, "I couldn't count. My rescuers placed me on the floor. While I was waiting for treatment, I saw dozens of wounded people lying around."

"They didn't treat you immediately?" Rachel asked.

"No, they had to save those more seriously wounded first."

His answer struck us dumb. For a long while the whole room remained in dead silence.

Then he told us about his life after the loss of his legs. The Communist authorities wanted him to tell the public that he'd lost his legs in a traffic accident, that they hadn't been crushed by a tank, but he refused to change his story and kept sharing the truth with others. Because of his refusal to cooperate, he couldn't find a job after graduation.

Rachel raised her hand, then asked, "You must have had many eyewitnesses, didn't you? Didn't the girl you saved stick up for you?"

He said, "No, she refused to get involved in my case. She just wanted to stay silent and keep a low profile. All of a sudden people were terrified into obedience and silence. Many even began to express their support for the government's suppression. It was so depressing to see a reversal of their attitude."

"What a bitch," Rachel said under her breath.

In 1992 Fang Zheng participated in the National Games of Disabled Persons and won a championship in both discus and javelin. There again, because of his non-cooperation, the government banned him from taking part in any international sport tournaments. That was why he had to leave China, where he could no longer survive.

"See, I am another Tank Man," he said calmly, indicating that the soldiers had been ruthless in using brute force and hadn't hesitated to crush him with a tank.

Jerek asked him what he thought of Wang Weilin, because we had just discussed the defiant hero in the previous class: how he was perceived and created by the public. We shared Loana's misgivings about the authenticity of the confrontation caught on camera between Wang and a column of tanks. Even the man's name might be fiction. We all knew that President Jiang Zemin had told ABC and *60 Minutes* that he didn't know who Tank Man was or his whereabouts. But he assured the West that the man hadn't been executed at all and that the Chinese government hadn't been able to find him afterward.

Fang Zheng smiled and said, "Actually I admire the man. He embodies the brave and defiant spirit of the demonstrators. It's good that he has gathered so much public attention. But we still don't know his real name. The truth is that after the confrontation, the Chinese government widely publicized the footage made by their cameramen to show the world how lenient and restrained the People's Army had been to the civilians—even if a man blocked a whole column of tanks, they wouldn't harm him. This indicates that the scene might have been staged. In reality, those tanks didn't hesitate to run over people. So many were killed by them. There was a graduate student at the Northern Aviation University named Wang Kuanbao. His pelvis had been crushed by a tank. He stayed in the hospital for years and the doctors couldn't repair the damage. I went to see him once. He had to go through one operation after another. So I believe Tank Man Wang Weilin may have been created for propaganda's sake, though later the image transformed into something beyond official control. Still, I am able to accept him as a hero, or as an embodiment of the Tiananmen spirit."

There was no bitterness in his voice, and I was impressed by his intelligent, nuanced answer. After class, Rachel and I chatted about Tank Man, who had become an icon in the West. We felt uneasy about this, of course, but we didn't see eye to eye on it. I thought there was no harm in the public embracing this iconic image, but as a historian, I didn't necessarily view the man as a hero because the creation of his public identity was ambiguous, to say the least. Rachel was more radical, believing the image should be suppressed, because it might be a lie. Indeed, numerous sources indicated that the Chinese propaganda cadres had intended to stage the confrontation. The man's name, Wang Weilin, was first mentioned by a small newspaper in England that had no connection with China whatsoever. In other words, the name could have been fabricated by Western media. More unusually, the man had worn a formal outfit, the standard mufti worn by plainclothesmen and soldiers (in contrast, most local men in the summertime wore shorts, T-shirts, and slippers). And he also knew semaphore, which he used to communicate with the tank operators. Most likely the scene was planned ahead of time, so his image, heroic though it later became, should be stopped from being disseminated further—that was Rachel's conclusion.

Equipped with the information we got from Loana's seminar, Rachel and I discussed Tank Man in the presence of her boyfriend, Joe. He was much more aggressive in his opinions and argument. He viewed Tank Man as a scar on China's face. If the man were a real hero, he should have stepped forward by now, because a number of former student leaders and preeminent exiles had been allowed to return to China, and no harm had been done to them. With the kind of international publicity Tank Man had garnered, he should have been safe if he had come forward, but to date, there'd been no trace of him. Joe had once attended a gathering in a local high school at which a traditional Chinese painter and calligrapher demonstrated his arts. Before the man wielded his brush, he asked the youngsters what they knew about China. A girl stood up and declared, "I know Tank Man." The artist had no clue whom she was referring to, and their teacher had to explain it to him. The man shook his head and couldn't say anything.

Joe felt outraged and believed that the Chinese government must intervene to counter the misperceptions generated by the icon of Tank Man, because the whole thing was based on a deception manufactured by stupid propaganda officials. It was further distorted by the Western media. The three of us were lounging on sofas in Rachel's living room and drinking coffee. I disagreed with Joe and argued that the iconic image should be left alone for the public, but in academia we must view it with a grain of salt, from a more rational perspective.

"Give me a break," he spit out. "The West means to utilize Tank Man to demonize China."

"That's a stretch," I said. "To many people, he symbolizes a defiant spirit against oppressive state power."

"More than that," Joe pressed on. "His image eclipses all the positive aspects of China."

"So what are the positive aspects, then?" His excessive patriotism made me angry. "You must have some demonic qualities for others to demonize you. You know what life is like in our homeland, where lies are so ubiquitous that every day is April Fool's."

Joe lost it. "Pei Lulu, you're speaking out of turn. You ought to remember who you are!"

"So go to the officials and squeal on me. You're pathetic enough to lapse into being an informer. You love Red China so much, you see red everywhere. You've got so high on patriotic propaganda that you eat China's shit like pastry."

"Damn it, you've done your best to trash China! If our country collapsed, who would benefit from it?"

"You're a national savior, huh?" I mocked.

"Cool it, both of you!" Rachel intervened.

"I can't stand this bitch!" He pointed at me. "She's too full of herself."

"I despise you too," I said and stood to leave, surprised that our exchange had exploded into such a fiery confrontation.

Rachel didn't stop me. She seemed eager to see me go away and to avoid more quarreling.

It was snowing sporadically, cars passing with their headlights blurred by snowflakes and with their wipers scraping their windshields. The street was still scattered with pedestrians. Turning a corner, I stepped on a patch of ice, slipped, and fell on my butt. An older man rushed over and asked, "Are you all right, Miss?" I said I was fine and thanked him while dusting the snow off my behind. I felt sad, breathing heavily, and continued toward my dorm. I wondered why Rachel hadn't stepped in to defend me. Maybe she shared Joe's view. She might also be a patriotic freak, a little red flag waver.

Later she told me that Joe had gone ballistic and demanded she terminate our friendship. He even declared, "You must choose between that bitch and me."

I was surprised, but didn't press her for an answer. I could see that she was reluctant to spend time with me, avoiding sharing my table in the cafeteria. In class we stopped sitting together. I could tell that Rachel must have caved to Joe and turned her back on me. The loss of her friendship hurt me, and for weeks I was downcast, but I managed to make it seem like everything was normal, especially when Rachel was around.

Though in pain, I was not disappointed. If someone could abandon you just because of another person's opinion, then you didn't need that friend. Loana sensed my low spirits and wondered whether it was because her

LOOKING FOR TANK MAN

class was too depressing. I told her in her office that I had quarreled with a Chinese student over Tank Man and for that I had lost a friend. She nodded, her tapered eyes flashing as if she was hurting herself. She told me, "This kind of hostility is unavoidable if you want to tell the truth. Nearly every time I presented the results of my research at a conference, some Chinese students yelled at me. Some even called me 'American Running Dog,' or 'Moron.' I'm used to being cursed and spat at. Once, at a conference in Chicago, a young man came over, about to attack me, but security intervened and took him away. He couldn't stop calling me 'stupid cunt.' Keep in mind, some Chinese students are spies and will report you to the officials if you say something against the government. Nationalism has clouded many of their eyes, and they view their country as God. God must always be right and beyond criticism and must never commit blunders or crimes. They can't see that a country is just a secular construct and can be mended and rebuilt like a house."

I nodded, my eyes hot, and realized that even though we were on the other side of the world, China still cast its long shadow over our lives, its dark, invisible hands still attempting to manipulate our behavior. I wondered if Joe was an assigned informer for the Chinese consulate. Perhaps he was. I had seen him rubbing elbows with some officials as if he were eager to become one of them.

I grew fond of Loana. Even though I was not taking her class in the spring semester, I still dropped by her office. From time to time we also had coffee together.

I once revealed to her that my mother had participated in the hunger strike in Tiananmen Square. Loana asked in astonishment, "What did she tell you about her experience?"

"Nothing. Whenever I mentioned the massacre, she'd say it was too complicated and I mustn't touch on such a subject. I didn't tell her I was taking your seminar last fall."

"Oh, but at some point, you ought to ask your mother about her experience. Any firsthand witness is invaluable."

"True, I just don't want to disturb her for now—she's a worrywart."

"There're things we must preserve. To remember is the most efficient way to fight the authoritarian power that makes people forget. A historian's business is remembrance."

"I can see why the Chinese government always urges people to look forward," I said. "They want to erase the traces of their crimes from public memory."

"Exactly. That's their way of reshaping history, making people avoid looking into the past."

"They want people's minds to be clouded with propaganda. That is their way of keeping the population ignorant and incapable of thinking clearly and independently."

Her eyes lit up. "That's right. Oblivion and stupidity always go hand in hand. A historian's job is to present the past truthfully and make others see it clearly. So if you want to be a good historian, you must look truth in the eye and reveal it. In China there is only one truth, which is what's provided by the government. Any deviation from the official view is regarded as a crime."

"So to tell the actual truth can be a crime?"

"Yes, keep that in mind. That also makes our scholarship more meaningful."

I enjoyed spending time with Loana and gradually viewed myself as a budding historian. Hanging around her became a kind of education for me, my most valuable experience at Harvard.

6

I SPENT A lot of time in the library, reading for my classes. Though I didn't have an assigned place in there for myself, I'd find a quiet spot to hide away from others. I envied the graduate students, who could apply for a carrel at which they could store the books they'd been reading and also work on their theses. The cubicles were so small, consisting of just a desk and a cabinet, both made of brown wood. At times, when taking a break from reading, I would pass Mark Stone's carrel on purpose. If he was there, we would chat for a while. On the door of his cabinet, opposite his desk, was Scotch-taped a poster of Tank Man. Obviously that skinny Chinese guy was his hero. I felt uneasy about that, since Mark was a PhD student in East Asian studies, writing a dissertation on the kung fu novels of Jin Yong (Louis Cha). I had read many of his novels—*Legends of the Condor Heroes*, *The Book and the Sword*, *Fox Volant of the Snowy Mountain*, and more. So Mark and I had a lot to talk about. He seemed amazed that I knew so much about the subject of his dissertation, which was a kind of outlier in Chinese literary studies. Even in China, Jin Yong is not regarded as very literary, though he might be its most popular writer, with

LOOKING FOR TANK MAN

hundreds of millions of readers in the world. He's similar to J. R. R. Tolkien but has a larger readership; his fiction is full of knightly adventures, sorcery, romances, spectacular kung fu feats, and they are mostly set in exotic spaces. They're entertaining and uplifting.

Another reason I often stopped by Mark's carrel was because it had a narrow window that looked out on a lawn. His was a bright spot on the cavernous ground floor of the massive building, from which, through the high window, you could catch a glimpse of the traffic on Massachusetts Avenue. He and I would chat for a long time, sometimes for a whole hour. I once asked him why he had picked a topic like that for his dissertation, he said, "I like it. There's a lot of fun in Jin Yong's fiction." I was amazed. I wouldn't build my scholarship that way, on a lightweight subject that was just for fun, but I made no comment.

I liked him, a lot. He was handsome, in his late twenties, and strapping, with deep-set eyes and with a high hairline that gave him a full forehead. His mullet gave him a carefree air. He reminded me of my American English teacher in high school, a man in his mid-forties, lively and kind and humorous in the classroom, whom I'd had a crush on. Mark spoke good Mandarin, a little stiff and accented, but we used English most of the time. I had noticed lots of girls hanging around him, though I wasn't sure who his girlfriend was. One day he invited me to dinner, and I accepted.

We went to a small French restaurant on Plympton Street, next to Harvard Book Store. I ordered duck and

61

he ordered lamb shank. He also wanted a glass of red wine, and I just had sparkling water. I could see that this was an expensive place, the tables covered with checked cloth and wineglasses stuffed with white napkins folded like birdwings. I enjoyed the dish very much. Back home, my father had taken me to a restaurant called Dadong Roast Duck every time he came to Beijing, but my mother had never joined us. I had to say I liked the confit de canard better than Beijing duck, because it was tender, less greasy, and less spiced, preserving the original flavor of the meat. Mark talked a lot about Hong Kong movies, another passion of his. From Hong Kong we moved to Taiwan, whose snacks and street foods he loved. Somehow he mentioned some Taiwanese girls we both knew. He said they were different from girls from mainland China. I felt odd, unable to see much difference, since we all spoke Mandarin and had similar cultural heritage and even shared some values, so I asked him how he compared the two groups.

He smiled with some embarrassment and said, "Well, with Taiwanese girls you can do anything except get them to be seriously committed."

"What do you mean by 'committed'?" I was puzzled.

"Taiwanese girls are more open to dating, but they rarely keep a long-term relationship."

"What do you mean by 'a long-term relationship'?"

"A step further than merely being boyfriend and girlfriend."

"Like an engagement?"

"Not that serious, but moving toward that stage."

I wondered how often he had dated Taiwanese girls if he had formed that strong an opinion of them. He must have been quite experienced, but he sounded pretty bitter. Perhaps one of them had just broken up with him.

When we were done with the entrées, he encourage me to have some dessert, which I didn't want. I said, "Thanks, I'm full. We Chinese don't eat dessert at dinner."

"Is that so?" he mused aloud.

"Have you ever seen a dessert menu in a Chinese restaurant? Some upscale places have fruit plates as a kind of dessert."

"That's true. Too bad they don't have a fortune cookie for you here." He laughed out loud.

I was a tad embarrassed, unsure whether he had meant to mock me. But he seemed amicable and was easily amused by his own wisecracks. He ordered a chocolate mousse and I got a decaf coffee, mainly to keep him company while he was eating his dessert. I put in a tiny cube of brown sugar and began drinking the coffee slowly. I did try a forkful of the mousse, which was delicious, but I was too full to eat any more.

I offered to split the bill, but he stopped me, saying "This is on me." He picked up the check and handed his credit card to the slender waitress, who was wearing a pair of French braids. She looked Vietnamese and may also have been a Harvard student.

It was warm outside when we stepped out of the restaurant. There was an author event in the bookstore. Next to it, on the sidewalk, people sat at small metal tables outside Bartley's, eating big hamburgers, onion rings, salads. The air smelled meaty, filled as it was with cooking oil. Turning onto Quincy Street, Mark invited me to go up to his apartment. Startled, I declined, saying, "I don't know you that well yet."

"Haven't we spent many weeks chewing the fat together? I feel I already know a lot about you."

"But it's still too soon for me to spend the evening at your place."

"Come on, we had a nice dinner and a great time." He smirked and went on in a jesting tone of voice, "What follows is just dessert."

"I can't be your dessert."

"This goes both ways," he said and kept grinning. "I can be your dessert, don't you think?"

"We Chinese don't eat dessert, you know."

"Okay, good night then." His eyes looked glazed with hurt. He turned and sauntered away, his square shoulders a little stooped.

I was offended and felt he had treated me too easily. It must be his habit to get a woman into bed just after having dinner together. But I'd heard that if you went out with a man, sex might become the next step of the date. I wished Rachel were still my friend so that I could have consulted her on this beforehand. She was far more experienced about dating than I was.

Two days later, when I ran into Mark in the Science Center, he was as friendly as before, as if nothing untoward had even happened the other day. I thought this guy really had thick skin and must be some sort of playboy, well accustomed to being rejected by women he dated. Though I noticed that he was always at ease with young women, especially Asians. When they were together, I often heard him laugh aloud.

Every time I passed his carrel in the library, I would peek into his neat alcove and see the Tank Man poster on the door of his cabinet. At its bottom "Wang Wei-lin" was written in Chinese characters. That was something new. Somehow the sight of this poster irritated me. One afternoon, after seeing Mark sitting there writing, I knocked on the top side of his desk with my knuckles. He lifted his head and smiled and looked happy to see me. I told him that the poster was so juvenile that he shouldn't display it so openly.

He was baffled and said, "This guy is my hero." He pointed at Tank Man. "Many boys in my high school had a poster just like this one. You can't ask me to take it down without giving me a good reason."

I said, "It's believed that he was staged for this footage, which was also used briefly for propaganda by the Chinese state media. Even Deng Xiaoping praised the tank for not running over this guy."

"Really, why don't you think he was the real thing?"

I went on to explain that many scholars, and even Fang Zheng—another Tank Man, but one who was legless—were convinced that Wang Weilin was just a fictional name. That sensational icon had actually been created by the Chinese government and the Western media, though originally nobody had expected him to become such an international sensation. Mark nodded, narrowing his gray eyes, but didn't look convinced.

I continued, "If a schoolboy hangs this poster, it's understandable and can be justified. But you're a scholar and must look truth in the eye and mustn't just follow the herd."

"Well, I see your point, but I'm not fully convinced. Even if Tank Man had been initially manufactured by the Chinese government, he has been transformed into an international phenomenon and become a public hero. I can't just abandon my hero because you told me there was something bogus about his origins. In other words, I ought to accept him as what he is now."

"Isn't what I told you already enough for you to view him in a different light?"

"No." He shook his long hair. "If you really want to change my view about him, you'll have to give me more than that. Maybe you should do some research and look deeper into his case. I'm eager to know about him and all the truth and facts about him so that I can form my own judgment. What you just said mainly reflects academic obsessions, which tend to focus on trifles and split hairs. You ought to think about things relevant to people's lives and to the real world."

"You're so arrogant," I said, feeling upset.

"All right, I can see that you might still have some feelings for me." He grinned. "If so, do some research on Tank Man. I'm open to being swayed by the results of your investigation."

I spun around and strode away. From then on, we would just nod our heads when we bumped into each other. I knew he probably thought of me as a little prude. The thought nagged at me, since that was not what I was. I didn't want him to take me for an angry woman, a killjoy, a sanctimonious, self-styled pundit in the making, even though there was no way I could get close to him again.

7

SINCE MID-APRIL LOANA had been organizing a conference, and she asked me and other students to help her. It was about the Tiananmen suppression and called The People's Liberation Army's Role in the June 4 Democracy Movement. The conference was meant to commemorate the massacre on its twentieth anniversary, so it was to take place in late May, when school was about to close for the summer. I was in charge of communicating with the speakers and panelists, one of whom had been a junior officer in the PLA and participated in the crackdown. So I was excited and looked forward to the conference, and I postponed my summer return to Beijing for it.

It happened that some Chinese students at Boston University were still on campus in late May, so their teacher, Professor Smerdon, wrote to Loana and asked if he could send them to the conference, because their school hadn't taught anything related to the Tiananmen democracy movement yet and most students from mainland China didn't believe there had been a massacre. Professor Smerdon wanted to have the few remaining students attend our symposium. Loana welcomed them.

LOOKING FOR TANK MAN

The conference was held on Saturday, and there were four sections in the morning and the afternoon, with a lunch break and a pizza dinner in the atrium outside the auditorium. I helped Loana order the food and soft drinks for that day. This was easy. There were local restaurants accustomed to catering academic events on campus. Some of the speakers didn't speak English, so Loana asked me and a few other students to interpret. I hesitated about doing it, knowing the conference would be recorded and Chinese officials would know I was involved, but I agreed to be an interpreter and believed I could justify my involvement as part of my coursework if I were made to explain my participation.

On the morning of the last Saturday in May, Loana opened the conference with welcome remarks, then introduced the speakers, including the former officer of the PLA. Because some in the audience were quite young and therefore unfamiliar with the tragedy, Loana gave a brief but comprehensive introduction, showing some photos and footage as well. She started from late April 1989, when people gathered on Tiananmen Square in memory of Hu Yaobang, the late, liberal-minded party secretary, to the violent killings in early June. After she was done with her presentation, a rotund man with a broad face got up in the middle of the sloping seats and said, "We all know June 4 was an awful tragedy, but it happened twenty years ago. Life continues, and we have to move on. What's the good of miring ourselves in the mud and blood of the past? Why not let bygones be bygones?" The man looked sleepy thanks to his heavy-lidded eyes.

Loana replied in a calm voice, "We want to remember in order to fight the Chinese authorities' efforts to erase the public memory of the massacre. Without knowing the truth of the past, how can we understand the present and look forward to the future? On top of that, if your child were killed in such a tragedy, would it be possible for you to come to terms with the loss without a truthful look at what happened? Then how can we stop this endless cycle of catastrophe? Moreover, we must not view the victims as a worthy sacrifice for China's development. We're human beings and have no right to decide whose life is dispensable."

The man pressed on, "I want to know the point of such memorial activities."

Loana said, "Those in power deny that such a tragedy even took place. They try to make people oblivious and unable to think clearly. How can we just let the memory evaporate like smoke? I'm a historian and it's my responsibility to preserve this part of history in unambiguous terms. Because of the Chinese government's banning of this topic, the Tiananmen Square Massacre is a gaping wound in many people's lives and in China's psyche. If the criminals remain at large and keep claiming that the victims were responsible for their own deaths and suffering, then how can we expect the victims' families to begin to heal?"

The man grunted, about to raise his voice to object again, but the audience booed. Loana seized the moment to announce a ten-minute break. People went to the front atrium to have coffee and mingle.

LOOKING FOR TANK MAN

The next speaker was Wang Chaohua, an elegant woman, close to fifty, wearing a pageboy haircut and black-rimmed glasses. In 1989 she had been a graduate student in modern literature at the Chinese Academy of Social Sciences, and she'd participated in the demonstrations in Tiananmen Square. She had been older than most of the other students there and served as a member of the standing committee of the Beijing Students' Autonomous Federation. She stayed in the square for many days and also joined the hunger strike, but on the afternoon of June 3, she collapsed and was sent to the hospital, so she didn't witness the massacre itself, which happened late that night and early the next morning. Nonetheless, she also landed on the wanted list afterward. After being in hiding for more than half a year, she sneaked out of China and came to the States, where she earned her PhD in modern Chinese literature at UCLA. Since graduation, she had been freelancing for magazines and had also written several books.

In a soft but clear voice she talked about recent scholarship in the study of "the June 4 democracy movement." She was articulate and good at summarizing various authors' arguments. She singled out a sociologist at the University of Chicago and criticized the man's critique of what he saw as the students' unreasonable intransigence, which according to him doomed the democracy movement and precipitated the tragedy, because no government could tolerate that kind of occupation in the center of its capital. Therefore, the students had undermined their own movement by their narrow-mindedness and

71

by their lack of a clear goal and self-restraint. Ms. Wang condemned the scholar by pointing out that although the students had made mistakes, the government had committed a crime by ordering field armies to shoot and kill unarmed civilians. The cause of such a massacre was clear and simple. How could anyone in his sane mind claim that those killed were responsible for their own deaths? No wonder that scholar had been recruited by China as a Thousand-Talent Professor and appointed as the dean of a college at Zhejiang University. Ms. Wang went on to criticize the documentary *The Gate of Heavenly Peace*, made by Carma Hinton and Richard Gordon. The film argues that the students, especially the radical leaders, were partially responsible for this historical eruption that led to the collapse of the liberal faction within the Communist Party. In her seminar, Loana had shown us the movie, which I thought was pretty good, balanced and reasonable in its narrative. To her credit, Ms. Wang was capable of self-reflection, and said that ever since the massacre, she hadn't been able to reconcile herself with the fact of her absence from the violent site and of the deaths of so many people, some of whom she had known well. That was why she had to speak up for those whose voices had been silenced.

The next speaker was Zhang Jian, who came from France and didn't know English. Samantha, the public health senior who had once broken down in Loana's seminar, served as his interpreter. Zhang had also been a former student leader in Tiananmen Square; he had been in charge of security, and later landed on the wanted list too, though he was only eighteen years old at the time. He shared his experience in the square during the early morning hours of June 4:

"Around one a.m. we were still gathering around the Monument to the People's Heroes. The army's loudspeakers kept announcing that they were about to 'clear the square at any cost and by any means.' So everyone must leave at once, or else they would treat us as criminals. In the square the soldiers set fire to our piles of tents and clothes. Against the backdrop of the flames, a swarm of troops was moving toward us from West Chang'an Avenue. When they got within one hundred meters, eight soldiers started to fire at us. The bullets hit the ground about one or two meters from our feet, and then bounced up and hit many people in their legs and torsos. Some students fell to the ground. Now the troops were coming closer, and I could see their faces, some of them wearing casual smirks. That outraged me. They stopped and stood there holding submachine guns and firing at our feet. The front row of soldiers fired simultaneously, the bullets hitting the ground with dull thuds. At times a few bullets were shot directly at people. For the first time I came to know what it was like to kill! People's lives were so easily snuffed out. Even if you were only hit in the arm or leg, you could still bleed to death. All of us got more outraged and shouted in unison to the troops, 'The People's Army loves people!' That stopped them briefly, then they resumed firing. We realized that things were too dangerous, so we began to retreat. By now about a thousand local citizens and students were already leaving the square, and we joined them. Our security team walked together with the local citizens. We often paused to rescue wounded students, but many of them had to be left where they had fallen—we couldn't get close to them. The firing was so torrential that we simply couldn't get close to the bodies and had to leave the square.

"Soon after we'd gotten out of the square, I went back to see if all the students had retreated. Some were still there, along with the local residents, gathering at a spot east of the reviewing platform under Tiananmen Tower. Nearby a tank was burning in flames. The troops and the local citizens and the students were facing each other in a stalemate. I joined the remaining students there, and we all held hands and belted out 'The Internationale.' The troops were arranged in a formation, ready to attack: the front row all stood toting AK-47s; behind them was a video camera on a tripod being manned by a soldier; next to him stood an officer with jug ears. If I remember correctly, he was a lieutenant colonel. He glared at us with fiery eyes.

"It was just past two a.m. now. A bus was being driven from the South Water Pools into the motorway at the front of Tiananmen Tower, running from east to west, toward us. At Golden Water Bridge it swerved right and stopped in between the troops and us. All at once bullets were unleashed on the bus and killed the driver. Then some soldiers rushed over and pulled five or six students off the bus. The soldiers smashed the windows with their rifle butts and found two cans of gasoline and some Molotov cocktails. Among the detained was Guo

Haifeng, the secretary at large of the Beijing Students' Autonomous Federation. They frisked him and found his ID, which said he was a graduate student of Beijing University, and they also discovered the master pass we had issued him, which meant he could go anywhere in Tiananmen Square. So they identified him as a leader.

"At this point I recognized him too; he was the last one dragged out of the bus. I rushed up to save him from the soldiers' hands. He was my friend and a good man. I cried out, 'I'm the general commander of the security team. The People's Army ought to love people. We have no weapons whatsoever, please let him go.'

"The lieutenant colonel came up and without a word, raised his Type 54 pistol and fired three shots at me. One of the bullets hit my thigh and shattered the bone. It didn't go through my leg, its melted lead spilled into my bone and some also stuck in the outside muscles of my right leg. My fellow students carried me to a quiet spot outside our broadcast station at the monument. I told them to inform Chai Ling, the chief commander of the students, that I was breathing my last. They put me and three other wounded members of the security team into a run-down jeep, which couldn't move by itself. There was a medical student wearing a white coat who told me that the other three on the jeep were wounded so badly that they might die soon. About a hundred locals and students pushed the disabled vehicle all the way to Benevolent Hospital.

"The doctors couldn't take out the bullet stuck in my thighbone, so they left it in there. I carried it in my leg for nineteen years. Not until 2008 did I have it pulled out at a hospital in Paris." He took out a squat, deformed slug and showed it to the audience. Due to the distance between us, I couldn't see it clearly, but people at the front could tell it was a hideous bullet.

After Zhang Jian's speech, there was a one-hour lunch break. In the atrium sandwiches and wraps were provided for all attendees, and there were also coffee and soft drinks. The group of students from Boston University sat around a low glass coffee table in a corner, eating in silence. Some of them looked upset, with damp eyes. I joined them, holding a cheese and ham wrap on a Styrofoam plate and an orange soda.

I asked them, "What did you think of the morning's talks?"

A tall young man with a buzz cut said, "How come I never heard of the Tiananmen Square Massacre? My dad went to graduate school in Beijing at that time, but he never breathed a word about the suppression. This is incredible." He held out his hand to me. "I'm Jason Wang."

I shook his hand and said to no one in particular, "Do you believe what the last guy said about the killings and bloodshed?"

They all nodded without a word. They looked like they were in a daze. A small girl sobbed, still munching on her turkey sandwich, "It hurts to know this! Those meaningless attacks on unarmed civilians, and all the official lies we were fed for so many years. I feel betrayed."

Jason said, "I'm going to call my dad tonight and demand he tell me the truth."

"I agree with the Tiananmen Mothers," another girl put in. "The criminals must be brought to justice or this whole thing will be a curse on the Communist Party."

I said, "Yes, it's like a malignant tumor—the longer they keep it, the more deadly it will grow."

A young man wearing glasses joined in. "The students were our age at the time. They were so brave and endured so much. All their hopes and dreams were shattered by the violent crackdown. I don't know what I might have done if I had gone through that kind of destruction and trauma."

"This hit me right here," another girl added, touching her heart.

They all agreed that it was shameful and outrageous to keep such an enormous tragedy under the rug. Sooner or later the truth would come out in broad daylight and haunt those who were responsible.

At one the conference resumed. The next speaker, Wu Renhua, was a historian and had also been a former leader of the student movement in Tiananmen Square; he had been in charge of the hunger strikers' petition and served as a picket. At that time he had already been a researcher at China University of Political Science and Law in Beijing. He had earned his master's in classics from Beijing University and specialized in editing and compiling historical works. After the events of June 1989, he was on the government's blacklist, which consisted of forty-nine dissidents. He fled to the south and moved around, staying in hiding until March 1990, when he swam for four hours from Zhuhai to Macau. His application for political asylum was granted, and he came to the States, settled down in LA, and became an editor of a dissident newspaper, the *Press Freedom Herald*. Then he took it upon himself to compile the historical records of the student movement in 1989. That became his vocation. For two decades he'd kept doing it. With his steel-rimmed glasses, Wu looked urbane and scholarly, and he had a bony face, with delicate features. He was from the coastal province of Zhejiang and spoke Mandarin with a southern accent, as well as some English. I stood next to him on stage, interpreting for him. It was intense work, and I had to concentrate to remember his sentences, but I managed.

He started by picking up the previous speaker's topic, the random killings. He said, "There was a student named Duan Canglong, a chemical industry senior at Tsinghua University. When the PLA began firing at people, Duan went out, biking around in search of his younger sister and his girlfriend. Soon he couldn't ride his bicycle anymore and had to push it through the crowds. Nearing the Cultural Palace of Nationalities at West Chang'an Avenue and Xidan Road, he saw a swarm of local citizens confronting troops of the Thirty-Eighth Army. The civilians were outraged by the killings in the city while the soldiers looked fierce, about to attack. It seemed another incident of bloodshed might break out at any second. So Duan went over to mediate.

He approached an officer, but Duan was hardly able to begin speaking before the officer pulled out his handgun and fired at his chest. He fell to the ground. A Beijing Medical University student picked him up and carried him on his back all the way to the Post Hospital. Duan Canglong died on arrival. The bullet had cut the artery in the left part of his heart. In the same hospital the people who had taken Duan there found many dead bodies, among them Wu Guofeng, an industrial management junior at the People's University. Wu had four gunshot wounds, one in the back of his head. Even more outrageous, there was a knife wound in his lower belly, about three inches long. According to eyewitnesses, Wu hadn't died right away after being shot three times. A soldier had stabbed him in the abdomen and twisted the bayonet. That had ripped Wu Guofeng's intestines to pieces. Then another soldier fired a round at the back of his head."

Loana stepped in and told the audience, "The Tiananmen Mothers have kept a full record of Duan Canglong and Wu Guofeng, including interviews with their parents, which give more details about them. If you're interested, you can go to our website and read about them."

A man in the audience stood up and asked the speaker, "Did you see dead bodies with your own eyes?"

"Of course," Wu Renhua replied calmly. "After rejoining the students outside of Tiananmen Square on the early morning of June 4, I went back to my work at the University of Political Science and Law. Thousands of students were sobbing on campus, seven dead bodies were lying in the lobby of the main building and covered with white sheets. Blood was flowing on the ground. The students were lamenting the deaths of their schoolmates and condemning the murderous army. Someone shouted, 'They don't have gunshot wounds on them! They don't have gunshot wounds on them!' He meant the dead had all been crushed by tanks. I lifted a sheet and saw a young woman whose arm had a bullet hole, but she looked calm, as if in sleep. In fact, she died of poison gas used by the army. But the rest of the dead were all crushed by tanks. My friend Liu Suli was teaching at the university at the time, and he and I dropped to our knees in front of the dead and couldn't stop wailing. It was at that moment when I made up my mind to become a historian and to fully record this crime against humanity. These words kept ringing in my mind: 'Never forget, never forget!' They later became the motto of my calling."

Wu had done a prodigious amount of work in his chosen field and had written several books. To avoid overwhelming the audience with too much information, he summarized whenever he could. He said there had been fourteen field armies that participated in the suppression in Beijing—all told, more than 180,000 troops, in addition to tens of thousands of armed police. He went on to describe briefly each army's task and route to downtown Beijing. He singled out two armies as the most brutal to the students and local residents: the Thirty-Eighth Army and the Fifteenth Army, the latter being China's only airborne force. It was the most violent of all. Every one of its troops held an AK-47 and would shout "No mercy to rioters!" and "Death to hoodlums!" They fired all the way through Hufang Bridge, Skywalk Overpass, Pearl Market Gate, Front Gate; it was a long way, at least a quarter of a mile, but they went through the length in just fifteen minutes, shooting and crushing whoever happened to be in their way.

The same rotund man who had challenged Loana in the morning stood up in the front row and spoke to Wu Renhua. "We all know that the commander of the Thirty-Eighth Army, General Xu Xianqin, refused to carry out the orders from the Central Military Commission and was later court-martialed and given a five-year prison term. How did his army become a murderous force? This is incredible."

Wu said with a rush of emotion, "Indeed, General Xu was a hero and suffered for following his conscience. He said to his officers, 'Even if they behead me, I won't be a criminal of history. This crackdown on the civilians has nothing to do with me.' He told his superiors that he couldn't execute the order of entering Beijing at all costs. Then he returned to the hospital, where he was being treated for a kidney stone. So his subordinates stepped in and took over the command, ordering the troops to move ahead. They intended to show their loyalty to the party so as to exonerate themselves. That was how the whole army turned murderous. People on the streets heard of General Xu's refusal to obey orders and assumed that his army, China's top force, which had been garrisoned in Beijing's eastern suburbs for decades, was going in to attack those who had turned on civilians. But that was wishful thinking. In truth, the Thirty-Eighth Army was the most vicious of all and killed countless demonstrators on the streets."

Wu paused, then continued, "Speaking of decent officers, I'd like to mention a few more. When Wu Jiamin, the Commander of the Fortieth Army, received orders that they break into the city by any means, 'including radical measures,' he understood that meant they could open fire. But he told his troops, 'I'm over fifty years old. This is the first time I've directed such an operation. But the military orders came like an avalanche, and we have no choice but to obey. Brothers, I beg you: after we get into the city, no matter what, always raise the muzzles of your guns an inch higher when you fire.' To date, throughout my research and investigations, I haven't come across a single case that showed someone wounded by the Fortieth Army. Also, I ought to mention a pair of top officers of the Twenty-Eighth Army, specifically its Commissar General Zhang Mingchun and its Commander General Ho Yanran. Their army was garrisoned in Datong City of Shanxi Province. When they arrived at a suburb of Beijing, they were ordered to enter the city and reach Tiananmen Square as soon as possible. But early on the morning of June 4, they were blocked by the civilians at Mu Xidi, near West Chang'an Avenue. The two generals didn't force their troops to move on. Somehow they appeared quite relaxed and even cracked jokes. Commander Ho pointed at the swarm of people and said, 'Thick and tall crops are everywhere.' He was referring to the anti-Japanese war, in which guerrillas moved around in crop fields to attack the Japanese invaders, who had sunk into the sea of the people's war. General Zhang picked up the joke and added, 'A hundred thousand youths have become a hundred thousand troops.' General Ho even said to the commissar that he wasn't sure which one of them would be court-martialed when this whole mess was over. The officers of the Twenty-Eighth Army emphasized to the local residents that they would never open fire on them, but some people sneered, saying that soldiers had already killed many civilians. The troops were incredulous and demanded proof. 'Show them the bloody clothes! Show them the bloody clothes!' some voices yelled in the crowd. A few people went to a nearby hospital and brought back a bundle of shirts, pants, and skirts, all drenched in blood. They displayed them, and the soldiers were stunned. Many hopped off their vehicles and stepped away, and some even surrendered their weapons. Then the civilians set fire to the trucks, armored personnel carriers, and even a communication wagon—in total, seventy-four abandoned vehicles burned to wrecks. Some soldiers even showed the civilians how to set an armored car alight. Around noon, a helicopter flew over and barked orders at the Twenty-Eighth Army: 'You must move forward. No more delay! The Central Military Commission orders you to reach Tiananmen Square at all costs, as soon as possible. Move ahead this instant!' But the whole army never moved. Around five they were withdrawn from Beijing. The Central Military Commission was furious and demoted both the commander and the commissar to provincial garrisons. General Zhang was so depressed that he died a year later."

The audience seemed surprised by the death of that brave officer as a hushed silence fell in the auditorium. Wu went on, "I should mention Division 116 of the Thirty-Ninth Army, in which our next speaker, Mr. Li, served at the time. That division was an esteemed unit in the PLA, ranked number two in the whole of the Chinese army. Its commander was Xu Feng. On the afternoon of June 3, the division was ordered to leave its makeshift barracks in Tongzhou, east of Beijing, and to reach Tiananmen Square 'at all costs and by any measure.' They had to get there and clear the square in the small hours of June 4. Along the way they were stopped by civilians time and again. In the evening, Division Commander Xu put on civvies and entered the city with a few scouts ahead of his men. They went downtown and got closer to Tiananmen Square to assess the situation. At this moment word came that the troops of other field armies ahead of them had begun killing civilians. The news disturbed the soldiers of Division 116. Commander Xu came back with a dark face and told his underlings, 'I can't get in touch with those above me or receive their orders, so don't bother me from now on.' He got into a communication wagon and wouldn't come out again. As a result, the whole division was stuck, just moving around outside the downtown area and waiting for instructions from above. In fact, according to one of their radiomen, the divisional headquarters could hear the

Central Command clearly—it kept calling to say 'Division 116, where are you now? Please reply.' But nobody responded to the request. They stayed put for the whole day of June 4. The next morning, around six, a senior officer from the Thirty-Eighth Army's Operation Office came to give orders in person. He got on a truck that had had two machine guns installed on top of its cab, leading Division 116 away to Tiananmen Square. Because of Commander Xu's passivity, he was discharged from the army shortly after the massacre."

After Wu Renhua's talk, we had a brief coffee break. I was so exhausted from interpreting for him that I found a quiet spot on the same floor and took a catnap. I covered my face with a campus newspaper, though some passersby might still have been able to recognize me by my dress, stockings, and slingbacks.

The conference resumed. The next speaker was Li Xiaoming, a former junior officer in Division 116 who had been involved in Tiananmen suppression. He was tall and slim, with bright eyes and a short, grizzled beard. He'd fled to Australia a few years ago, and that was why we were able to fly him over for this conference. Loana interviewed him onstage, while David, a Taiwanese graduate student, sat next to him, serving as his interpreter. Loana said that to date, Mr. Li was the only PLA soldier who had dared to speak about the tragedy publicly. Then she began the interview. Loana first asked her questions in Chinese, then translated them herself. She asked him to describe how he had participated in the suppression of the democracy movement.

Li seemed to already have in mind a draft of what he was going to say. After every five or six sentences, he would stop for David to translate. The interpreter held a yellow writing pad and jotted down notes while Mr. Li was speaking. Li said, "That year I was in charge of a radar station of the First Battalion in the 166th Division's antiaircraft artillery regiment. Our barracks were outside Shenyang City. In late May we received orders to head for Beijing, leaving behind our radar equipment. The soldiers were baffled and unhappy, because we were radarmen, not foot soldiers. Obviously we were used as infantry. Our division stayed in the suburbs of Beijing and didn't enter the city, although we were given full ammo, and once in a while, we saw tanks roaring by, heading toward Beijing. On the morning of June 3, while I was napping, I was woken up by the noise of an engine. I saw an armored personnel carrier knock aside a bus that had blocked the road, and then a machine gun on the turret started shooting. The personnel carrier was heading to the city at full speed. Our division could easily have followed the armored vehicle and gotten into the city, but we didn't move. Instead, we just lingered, as though we had bogged down. On the evening of June 4, our trucks were still parked alongside paddy fields in a suburb. Everyone was troubled and stayed quiet; nobody wanted to chat. We couldn't doze off either, because in the distance, beyond the steel plant, the sky was scarlet with flames. The view reminded me of the chimneys of crematoriums in Nazi concentration camps that I had once seen

LOOKING FOR TANK MAN

in a documentary. We were the People's Army. How come all of the sudden some of the troops were butchering the city's inhabitants? How could we justify such a use of force? Thank heaven our division had a decent commander. He didn't plunge us into the violence."

"When did you enter Beijing and reach Tiananmen Square?" asked Loana.

Li replied, "Around six o'clock the next morning, a senior officer from the Thirty-Eighth Army came and forced us to move forward. He got on a truck that had a pair of machine guns mounted on the roof of its cab. We had to follow him. Along the way, I saw a lot of burned army vehicles, and angry crowds of local residents shouted slogans at us. That was how we eventually reached Tiananmen Square."

Loana said, "Did you fire your guns?"

"I didn't fire a single shot, but some soldiers got incensed when people in some residential buildings yelled 'Fascists!' and 'Murderers!' at them. They fired at some of the apartment buildings the voices came from."

"Did you see dead bodies in Tiananmen Square?" Loana asked again.

"I didn't see dead bodies in the square. Actually, I didn't join the other troops in clearing the square, because we arrived almost a day late. My task was to stay with our vehicle, but I saw splotches of blood. Some of my comrades took part in the clearing. They came back and told me they had seen some pants, shirts, and underclothes with bullet holes on them. Evidently there was bloodshed."

Loana pressed, "So your division didn't kill any civilians thanks to the brave Commander Xu?"

"I wouldn't say that. Our superiors told us to fire above people's heads if they cursed at us, just to scare them. But there were soldiers who actually fired at people. Everyone was angry and mad. Things got out of hand. I heard from a soldier in our battalion that he had fired a clip into a crowd. Hearing that, my heart dropped and my vision blurred. The crowds were so dense. Imagine a whole clip, thirty rounds, how many people were killed by that? I know the man in person, but I won't name him here. If in the future he is tried at court, I'll be willing to serve as a witness."

Following the interview was a short Q and A, but I didn't stay for it, since I had to make sure that the pizza and soft drinks were delivered and arranged properly in the atrium.

8

AS SOON AS the conference was over, I left Boston and headed to Beijing for the summer. A couple of days later, I heard from Jason Wang, the student at Boston University. He emailed: "My friends and I greatly appreciated your conference and felt overwhelmed by the experience. In fact, we were quite shaken and often broke into tears when we shared the contents of the conference with our peers at BU. We all feel we were tricked by our education back in China, because none of us knew what had really happened in Beijing in the spring of 1989. But after the symposium, I now believe that the government went overboard, and that it was a huge blunder. I did more research and came across the long list of those killed that has been compiled by the Tiananmen Mothers. There are 202 deaths on the list, which supplies each victim's name, a brief bio, and the manner and place of their death. I was horrified by the large scale of killings, which in every sense was a massacre. The youngest victim was just a young boy, nine years old, a third grader. After the research, I changed my mind. The violent suppression was not a mistake but a crime. Even worse, for twenty years the government has been trying to cover up its crime. This simply increased the monstrosity of the violation. The longer they do this, the deeper they will sink into the depths of their atrocities. Thanks to Professor Hong and you for opening our eyes and making us reevaluate our past and ourselves. Please keep us posted on your future events."

I forwarded Jason's letter to Loana. She was delighted, saying she would share it with some of her colleagues, specifically those who had misgivings about her "obsession" with making the Tiananmen movement an essential part of her scholarship, because they didn't see it as intellectually substantial. I wrote to remind her not to reveal Jason's name. She responded, "Of course, I'll keep his letter anonymous and won't reveal his email address. I will refer to Jason only as a student of a local college."

Loana got a summer grant enabling her to travel to France and Germany, where she planned to meet some dissidents in exile and interview them. Summertime was supposed to be restful for me, but in spite of that I read a lot, preparing for the coursework in the fall. When school resumed, I'd be a senior, and after the last year of college, I'd have to either go find a job in China or continue to study for a graduate degree.

My mother said to me, "Why work so hard? Find a good young man and get married. Then I can feel at ease about you."

She placed a bowl of seaweed soup in the center of the round dining table for both of us. We were having buns stuffed with turnip slivers and eggs for dinner, bought from an eatery at a street corner nearby. Mother was happy to have me home. I could see that she was proud of me, especially when she was talking with our neighbors. But I'd feel uneasy whenever an "auntie" or "uncle" told their kids about me: "See, she's the elder sister going to Harvard. You must take her as a model."

I complained to my mother one evening, "I wish people in our neighborhood would leave me alone. In America, nobody notices me and I have a lot of privacy, but here everyone thinks of me as a success. I'm just a struggling college student like everyone else."

"But the truth is that with your kind of education, you can easily find a good job in Beijing." She grinned, smiling a bit indulgingly. "That's why people consider you a success."

"That's not true, Mom. It's hard to find a job I really like."

"Lulu, you ought to have the right attitude." She lifted her teacup and took a sip. "How many people truly enjoy their day jobs? I wanted to be a medical doctor when I was young, but I have to work on fragments of ancient objects every day, sometimes on bones collected from ancient tombs. Still, people admire my research job."

"We don't live for others. One's life belongs to oneself, and one must live it well and make good use of it."

"That's very American. If you come back to China, you won't be able to thrive here with that type of mentality. We have to think of others first."

"Then what should I do, come back or continue to study in the States?"

"By any means come back."

Usually I didn't agree with her. It seemed to me she tended to lack sound judgment when dealing with matters outside the household. Within our family, she was an expert in everything, always knowing what to get and how to get it. She was good at balancing our budget and managed to save quite a bit. But outside our household her vision was rather limited. She had been a good wife for my father, cooking for him every day and keeping the home clean and neat, but she couldn't see how the world operated beyond the domestic sphere. For many years I had been angry at her poor judgment about dissolving her marriage and agreeing to the divorce proposed by my father. Living and working away, unable to join us in Beijing due to his residential registration in Tianjin, he had started an affair with a graduate student of his and then wanted to marry the young woman. He confessed to my mother to sound her out about the possibility of a divorce. She was outraged, her self-respect and pride wounded. To everyone's surprise, she filed for divorce, saying she could easily find a man better than my father. Her parents were mad at her, calling her a bookish fool with no sense of reality. She was already getting close to forty. Worse still, she had me, a child, in tow. Most Chinese men were reluctant to marry a single mother, calling their children "soy sauce bottles," which meant they were redundant, since you can always get a new bottle when you buy soy sauce.

The divorce went through, and my father was pleased. After that, Mother often wept in silence at night. I overheard her but didn't know what to say. I was angry at both of them but sided with her because he had betrayed her in the first place. My mother's self-confidence had been based on an illusion. She was pretty for a woman her age, with still-vivid eyes and a shapely figure in addition to her soft, urbane voice. Before the divorce, men would drop by her archaeology institute to see her. They chatted with her and must have ogled her as well. Perhaps she enjoyed all the attention from the opposite sex. After my dad had left, she often asked me, "What do you think of Uncle Liu?" Liu was one of those men who seemed to be after her. Or, "Do you like Uncle Jia?" That was another one who used to flirt with her, although the men all had their own families. I told her that they were all right, but in reality I disliked all of them. Behind her questions lurked a secret desire to see them going after her seriously now that she was finally available. She began to dress more brightly, as if the divorce had shaved off a few years of her age. Yet to her disappointment, all the frivolous men disappeared from her life, and none of them showed up at her workplace anymore. They even avoided her when they bumped into her, as if she had a disease they could catch. I once overheard her telling a friend of hers that those men were all cowards, with hearts of mice. I often wondered how much my mother must hate herself when she turned and tossed alone in bed at night.

But she seemed to lack self-reflection, like most other Chinese of the older generation. They believed in the collective and rarely gazed into themselves. Even their souls had to belong to the country, as they had been indoctrinated. In recent years, whenever I was back in Beijing, I was troubled by the surveillance cameras ("dragonfly eyes") that kept a close watch on you wherever you went. My mother had read *1984*, in a somewhat censored Chinese translation. So I complained one night, saying "Big Brother is watching you all the time. But it's getting worse in China. Soon they'll keep an eye on your butt when you sit on a toilet."

"You have a tongue sharp like a knife, Lulu," my mother said, and then sucked her teeth, twisting her mouth, which had thin lines around it now. "I'm not bothered by the surveillance cameras. At least they deter thieves and hoodlums. They have really enhanced the security of our society. Don't you know that the crime rate has dropped precipitously, by more than 30 percent, since the installation of those cameras? Even foreign visitors praise Beijing as one of the safest cities in the world. There's a real advantage to having electronic surveillance. It doesn't bother me that much. If you have a straight posture, you won't mind the slanting shadow it casts. No worries at all."

"People are not domesticated animals and shouldn't be kept like this. Freedom is essential for a decent life, and it might preclude security."

"I can see that you have accepted American values too easily."

I thought, What's wrong with that? But I didn't let it out.

She and I didn't argue anymore. I felt she was pitiable, but I loved her and was also worried about her lonely life. Unlike the older people in our neighborhood, who went out to dance in parks and squares and gossip at tea stands, she spent her free time reading and watching Korean TV plays. Indeed, if I came back and got a job, I could live with her. That might make her life less desolate. I was sure she was afraid I wouldn't come back.

Ever since early June, she had urged me to become an intern at a company. I was not that interested, because deep down, I felt I could always find a way to earn my keep. My written English was quite good, and I could freelance, translating Chinese books and documents into English. Such work pays well, at least twice as much as translation from English into Chinese. There were not many people who could do such work here. Recently I had come across an interview given by a publisher who complained that there were few capable Chinese-to-English translators now. "In all of China only five or six people are good enough for this kind of work," the man told the interviewer. "Surely a lot of young people have learned English since childhood and many have gone abroad for education, but they can only speak the foreign tongue, and few can write it well. Written English is an art that few Chinese have mastered."

That gave me the idea that down the road I could freelance for a publisher if I returned to China after college. I was confident I could become a decent translator if it came to earning a living with my pen.

I told my mother, "I have so many books to read for the fall that I shouldn't go out working in the summer. Don't worry about my future. I might not look for a nine-to-five job. Maybe I can be a freelance translator."

I had shared this idea with her before, so she knew what I had in mind. She said, "Even for such work, you need to know some editors and publishing companies. Else how can you find work? They won't let you participate in their projects otherwise." She snapped a pole bean.

I picked up another bean from a bamboo basket and pulled off its string. For dinner, we were going to stew them with potatoes, one of my favorite dishes. I told her, "My English is much better now and I'll be useful to many publishers when I'm back. Don't worry about me."

"You'd better expand your orbit for your future," she said.

"Our family is my orbit."

"You don't understand. You have to build a network and make people like you. Otherwise, how will they know and trust you?"

I didn't want to argue with her. To some extent she was right. In China networking is a matter of survival. I remembered what an author had written recently, declaring in a powerful official's voice: "If I say you're capable, you are capable, even though you're incapable. If I say you're incapable, you are incapable, even though you're capable." That's how officials judge people. Indeed, ability and talent could hardly help you survive in China—finding the right people and getting to be liked by them were the way to success. But I hated networking, which was an abnormal way of life to me. I didn't want to attach myself to anyone.

Mother and I talked about my father. I was supposed to see him soon. She didn't like the idea but still let me go to Tianjin, probably because he had been paying my living expenses at college. I promised her that I'd come back the same day. She was pleased by my concern about her feelings.

9

I LIKED TO visit my father's family mainly because I love my two younger brothers, Yawei and Yasheng, who were twins and already in second grade. People all said my father was a lucky man because he had had two sons at one attempt (one shot that lands two birds), given that he and his young wife, Meichin, hadn't been allowed to have a second child. Yawei was one hour older than Yasheng, but the younger boy was bigger and stronger, and also more rambunctious. Whenever I was with them, they wanted me to take them to snack bars or play video games with them. Being an only child when I grew up, I had often longed for siblings. And if I got married someday, I also wanted to have a couple of kids of my own.

It was Tuesday, and my brothers were at school, which didn't let out for the summer until mid-July, so I left the ten bars of milk chocolate, which I'd brought back from the States, with their mother. Meichin smiled appreciatively, two lines bracketing her thin nose. "The boys will be thrilled to have these. Thank you so much, Lulu!" she said. She had aged some, no longer the young beauty who behaved with studied ebullience, though I wouldn't say she'd lost her looks. Now in her thirties, she still had a willowy figure with a narrow waist, and she was wearing hoop earrings and jade bangles.

"When will they come back in the afternoon?" I asked.

"Around three o'clock."

"So I'll be able to see them before I head back."

"Of course."

I had mixed feelings about Meichin, who had broken up my family, and my mother hated her. But I could see that she was quite devoted to my dad and had managed to give him a comfortable, thriving home. Their townhouse was spacious, with six rooms, and it was stylishly furnished. The sectional sofas alone, made of deerskin, must have cost a fortune. My father's studio was in the loft, and there was also a garage in their basement. This place might be worth about three million dollars now. Small wonder he had to work hard to make money, since there must be a sizable mortgage to pay.

Around noon my dad and I went out for lunch at a place nearby. As usual, Meichin didn't join us. She wanted to let us spend some time alone. She was smart and understanding. I could see that when she'd been young and beautiful, she must have been chased by many men, so I didn't hate her like my mom did. She must be a loving mother and a devoted wife.

My dad and I went to a restaurant called Yummy, Yummy—Every Bite, which had excellent seafood noodles. We each ordered a bowl. "Would you like something else?" he asked, turning a menu open to me. "They have excellent cold cuts and pot stickers."

"No, the noodles are enough for me," I said. I didn't like to eat too much.

When our orders had come, I told him about my concern about what to do after college. "My mom wants me to come back, but I'm not sure of that," I said.

"Why rush back so soon?" he asked, his chopsticks twiddling a small bundle of buckwheat noodles. "Are you already tired of America?" He had been to the States a couple of times for art shows, and once in a while a few pieces of his work had also been exhibited in group events there.

"I like America a lot," I said. "But I'm worried about Mom. She's getting on in years and must be feeling lonely, thanks to you and Meichin."

"Come on, don't start this again. I know I let your mom down, but we're talking about you. I don't think you should be in a hurry to look for a job here. There might be other opportunities for you, so you shouldn't think of rushing back. It's always better to study than to work."

"Mom wants me to find a suitable man and get married soon."

"Is that what you want?" He was eating with little slurps, like most noodle lovers here.

"Not really," I said. "I'd like to continue to study."

"Toward a graduate degree?"

"Probably, but that'll take several years and a lot of dedication."

"What would you study if you got into a graduate program?"

"Probably the Tiananmen Square Massacre."

His face twitched, as if he were stung. Then he said, "That's not a bad subject, actually, but it's not something you can study here, so it would probably be a good choice. Because of its rarity, the subject might become more valuable in the long run."

"So you think I should study the democracy movement in 1989?"

"That's not what I meant, exactly. You must always follow your own heart. What I'm trying to say is that the choice of your subject will affect your future and your life. But then what the hell? Who's to tell what will happen when you come back? You shouldn't be too pragmatic about this. Being a history major is already not a practical choice. To tell you the truth, I always admire impractical people. We Chinese are too pragmatic, too clever, too calculating. That's why we don't have many great philosophers or master artists. The world is improved by impractical people. Don't be too practical."

"So you don't mind if I work on the Tiananmen Square Massacre?"

"If you like it, then do it. I don't believe that with a degree from Harvard you will ever starve. Don't worry too much about your future." He waved his left hand, which was missing its pinkie; once he'd told me he lost the digit to an electric saw when he was a rookie sculptor.

What he'd said about my future was reassuring. I was heartened, but knew my mother would be mad at me if I told her that the Tiananmen Square Massacre was going to be the focus of my future study. She had even opposed my applying to graduate school, believing I had already spent enough time at college. I told my father, "I worry about Mom. Life isn't easy for her when I'm away from home."

"She's much stronger than you think. We mustn't be nearsighted. In the future, if you settle down in America, she might be able to go and join you there. That way she can have a better life than she has here."

"She might never leave our apartment, which has become her home."

"I'm saying she'll have more choices if you live in America or someplace outside China. Above anything else, if you're an eagle, you must fly as far and as high as possible."

That felt like a cliché and gave me a sour taste in my mouth. I giggled, remembering those clay eagles he used to sculpt.

"What's so funny?" he asked.

"Nothing. You don't make eagles anymore?"

"No, the market for that kind of bird sculpture is dead. For now I've been making dragons and Buddhas."

I appreciated his encouraging words. In many people's eyes I might have a bright future, but I'd never felt that way. Even my admission to Harvard might have been a fluke. I had been an outstanding student at Tsinghua University High School, but I wasn't one of the top five. I got lucky at the interview, which was conducted by some Harvard professors in the downtown Hilton Hotel. They had asked me why I applied to their school and what I expected to learn at Harvard. I said, "I want to study social sciences or the humanities so that I can change myself and eventually improve our society." Professor Daniels, a small old man with a kind, smiling face, asked me to elaborate. I told them about a peasant family in Henan Province that had contracted HIV because they have been selling their blood. The parents both died, leaving behind a girl and a young boy, who also suffered from AIDS. The girl had to beg in order to feed her four-year-old brother. Someone posted their suffering and predicament online, which caught a lot of attention. A few of my schoolmates, myself included, asked for donations. We collected more than half a million yuan, nearly seventy thousand dollars, but to our horror, none of the money actually reached the girl and her brother. The people and organizations in between kept the funds under various pretexts. Even worse, the girl appeared online begging people not to worry about her and her brother anymore, because, in her own words: "Our country will take good care of us. We have been treated by the best medical personnel. We trust our government. We don't need your help, especially the help from abroad. Please leave us alone." I sensed something terribly wrong with the girl's mindset and with the society we were living in. That was why I wanted to study social sciences or the humanities and eventually figure out the problems in our society and find solutions to them.

I later learned that I was the only interviewee who expressed a keen interest in the liberal arts. The others all wanted to specialize in the hard sciences. That might have given me an edge in my application. In fact, when I later ran into Professor Daniels on campus, he smiled and said he remembered me, impressed by my "bold and heartfelt answers" in the interview.

Yawei and Yasheng came back around midafternoon. At the sight of me, they rushed over and hugged me, pressing their faces against my waist and beaming with happiness. I went with them to their room, in which they each had a computer that sat on a desk beside their identical beds. Even their lamps were identical. They showed me a war game that had a lot of monsters and flying creatures. I pretended to be interested, just to humor them. An eviscerated laptop sat on the floor in a corner of the room. Yawei, bespectacled and half a head shorter than Yasheng, was a computer whiz. He had been assembling his own laptop. They had started learning English at school this year. They showed me their textbooks, which were full of platitudes, such as "I love my motherland! We must work hard to build a harmonious society!"

"What does 'a harmonious society' mean?" I was amazed that such a slogan, coined by the party's Propaganda Department just a few years ago, appeared in a children's English textbook, where a word like "harmonious" was too big, too much of a mouthful for beginning learners.

They both shook their heads and couldn't answer. I said, "If your teacher asks you to read out this sentence again, you should ask her what 'a harmonious society' is like."

More surprisingly, their pronunciation was deplorable, incomprehensible, as though their tongues had been crippled. If they continued to learn English this way, they might become messed up, never able to speak the language clearly and fluently. I told Meichin, "English is taught differently in Beijing, where the teachers are much better. In my high school, we actually had two American teachers." I knew it would cost a fortune to have private English tutors, but it would be a better investment than the money spent on luxury cars, brandname bags, jewelry.

"I wish I had known this earlier," she said, genuinely worried. "What should we do? Both your dad and I want the boys to speak English like you in the future."

"Maybe hire a private tutor to help them with English. Today I can record a few lessons for them so they can follow my way of speaking when they practice."

"That's great. We can't thank you enough, Lulu."

I read out eight lessons from their textbook. The recording was clear and crisp, so Yawei and Yasheng were impressed. Yawei said, "I've never met anyone who speaks English as well as you, sister."

I told them that actually my oral English was just so-so, but I could write better. Next year, when I came back, I'd teach them more. They loved that idea.

In fact, Meichin seemed eager to have me more involved in the two boys' life. She often urged them, "Try to learn from your sister Lulu." She might mean they should follow in my footsteps. I didn't tell her that I wasn't really a top student—my admission to Harvard was largely due to luck.

My father was pleased to see that his young wife and I could get along. Before I returned to Beijing that evening, I asked him to keep an eye on my mother when I was away in America. He said, "Rest assured, even though your mom might still hate my guts, I respect her and will watch after her."

I blurted out the proverb, half in jest, "One day spent together as man and wife guarantees a lifelong affection, doesn't it?"

He smiled with a nod of his head, though he looked uneasy and sucked his teeth.

On my way to the train station, the bus had to be stopped on Huachang Road, near Walmart, because a top official came from Beijing and his motorcade needed to go before others. There were traffic cops everywhere. All the pedestrians and other vehicles had to halt to give way to the leader's retinue. Our bus stayed where we were for more than half an hour. That made me restless, worried that I might miss the train home, but people around me seemed untroubled by this delay. Everybody must be used to this kind of abuse of official privilege. Fortunately, even though I missed my train, there was another one an hour later and I was allowed to get aboard since it was a slow train. Most passengers on it were daily commuters, and their tickets didn't have the assigned seats that a fast train had.

10

IN MID-AUGUST, RACHEL'S father, Guo Huan, appeared in the news. Numerous customers had complained that they had received knockoffs and counterfeits in place of the genuine products advertised by his company. Although Mr. Guo was not the owner of Baobao, the online retailing business he worked for, it had to respond to the barrage of criticism. So Guo Huan, as a top manager in the company, was dismissed from his position. Apparently he had been chosen to be the scapegoat, and the unfair treatment he received was pointed out by the public. Many people argued that firing him wouldn't get rid of the fraudulence rooted in the company's system and culture.

The news made me think a lot about Rachel these days. Her father's dismissal might make her family regret having donated six million dollars to Harvard, and her life might change. She could no longer be a superrich girl. It might do her some good if she began to taste hardship like others. On the other hand, even if her family didn't have a prodigious income anymore, they should be able to manage. An emaciated camel is still larger than a horse—they might have other kinds of earnings. I didn't think I needed to worry too much about her.

Back on campus, I ran into Rachel at the Fogg Museum. She was having coffee alone in the vaulted-ceilinged lobby, with a half-eaten quiche next to her cup. I forced myself to say "Hey, can I join you?"

"Sure thing," she said with a grin and removed her tote bag from the metal chair next to her.

I bought a latte and came back to sit across from her. There was a palpable barrier between us, even though we both tried to pretend that everything was normal, like before. She hadn't returned home for the summer and instead had gone to Wall Street for an internship. I asked her if she had liked it there.

"I hated it," she said. "I told my parents I'd never do trading for a living."

My curiosity was piqued. I said, "Does this have something to do with your dad? I read about his trouble in the newspapers back home."

"I know he's notorious now, but that made me more determined to stay away from the bloody business world."

"Can your parents manage now that he lost his big job?"

"They're doing okay. They've accumulated some of the company stock. Compared to others, they're still well-to-do."

"I heard that your dad is just a scapegoat. He must be very upset."

LOOKING FOR TANK MAN

"He's unhappy about having lost his job, but he's already in his late fifties, close to retirement age, so he feels at peace with his situation now. He wants to do something he really likes. For years he kept grumbling that he was wasting his life making money. Now's the time for a change."

"What's he going to do?"

"He wants to paint. He always wanted to become an artist. I told him to take it easy and do it just for fun. The truth is that he spent his prime years building wealth. He no longer has the fresh creative energy an artist needs for his work. That's why I don't want to repeat his mistake."

"So you plan to go to graduate school?"

"I'm thinking about it."

"What will you study?"

"I don't have a practical field. Probably literature."

"That's bold, but I admire it," I said in earnest.

"I don't think a well-educated person will starve in America, so my parents don't mind if I pick a field that doesn't make money." She batted her round eyes as if smiling to herself.

"I've also been thinking of graduate school, but definitely not to study literature. That would be too hard for me."

"What do you want to study?"

"Nothing's certain yet, maybe history."

"That will make us a pair of rare birds in the humanities."

"History is often treated as a social science."

"But many schools list it as a branch of the humanities too."

That was true. I was pleased that Rachel seemed more than willing to reconnect with me as a friend. We also chatted about others. At my mention of Joe, Rachel sneered, wrinkling her turned-up nose. She said, "He's going to become a PhD candidate at MIT, he's already been accepted by a professor there. Once he starts full-time, his boss will pay him a big stipend for lab work, thirty-five grand a year."

"That's impressive. I might never pull in that kind of income." I wondered whether to pass my greetings on to Joe, but decided against it. I still didn't like him.

Rachel sighed and confessed, "He's opposed to my doing graduate work in literature. He said the humanities were useless, and that he had no use for fiction or poetry. He's only interested in sciences."

"So you two are still dating?"

"Yes, but Joe is a difficult person, you know that."

I didn't press her for more information on him; I wanted to leave someone that was so arrogant and zealous out of my orbit. Later I heard that the two of them had split, in part because Rachel wasn't as openhanded as before and no longer could afford to take him on cruises or to Europe for skiing and sightseeing. She must not have been fun for Joe anymore. Then I heard he had another girlfriend, one from Singapore. He was nasty about Rachel, badmouthing her behind her back, and even said she was a nympho, "broad like a city gate," meaning that everyone could enter. Such a sordid end to their relationship disturbed some of us who knew them. I could hardly imagine that an educated young man could be so crude, so unfeeling, so malicious. When I bumped into Rachel the next time, she had red eyes and a puffy face, and was apparently suffering from sleep deprivation. She claimed she'd never date a Chinese man again; to her, every Chinese man was potentially a wife or girlfriend abuser. Though I didn't share her bias, her quandary unsettled me and made me see that a bad boyfriend could easily mess up a girl, so I'd better not have such a relationship at college. That was what my mother had admonished me to avoid in America. For senior year, I'd better devote my energy and time to my studies. I also had to figure out what to do afterward.

11

I DROPPED IN on Loana and talked with her about my concerns and future plans. I wanted to do graduate work after college, but wasn't sure if I should go for a master's or a PhD in history. Loana was warm and always helpful. Smiling with pinkish cheeks, she explained, "You ought to go for a PhD, because most scholarships are given to doctoral students. Schools usually use master's students to make money for sustaining their PhD programs. Also, a master's can be awarded while you are completing your PhD."

"Doesn't a doctoral degree cost a lot?" I asked.

"No, you'll be paid to do the graduate work," she said.

"I don't understand. Why pay me for my study since I'm the beneficiary?"

"Because history is a branch of the humanities or a social science. Unlike a law or business degree, a PhD in an impractical field won't make you rich. But society needs some people to specialize in social sciences and the humanities. That's why they pay you to study. In general, a good graduate program gives a PhD candidate a financial package of five or six years—full tuition plus a substantial stipend. It's a lot of money, more than a regular worker can make. That means you'll be financially secure during your studies."

"It's great to know this. Then I can tell my parents that I'll be on my own if I get into a PhD program."

"Yes, you can assure them of that. What do they want you to do after college?"

"My mother wants me to get married and raise a family."

"Is that what you want?"

"Not really. In fact, my parents won't have a problem if I decide to do graduate work, but I just don't want to become a financial burden to them."

"Most people don't understand that as a rule, you don't spend your own money if you do a PhD."

"How long does it take to complete such a degree?"

"It depends. I finished mine in seven years. I have a friend who did his doctorate in history at the University of Chicago. It took him ten years, which is the average there."

"What? That's tremendous dedication, ten of your best years."

"Of course, it means you must love what you study. So don't rush to a decision. Think carefully. If you decide on a field, you should treat it as your lifelong calling."

Loana agreed to write a letter of recommendation for me if I decided to apply to graduate school. She also said I would need another letter from a professor, since as a rule most programs require at least two recommendations. I'd gotten an A for Professor Jeffrey Snelling's seminar on modern Japanese history, so perhaps I could ask him for a letter. Loana said, "That's a good idea. Jeff is a great guy, well respected in the field."

We also talked about what one could do with a PhD in the humanities or social sciences. Loana said most people became professors. "Do you like teaching?" she asked.

"I'm not sure. I've never taught," I said. "What else can I do if I don't like teaching?"

"You can do research or become an editor. There are other options. Above all, you must love what you study. Treat it as fun and eventually make a living out of it." She looked at me searchingly, narrowing her eyes a little, as though to assess my earnestness.

I was intimidated by the length of time needed for completing a PhD. I wasn't sure I was willing to spend many years at a desk in a carrel like Mark Stone, who seemed to enjoy his life in the library, poring over kung fu novels by Jin Yong and working on his dissertation. His life was like that of a book louse, though he looked happy and content. If I went for a PhD, I'd want to finish it within five or six years.

Speak of the devil—as I stepped out of Loana's office building on Divinity Avenue, I caught sight of Mark with Rachel. They were heading toward Oxford Street, Rachel's hand holding his upper arms, her big earrings jiggling a little. Their body language showed the close intimacy that only belonged to lovers. They must have been sleeping together, given that for Mark, going to bed with a woman was just like having dessert after an entrée. Somehow I couldn't tear my eyes away from them. Observing them from behind—Rachel shaking a bit with her head bowed while laughing—I couldn't help but feel a touch of bitterness. She was really a slut, I muttered to myself. From now on, I'd better give her a wide berth.

But whenever I went into the library, I passed Mark's carrel, in which the Tank Man poster remained on the door of his cabinet. I wanted to tear it off, but I checked my impulse. One afternoon I saw him bent over his desk, typing away at his laptop. He lifted his head and saw me, his face breaking into a smile. I said hello and pointed at the poster, saying, "You shouldn't keep that up."

"Why does it bother you so much?" he asked and grinned. He stood and seemed eager to chat some.

"It makes your workspace seem immature," I said.

"Don't be a bigot." He made a wry face and began twisting the small beard he'd been growing lately.

"We all know Tank Man might be fake."

"Who are 'we'?"

"If you don't believe me, ask Rachel. She also took Dr. Hong's seminar and can tell you about it."

"Rachel has no problem with this poster at all. I have another one in my living room. She's more easygoing than you."

"Of course she's easy."

"Whoa, whoa, she thinks highly of you and values you as a friend. Why are you so bitter?"

"She and I are friends, for sure, but I'm talking about the Tank Man poster."

"Like I said, if you want me to stop adoring my hero, you ought to explain your reasoning. Do some research and write a paper or even a book on him, so I can see why he's so problematic to you. You can't just stick your pretty nose into others' business and dictate to others what to do."

"Okay, I'll give you my reasons," I huffed.

"I can't wait to hear about it." He put on a practiced smile again.

I swerved and hurried away, flustered. I shouldn't have engaged him in that argument in the first place. I was amazed that Rachel may have accepted him completely as a boyfriend.

Yet intuitively I felt Tank Man could be a good point of entry if I wanted to study the history of political suppression in contemporary China. Because my mother had joined the hunger strike in Tiananmen Square, my exploration of Tank Man could become something personal and intimate, and Mark's casual remarks had prompted me to think seriously about Tank Man as a dissertation topic. On the other hand, it gnawed at me. I couldn't help but wonder if I was jealous of Rachel and intended to do something that might exert my influence on Mark. I was bewildered by my obsession with Tank Man, unable to sort out my feelings and thoughts.

I talked to Loana to see if she felt that Tank Man could be a serious subject for a dissertation. She thought a moment, then said, "It's a rich and important topic. You can study various facets of the Tank Man issue, like the origin, the dissemination, the public consumption, the transformation of the image into an icon, and China's official efforts to erase it from public view and memory. Tank Man could be a central topic in the study of the democracy movement in the spring of 1989."

"So you think I should mention Tank Man in my statement of purpose if I apply to graduate schools?"

"You don't need to be too specific in your statement. You could say you wanted to study the contemporary political history of China and East Asia. Once you become a PhD student, you can talk with your advisor, who will help you decide on a topic. What I'm trying to say is that Tank Man could be an excellent dissertation subject, and that you should feel confident about it."

That was reassuring. I began to prepare the materials needed for the PhD application. Luckily Professor Snelling agreed to write on my behalf, and I had polished a long paper—twenty-seven pages—as a writing sample. At Loana's suggestion, I focused on schools in New York City, where many democracy activities took place. What's more, there were several communities of exiles and dissidents in that city, and from contact with them I might get more firsthand data and information. Loana said I should keep her updated, so that she could put in a word for me personally if she happened to know the professors.

12

IN MID-OCTOBER A large delegation, formed by representatives from several conglomerates, came from China to recruit students from universities in the Boston area. Though they seemed more interested in grad students and postdocs, they were also considering some undergraduates, particularly those majoring in the sciences, finance, and economics. A couple of my friends went to the Four Seasons Hotel in downtown Boston for the job fair, but they were underwhelmed, saying that without a doctoral degree, you couldn't possibly find a good job with the multinational companies that were there, like Alibaba, Tencent, and Baidu. As a history major, I didn't bother going to their receptions at all, which, according to those who had attended, provided excellent finger food and beverages, even margaritas and sangria. I had no plans to return to China after college anyway.

Strangely enough, I heard from my mother about a job offer. She treated it like a godsend, a once-in-a-lifetime opportunity. She mentioned Uncle Chang, who lived in our neighborhood and who owned an international education agency in Beijing that helped high schoolers apply to American and European colleges. His

LOOKING FOR TANK MAN

kind of business was one of the most lucrative in China today, since most well-to-do families tried their best to send their children abroad for college. In most people's view, the Chinese education system was already bankrupt and had failed, because it was meant to turn every youngster into "a brick or tile in the Socialist Mansion." I knew Uncle Chang and his son Gourd, who was my age, maybe one or two years older than me; we had gone to the same high school. In spite of his rustic nickname, the young man was handsome and tall, with an elegant bone structure and delicate features. But he wasn't a good student and couldn't get into a real college. He had enrolled in a two-year drama school in hopes of breaking into TV plays. He was proud of his good looks and dreamed of becoming a movie star someday. Whenever we ran into each other, he would nod and smile. Once he even invited me to have ice cream with him in a nearby snack bar. I was reluctant to meet him alone, but he was a neighbor, and we had practically grown up together. I knew he was harmless, that at worst he was a skirt chaser, so I went and had strawberries à la mode and chatted with him for less than an hour. He said his father was a fool, because the old man had returned to China after teaching at Yale as a lecturer in Chinese for only three years. He should have stayed on so that their family could have immigrated eventually. I listened to Gourd complain about his dad without comment. I didn't enjoy the time I spent with him that much. He was too vain and self-centered. After I had been admitted by Harvard, he seemed eager to get close to me, but

I wasn't that interested in him, even though I knew a lot of girls couldn't wait to go with him. For them, he was like a prince on a white horse, even though he actually rode a red scooter. This made him more attractive to girls, because he could offer them a ride, but my view of him had remained the same. I had once read in a letter by Chekhov: "A man is what he thinks." Chekhov might have been a sexist—he had even said that as far as writing was concerned, women and cows were alike. But he was right about the inner quality of a person. I would say, "A woman is also what she thinks." I was more interested in the inner life of a person.

Now my mother was excited about the job offer from Uncle Chang, who even made it clear to her that I could become a partner of his business eventually. I felt uneasy about such an extravagant offer. In a roundabout way, he might be intending to tie me to his agency for the sake of his son, and my mother's excitement might also reflect that possibility. To her, once I had a high-paying job and settled in with my future boss's son, I would be set for life. But that was not what I wanted.

Because Uncle Chang had once taught Chinese at Yale, he named his education agency "Teacher Chang from Yale." Such a title greatly enhanced the popularity of his business, since the smartest high schoolers were all eager to get into the Ivies if their families could afford it. In the applying season his agency got more business than it could handle. For admission to a top Ivy school, the applicant's family was supposed to pay him more than one hundred thirty thousand dollars. Even getting someone into a top-50 U.S. college, he could rake in sixty grand. His service included helping the applicants fill out the forms and prepare their essays, giving mock interviews, and providing strong letters of recommendation. I could imagine how I might fit well in Uncle Chang's business. If I worked for him as a consultant, his agency could hang another placard: "Teacher Lulu from Harvard." (Compared to him, I would be more genuine in regard to the Ivy League.) That could double the profit of the business, and might make me flush with cash.

I didn't make that clear to my mother, who couldn't see Uncle Chang's ulterior motives. She was easily swayed by men. I just told her that I would seriously consider the job offer. That weekend I called my father and asked him what he thought of the opportunity. He didn't like it and said, "Why should you worry about money at this point of your life? Money has little to do with the quality of your life. If I didn't have two young kids and a young wife to support, I might have become a better artist."

I asked in surprise, "You mean you regret raising another family?"

"It's not a matter of regret. But for some years I forgot my original aspiration to become a spectacular and original sculptor. I spent too much time making money. You must follow your ambition and go as far as you can, especially when you're young. Don't settle with what life can give you at this moment."

"So you want me to just ignore my mom?"

"Try not to hurt her feelings. You know how to explain it to her, I'm sure. She's a good woman but she tends to be nearsighted and doesn't know how the world works. You have more common sense than her."

"All right, thanks for the advice."

In some respects he was right about my mother, who was typically book smart, but I loved her for that. There was an uncorrupted innocence in her that made her a kindhearted person, but one who could be too credulous. On the other hand, she often said that most rules and standards had been made by men, so as women we really didn't have to go by them.

Although certain I would decline Uncle Chang's offer, I was still nagged by uncertainty about my plan to do a PhD in history, particularly because I couldn't see how useful my endeavor would be. And I didn't know how to pacify my mother about pursuing the study of contemporary Chinese history. One day I ran into Professor Daniels, who had retired the previous spring but who still came to campus on weekdays. He was so distinguished that the college allowed him to keep his office without teaching. We chatted briefly, and I asked, "Can I invite you to coffee? I'm eager to hear your advice."

"Of course, I'll be happy to be of any help," he said. His small, lined face broke into a kindly smile.

He agreed to meet two days later at Café Pamplona on Bow Street, a quiet, cozy coffee shop with tiny tables and old chairs (metal frames with wooden seats) in it, where we could converse more comfortably. I arrived ten minutes before the appointed time, anxious about whether he would show up. At three sharp, he stepped

LOOKING FOR TANK MAN

in with his splayed feet, nodding at me. The moment he sat down, I handed him the coffee menu, and he ordered a double espresso and I a latte.

I talked about my plan to do graduate work in contemporary Chinse political history and also about my anxiety. He said, "I've heard you're an excellent student. To become a historian is a great career choice. Why are you so worried? Life is unpredictable, you shouldn't worry ahead of time."

I said, "Remember when you interviewed me in Beijing? I said I wanted to study social sciences so I could change society."

"I remember that. That was why we were all impressed by your wonderful ambition. There're a lot of smart kids, but it's ambition or aspiration that eventually make one different from others."

"Now I'm not sure how a PhD in history is related to that ambition. How can my career choice be useful and serve that purpose?"

He smiled and said, "It's normal for young people to have your kind of anxiety. A lot of our scholarship might not have practical value at first glance. That's the beauty of it. We do something that can sustain our humanity and sanity. Just by being a decent, intelligent human being, you can influence people around you. Of course, by studying contemporary Chinese political history, you'll automatically touch on some taboo issues, which the Communist authorities want people to forget. So your scholarship is also to fight against the collective amnesia the authorities attempt to produce. Your scholarship could be very useful in that way, don't you think?"

"I see, you mean we must preserve the truth so that people won't forget it?"

"Exactly, you're a smart girl and know how powerful truth can be. That's what those in power fear most. They always do their damnedest to keep people ignorant so as to make them irrational."

I was touched by his wise words, which reassured me of my plan. The hour I spent with him reminded me of what my father had once told me. He said, "Hang around professors as much as you can. You'll learn a lot from just observing and listening to them."

My dad was right. A fine education also means learning how to look at things differently, in one's own perspective. My conversation with Professor Daniels cemented my resolve to pursue a PhD. Loana was delighted to hear my final decision, saying she wished she could take me as a graduate student. But she was a postdoc, and not entitled to accept graduates, and in fact she had to look for a permanent teaching position elsewhere. I assembled all the application materials and submitted everything online at the end of December, including the eighty-dollar fee for each school.

13

IN EARLY FEBRUARY I heard from NYU and Columbia about my admission to their history programs. Both schools gave me a five-year package, which included full tuition, a monthly stipend of more than two thousand dollars, and medical insurance. I pinched myself, not having expected they would accept me as enthusiastically as their letters stated. Although stupefied with happiness, I couldn't decide which offer to take. In my statement of purpose, I mentioned the professors under whose tutelage I'd like to study. Now I was given both opportunities, and that overwhelmed me.

Professor Wilson, at NYU, was a political historian, and he had worked on a history of the Chinese Communist Party and published extensively. His book on the Long March was a textbook and had been translated into several languages. In contrast, Professor Bailey at Columbia was a cultural historian and had published books on contemporary China. His Mandarin was so impeccable that he had even performed crosstalk (comic dialogue onstage) to large audiences in Chinese cities, where he used to be a minor celebrity. But after the Tiananmen Square Massacre, he'd left China and resumed his teaching career in the States. Both of them were major scholars in the studies of contemporary China, and I'd have been happy to work under the guidance of either. Unable to decide which offer to accept, I spoke with Loana again.

She suggested that I go to New York, visit both programs, talk with the professors and some of their graduate students, and find out which place suited me better. I was unsure whether Wilson or Bailey would be willing to meet me, a mere prospective student.

"Of course they will," Loana said. "Every professor is eager to meet the students they have admitted. That's a common practice. They want to see what kind of candidates they have accepted. To produce significant scholars is an essential measurement of a PhD program's caliber. In fact, many programs fly in their admitted candidates for a mutual introduction."

"What if they don't like me?" I asked.

"That's unlikely. If they hadn't liked you, they wouldn't have admitted you and invested in you. An admission letter is an official document the university has to stand behind, and it can't be retracted. Don't worry about that. The ball is in your court now. Besides, everyone can see that you're a gracious person."

"Should I tell each of them about the other offer?"

"Don't volunteer information. You might say you have a similar offer and you'll have to decide which one to take. If they press you for more information, you should be candid, telling them the truth. And after you decide which program to join, you should let both programs

LOOKING FOR TANK MAN

know right away, so that the offer you have declined can be given to another applicant. Every program must have a long waitlist at this stage of admissions."

I could see the soundness of her advice, so I told Loana that I'd go to New York and visit Columbia and NYU to see which I liked better. She was pleased and said she had a favor to ask me. A friend of hers, a noted dissident, needed a laptop. Loana had just bought a new one with the research funds provided by her department and had retired her old laptop, which was still a solid machine. She wanted me to deliver it to the dissident, who lived in Flushing. "In fact," she said, "you should go to that part of Queens for lodging. There are many family hostels that are much more affordable than elsewhere, usually at a third of the price for a hotel in Manhattan."

The following week I took the Chinatown bus to New York, paying fifteen dollars. From Port Authority I boarded the 7 train to Flushing, where I had booked a bed in a family hostel for forty-six dollars a night. The next day I went to Columbia, whose campus I was somewhat familiar with, having visited it twice before. Professor John Bailey's office was in a brick mid-rise building whose foundation was built of huge blocks of whitish granite. He was there waiting for me. At the sight of me, he put away a book he'd been reading and moved to the coffee table, around which were a short sofa and two armchairs. He was a tall man in his mid-fifties, with thick shoulders but loosely built. He sat in a chair and pointed to the sofa for me to sit down. "Welcome, Lulu," he said. "We're thrilled to have you and hope you'll come join us in the fall."

He seemed quite sensitive, with an intelligent face and an inviting smile. When emailing with him, after he pressed, I confessed that I had also received an offer from NYU but that I couldn't decide which school to accept until I came to see both programs. I had read some of Bailey's papers and books, so I told him that it would be an honor to study with him. He was pleased, and assured me that he and his colleagues could help me a lot in my graduate work. For the first year and a half, I'd take courses, and then I'd spend another year or so preparing for the qualifying exam; after passing that, I would concentrate on writing my dissertation. I told him that I wanted to work on democracy movements in contemporary China, but right now I didn't have a specific topic for my dissertation yet.

"That's normal," he said. "Once you start here, you'll figure it out gradually. My colleagues and I can help you with that."

I also mentioned I had watched his crosstalk performances online and enjoyed them very much. At that, he gave a hearty laugh, tipping back his head, where there was a shiny bald patch encircled by curly reddish hair. His hazel eyes twinkled.

I was happy to meet him, and he gave me a positive feeling. I also wanted to visit the East Asian library and take a look at the materials I might have access to.

"Let me see if Andy is here. I'll be back in a second," Bailey said and headed out.

Outside, the traffic on Amsterdam Avenue surged and a truck honked, followed by a few spasmodic bleats of cars. A few moments later Professor Bailey brought in Andy, a fourth-year graduate student, and told him to show me the library. I said goodbye and left with Andy, who was of medium height and thickset, and quite talkative. He was going to give me a tour. As we were strolling out of the building, he said he was fond of New York, though he had grown up in the Bay Area and sometimes, especially in winter, missed Northern California. But he loved Columbia, saying the department was very helpful and generous to its graduate students. As for the placements of the recent PhDs, most of them had found tenure-track teaching positions, although good jobs were getting scarce nowadays. Andy led me to the Starr Library, at the center of the campus. The library was cozy and neat. Its holdings were impressive, including all the major newspapers published in East Asia, with the current issues on poles and the back ones in stacks. There was also an abundant collection of manuscripts and some dignitaries' personal papers. Everything was in order, and I could go to the shelves directly, the same way I could in the Harvard-Yenching Library. I was pleased to see such a trove of old books, personal papers, and recent publications.

Professor Wilson at NYU kept office hours in the afternoon, so I went there directly from Columbia. But it was almost noon, so for lunch I picked a couple of items in a delicatessen and ate in the store. New York was so convenient, you really didn't need to cook, I realized, though every now and then I'm sure I would want to make a fine meal, even just for myself. Professor

Wilson's office was on the fourth floor of an old brownstone building on Washington Square North. It was easy to find, and he was expecting me. He stood and held out his hand. His palm was thick and strong, and I thought that he must go to the gym a lot. He was close to fifty and looked robust, with a high, square forehead. He had a British accent, which reflected his Oxford education. "We all hope you will come and join us, Lulu," he said with a shy smile. "Personally I'm fascinated by your statement of purpose. My colleagues are impressed too. We believe that the kind of scholarship you plan to do will be important and useful, so we're eager to have you in our program."

I knew his work on the CCP's history, and we talked about the possibility of real political reform in China. He was optimistic about the party's ability to adapt to the times. "If it doesn't change, the CCP will implode," he said, smiling and displaying his white, square teeth.

"I hope you're right," I said, but deep down I was not that hopeful about the CCP's will to catch up with the times. Those in power seemed desperate to hold on to it at all costs. For them, to lose power meant to lose everything, even their lives, so they'd fight tooth and nail for survival. I didn't contradict Professor Wilson's view and just nodded. He did impress me as a vigorous and perceptive scholar who would be able to help me with my work. I mentioned I'd love to visit NYU's East Asian library. He confessed that they didn't have a special library for East Asian studies, but there were various collections and all sorts of materials kept in different schools at NYU. They were accessible to the faculty and graduate students. Nowadays, most publications are available online, and they had subscribed to everything they could. Also, there was the vast interlibrary loan system through which one could borrow books from other universities. After meeting with Professor Wilson, I went to their main library to look at its East Asian studies collection and was underwhelmed by the holdings. When it came to books and old periodicals, I could see the advantages of being a graduate student at Columbia; besides the Starr Library's rich collections, it could borrow from other Ivy League libraries, which didn't share their vast holdings with non-Ivy schools.

On the other hand, NYU's annual stipend was $2,600 more than Columbia's offer. For a graduate student, that extra amount was a lot of money, nearly enough to cover my food expenses. In the department's lounge at NYU, a Vietnamese grad named Kimberly told me that my package was the most generous one that their program had offered. That reminded me that their admission letter said my stipend was a fellowship directly from the provost's office, so I ought to cherish such an opportunity. Amy Shields, an art history PhD student at Harvard, had advised me to use NYU's offer to bargain with Columbia for more funding, but I didn't think that was a good idea. I didn't want to appear greedy. On the train back to Flushing, I weighed the pros and cons of both schools and began to lean toward Columbia, believing it suited me better. I didn't tell the two schools my decision right away, preferring to wait two or three days to give them the impression that I had deliberated carefully.

Before returning to Boston the next day, I met Wentao, the man to whom I was to deliver Loana's used laptop. We met at a teahouse on Roosevelt Avenue, near Macy's. Wentao was in his mid-forties and looked urbane, with long eyelashes and bony hands. Before leaving China in 1993, he had been imprisoned for three years for his participation in the Tiananmen demonstrations. Although he had been in the States for almost two decades, he didn't have a regular job. He was so obsessed with China's violations that he had become a full-time fighter for human rights.

"Loana wants you to know this laptop still works well," I told him, lifting the cup of Icy Peak oolong and taking a sip. "The tea is delicious."

"It's Taiwanese," he said and grinned. "Please thank Loana for me. She's such a nice lady, smart and kindhearted."

"She's a great teacher too."

"She mentioned you in her email, saying you're her best student. If you go to graduate school in New York, I hope you'll be able to help us with our work."

"What kind of work are we talking about?" I asked.

"We've been keeping an eye on the Chinese government and trying to deter those in power from abusing human rights." He smiled, almost diffidently, his pale, delicate face a little creased. I could see that when young, he must have been quite handsome. But even though

LOOKING FOR TANK MAN

a man in his forties was supposed to be in his prime, Wentao looked tired, as if suffering from malnutrition.

I told him that I was going to start graduate school at Columbia in the fall and would be happy to help his group if I could. He said they needed young people badly, especially those fluent in both English and Chinese. In our conversation, he tossed out an English word now and then, but his pronunciation was flawed. He tended to add an *a* to the last syllable of some words, like "experienceda," "speciala," "White Housa." That made him sound a little silly, but I could tell that he was intelligent and probably well learned. He had been eking out a living by contributing articles to dissident magazines, which paid peanuts. "I wish I could write in English," he said, his Adam's apple protruding. "Without enough English, you can never feel at home in America."

"Is this your personal view? Or are you talking about the exiled life in general?" I asked.

"Most Chinese exiles have been somewhat hamstrung by their lack of English. It makes one feel like a fish out of water. That's why we badly need young people like you."

"And also scholars like Loana," I added.

"Of course, her work helps give us a voice in academia. That is most valuable in the long run. The exiles like me and my friends have to struggle for survival, so we tend to plan things only in the short term. I wish I had gone to graduate school when I came out of China. I was stupid, possessed by a longing for our homeland,

and thought that China would have to change its policy regarding the Tiananmen Square Massacre pretty soon. I began waiting for that ruthless country to change its course. It's like waiting for a wolf to turn vegetarian."

Perturbed by his words, I asked, "If you could choose again, would you live differently?"

"I'd still keep working on the improvement of human rights in China, because I promised my friends that I'd continue the cause they had lost their lives for, but that first I had to educate myself some more. That's a better way to live an independent life." He sounded wistful, his voice tinged with sadness.

I didn't press him more on this, realizing that I was in a more privileged position by far. I was glad that Loana had put me in touch with Wentao, behind whom there must be a large dissident community, which could be valuable for my graduate work as well.

14

BACK FROM NEW York, I reported my decision to Loana. She was pleased, saying that Columbia should be a great place for me, and that under Professor Bailey's guidance, I would accomplish significant scholarship. We were having coffee in the department's common room, both of us seated on a long sofa. She told me more about Wentao, whom she deeply respected. He and his wife had just divorced. That had crushed him, and it explained his moody air when I had seen him two days before.

Loana said, "I met his wife, who is beautiful, eight or nine years younger than him. They also have a lovely boy."

"What happened to the child?" I asked, sipping the French roast coffee.

"She has custody."

"Was Wentao willing to give up his son?"

"It was complicated. She offered to marry him when he was imprisoned. I have to say she was a brave woman and knew what she was getting into. For marrying a political criminal, she lost her job. After he was released on medical parole, they managed to come to the States together and were granted political asylum. She did all kinds of odd jobs, because she couldn't speak English, while he became a full-time democracy activist."

"Does that mean they only lived on her wages?" I asked.

"Yes, that helped break up their marriage, and they often bickered. You see, brutal, oppressive power couldn't stop them from loving each other, but the reality of everyday life here, in this free capitalist society, wore them down and dissolved their marriage. She gave him an ultimatum: if he didn't mend his ways and stop being a full-time, unpaid human-rights watchdog here, she'd leave him."

"He didn't change?"

"No, he said he had promised some friends killed in June 1989 that he would carry on the cause they'd left behind. He had to devote himself to the improvement of the human-rights situation back in China, and he wouldn't quit the battle he started long ago. His wife couldn't take it anymore and filed for divorce."

"Why did he allow her to keep their son?"

"He loves the boy but believed the child could have a better life with his mother. On top of that, she was going to marry another man, who could give her a stable life."

"An American?"

"No, a Taiwanese fellow who was an accountant in a pharmaceutical company and had been running after the wife for some time. She simply couldn't endure the precarious life that her husband had imposed on their family anymore. She wants a stable income for their household. Wentao told me that the Taiwanese man was decent and would treat his son well."

"Still, he gave up his child," I said with a sigh.

"That was why Wentao has been depressed these days."

I viewed Loana as a friend now, so I half joked, "He must be a capable man and is also somewhat handsome. Are you not interested in him?"

"I respect him, but I won't go further than that. My life is unsettled yet. I might have to take a job in another college when my stint here is over. I want a normal life, an ordinary family life. A full-time democracy activist, a professional revolutionary, won't work for me."

"That's true," I agreed.

I remembered a well-known dissident had once said in an interview that for an exile, first and foremost, you had to be self-sufficient and live a free life with dignity. Such a life could become a small torch, because it showed that a true individual could thrive without depending on their home country, and a good life like that could dispel the lie told by propaganda officials and bought by the multitudes: "Without your country, you would become nothing." Indeed, too many dissidents had blindly allowed their country to form the underpinnings of their existence. Few had attempted and realized self-reliance. To be free one has to be self-sufficient.

I appreciated Loana's candor and her treating me as a friend. What she said made me think more about the plight that trapped many Chinese exiles. I realized that the most challenging task for them outside China was how to find regular employment and how to give their families a stable life, which ought to be totally independent of the politics of their homeland. A man like Wentao basically existed in the past, even though it took guts to live his kind of monastic life.

Jason Wang had included me in his Weibo group. There were more than twenty Chinese students in that circle, most of them attending BU and a few back in China, but they all seemed to be our age, in their twenties. They often argued and quarreled; I never joined in and just remained a bystander. My reticence was mainly due to my awareness of the Chinese internet police. To become active on Weibo was like streaking. Any radical or politically unacceptable views expressed on it could easily get your account canceled. Worse yet, the mainland police could easily shadow me if I expressed any strong opinions. On the other hand, my voyeurism was gratified by following the BU students. I was eager to see what pleased and upset them. Jason was an active member on Weibo and kept reporting his own activities. I was delighted to know that he was accepted by Stanford, where he was going to do graduate work toward a PhD in political science. I hadn't shared the news of my graduate admission with anyone on Weibo, but I was excited about Jason's success, given that two years ago he hadn't known anything about the Tiananmen Square Massacre. Now he was eager to become

LOOKING FOR TANK MAN

a political scientist. I got in touch with him through email and congratulated him.

He said he was coming to the Harvard-Yenching Library to look at some old magazines and wondered if we could meet. I was eager to find out more about his studies and academic track, so I met him there and invited him to lunch, since it was already noon. Together we went to the food trucks parked in the small plaza in front of the Science Center. As we were walking, he shortened his long strides to keep pace with me. He was carrying an accordion folder that contained the photocopies he had just made. At a yellow van I bought two clamshells of Mediterranean food—roast chicken breast, pita bread, tossed salads mixed with feta and halved olives. Together we went into the café inside the Science Center and sat down at a table. I went over to the counter and bought two cups of pea soup, which Jason enjoyed a lot.

Over lunch we chatted about graduate school. I told him I had been accepted by Columbia's history department. At that, his face shone with elation. I was pleased to see he was happy for me.

"Why are you going to the West Coast?" I asked him.

"For the gorgeous weather. Besides, Stanford gave me a lot of money," he said with a grin, the ends of his walnut-shaped eyes tilting to his temples. A sprinkling of pimples dotted his forehead. Then, as if to correct himself, he added, "It has lots of materials I need for my study, specifically those at the Hoover Institute. It's full of primary sources. For example, Chiang Kai-shek's diaries and papers are there. I want to work on the historical relationships between the Nationalists and the Communists."

"That's an unusual topic, isn't it? What drew you to it?" I cut a wedge of the chicken and dipped it into white sauce.

"I realized over the past few years that there had been too many lies in what schools had taught us back in China. So I want to go to the primary sources and find out the truth on my own. How about you? What are you going to work on at Columbia?"

"Nothing is certain yet, but I might do research and write about Tank Man." I laughed, a little uneasy about my confession. Unconsciously I shielded my mouth with my palm as if to stop myself.

"That's a great topic. You must do it. I'm glad our studies will overlap some."

"We must stay in touch and inform each other of our progress."

"Sure thing, there're not many people who share our academic interests."

He told me that this year he was the only one among the hundreds of Chinese students at BU doing graduate work in social sciences. All the other seniors were going to professional schools, mostly in finance and management, or just returning to China, where their families could help them find jobs. In a way, this thrilled me, because our rarity could make us stand out in the long run. I told Jason my thoughts, at which he nodded his agreement. He confessed that he hadn't told his parents

LOOKING FOR TANK MAN

what kind of research he was going to do at Stanford. They didn't have a clue what political science was and were just pleased to know he would be working toward a PhD at that prestigious school.

One afternoon the following week, I ran into Rachel in the campus quad and told her I was going to do graduate work in New York. She looked amazed, her smile on the verge of a grimace, her eyelids a bit puffy, though I was certain she had heard I'd been admitted to Columbia. I asked her what she was going to do after college. "Well," she said, "I'll take a year off, maybe two years, just to see what I'll do. I wish I were as clearheaded as you. Do you have any idea what kind of dissertation you're going to write?"

"It's too early to decide. Probably I'll work on Tank Man. It sounds nuts, doesn't it?"

Her eyes blazed. "Actually, it's an excellent topic. I admire you for your madness and perseverance."

I was unsure if she was serious and looked her in the face. She sensed my perplexity and added, "'Much madness is divinest sense.' I meant what I said." That was typical of Rachel. She often waxed poetic, which usually didn't jibe with my temperament. But this time I was pleased. She could quote from English-language poems off the top of her head.

"Thanks, Rachel," I said. "That means a lot to me. So will you be going back to Nanjing for the summer?"

"It depends. If I can find a job in the Bay Area, I'll work there for a while."

"What kind of jobs do you have in mind?"

"Probably PR. I like working with people. As a matter of fact, I also thought about going to graduate school, but I don't think I can sit down and read and write for five years while life flows past me. I would be bored stiff. But heaven knows I might change my mind."

I was surprised. She was an English major, knew a lot about modern poetry, and loved Emily Dickinson, Sylvia Plath, Elizabeth Bishop, and Louise Glück. Why would she decamp for San Francisco to look for an office job? Her family was probably eager to make her go into a lucrative profession. What was more baffling was why wasn't she staying in Boston if she and Mark Stone had been dating? Maybe it hadn't worked out between them. I refrained from asking her about this.

15

MY PARENTS DIDN'T come for my commencement, but that didn't bother me. The flights were so expensive. Worse, they wouldn't have wanted to share a room in a hotel. That would have made a joint trip to Boston more cumbersome. If my mother had come, I'd have taken constant care to keep her from blowing her top when she rubbed shoulders with my father. She may have just been starting menopause, and her temper was quite volatile. I told her that I would head back in early May, before commencement, which I didn't mind skipping. I would receive my diploma through the mail anyway.

My mother loved to have me home. I planned to take a part-time job and to rest some to get ready for the fall. Schools and colleges didn't let out until mid-July in Beijing, so I was allowed to teach a short English class in my former high school. I taught tenth graders, not a class of rising seniors, who would have been taking the national entrance exam the next year, so I didn't have serious responsibilities. As long as I could hold the students' interest and make them learn some English, my duty would be fulfilled. So I felt comfortable about the arrangement and pleased that I could have a few weeks for myself before I started graduate school at Columbia. I didn't use a textbook in my teaching, since my course was a mere supplementary class, "listening comprehension." I used some English magazines and newspapers and mainly read out the articles to the class. I read loudly and slowly and whenever coming upon a word or phrase that might be hard for the thirty-four students to follow, I would pause to ask them if they understood it. If nobody knew, I would clarify its meaning for them. They seemed to like my casual way of teaching, and I was careful to exclude articles that might be politically sensitive. But because the class was taught in English, I could get away with a lot. From time to time I would slip in some words that expressed novel or radical concepts and entities to the students, such as transgender, the Senate and the House, affirmative action, age discrimination, same-sex marriage. About the last phrase the class got into an argument. At first, most of my students didn't think such a marriage was appropriate. The grounds for their objection were that a couple of the same sex couldn't make babies, so the marriage defeats the purpose of such a union. I said, "Let us think about this in a different light. What if someone argues that the purpose of marriage is not to produce babies but to make two individuals more able to love and help each other? In other words, what if the basis of marriage is not procreation but love?" That stumped the class. Later, a few of them told me in private that they had changed their minds about the issue and that if two persons really loved each other, they could get married and the marriage should

LOOKING FOR TANK MAN

be their own business and be justified. On another occasion, I talked about various uses of the word "office," from which I gave them the phrase "run for office." They were fascinated, and then more questions came up. So I included words more related to elections, like "electorate," "ballot," "constituency," and "gerrymander." Luckily, nobody told on me to the school leaders.

The high school was near Tsinghua University, which I passed by on my way to work. Though I was certain that for my graduate work I would concentrate on the democracy movement in 1989, I hadn't brought back many books because I was no longer at Harvard, having no access to its libraries anymore. I owned a few titles that I ought to read as an aspiring historian, but I hadn't brought them back, afraid that customs might confiscate them. Unfortunately, in this place there were no useful books or periodicals available on the Tiananmen movement, which was treated as a suppressed riot in all publications here. Even at Tsinghua University, where I could use my mother's employee card to access its libraries, I couldn't find anything useful for the study of my future field. This scarcity of information pained me and made me feel deprived. It indicated how the facts and truths had been erased from people's minds or revised to avoid tarnishing the party's image. The city seemed to still be bathing in the afterglow of the successful Olympics that had taken place here three years back. But I couldn't help wondering, Have people really forgotten what broke out just two decades ago? Was it so easy to tailor or blot out history?

I had brought back a photo of Tank Man. It was a bookmark handed out at the Tiananmen Square Massacre conference organized by Loana two years before. Placed between the pages in a dictionary, the picture had slipped through customs at the Beijing airport, though a woman officer had seized my copy of Jonathan D. Spence's *The Search for Modern China*. I was perplexed and outraged, explaining to her that this wasn't a reactionary book and that it was written by an author regarded as a friend of China's. As hard as I argued, she wouldn't give it back to me. Probably one of the officers knew English and was eager to get hold of a book like that for personal use, or maybe they were going to present it to a superior who happened to know the foreign tongue and loved forbidden books. In China, a lot of outrageous things were done for personal reasons under the pretext of law, regulations, patriotism.

One afternoon, as I was walking home after teaching, I saw two female students coming out of Tsinghua University's side entrance, I went up to them and pulled the photo of Tank Man out of my skirt pocket and said, "Excuse me, Miss, do you happen to know what this picture is about?"

At the sight of the bookmark, both girls gasped and recoiled, as if it were a contaminated object. They shook their heads no, but their faces twisted with fear in spite of their efforts to smile. One of them said, "I have no idea who he is. Maybe it's part of an ad?"

The other one took the photo from me and said, "I can't see his face here. Of course I can't tell who he is. Maybe it was made on a computer."

As they were hurrying away, they turned their heads to observe me. I could see that to them I must be a crazy woman, but I could also tell that they knew who Tank Man was. Their denial upset me.

Feeling bold, I entered the gate. A young man wearing sunglasses turned up, heading out of campus. I greeted him and asked, "Excuse me, do you recognize who this is?" I flashed the photo at him.

"No, I have no idea." He looked blank, shaking his head of thick hair. "Let me see it again," he said, and took the bookmark from me, removed his shades, and looked at it more carefully. Evidently he didn't know who Tank Man was.

"He's an international icon," I said. "Probably the most popular Chinese man in the world. This photo shows how he singlehandedly stopped a column of tanks at Tiananmen Square."

"When was that?" He looked incredulous.

"On June 5, 1989. You've never heard of the Tiananmen Massacre, in which hundreds of people or more got killed?"

"Not really. Oh, I remember in my high school's politics class, a teacher once mentioned an uprising in Tiananmen Square, but she referred to it only in passing, so I didn't register it as a significant historical event that involved losses of lives."

More people were stepping out of a nearby building. A girl called to him, and he turned away to join her. I thought of going up to the crowd and showing the photo to them, but thought better of it.

As I was leaving, I saw a woman in her thirties. She must have been a graduate student or a junior faculty member and might have a clearer memory, so I went up to her and said, "Miss, do you recognize this man?" I raised the photo to her.

She nodded calmly. "Yes, I saw a picture like that long ago, but I don't believe it was based on a real event."

"Do you remember the Tiananmen Square Massacre?"

"It was not a massacre. Yes, some people died, but the government had no choice but to suppress the rebellion, or the country would have lapsed into chaos. As for this photo, it was a product manufactured by the Western media to demonize China."

"You really think so?" I was amazed.

"Beyond a shadow of a doubt. There was simply no other way for the government to restore order, so it had to use force."

"Even field armies, tanks, and machine guns?"

"Look, the government was not experienced in dealing with such an insurrection, so mistakes were unavoidable." She fixed her thin eyes on my face, looking daggers.

I realized we were talking at different frequencies, unable to communicate at all, so I stepped away and went out the front gate and headed home. I hadn't walked for more than three minutes when a jeep pulled up ahead of me, as quietly as a shadow. Two cops stepped out of the vehicle and blocked my way.

One of them said, "Hey, you must come with us."

I saw "Tsinghua Police" on the car door. "What for?" I asked. "What crime did I commit?"

"You just displayed some reactionary material on campus. We must bring you in so you can answer a couple questions."

"What if I don't want to answer?"

"Then we won't let you go."

I realized there was no way to wriggle out of this, so I agreed to go with them. The moment I got in the backseat, the jeep swerved around and pulled away. The cop in the passenger seat asked me, "Are you a student here?"

"I won't answer you now. I must see my attorney first." In spite of saying that, I had no clue where to find a lawyer here.

They both cracked up. The one at the wheel, who I noticed kept observing me in the rearview mirror, told me, "We can send you to a jailhouse without bothering to involve your lawyer. You'd better be more polite to us and more obliging."

I did my best to keep mum all the way, though my throat tightened with panic. The cop in the passenger seat phoned their headquarters, saying they were bringing me over now. We stopped in front of the police station, a white house with tall windows, and they ordered me to get out. They led me into an office, in which an older officer pointed at a chair for me. The instant I sat down opposite him, he began to question me. He asked my name and age and my home address. I answered truthfully.

"Are you a college student?" he continued.

I nodded and tried to stop squirming. I rubbed my hands, the palms wet with perspiration.

"Yes or no?" he said.

"Yes."

"What college?"

"Harvard."

"Are you making fun of me?" He looked cross, pulling a long face and wrinkling his forehead.

I took out my Harvard ID and handed it to him. He looked at it, then leaned in and held the photo up closer to my face, peering at me as if to make sure I was the person on the card. "Truth to tell, you look better than in the picture," he said.

"Thanks. I wish I were photogenic, I'm sorry."

He giggled, then laughed. "You must be a good kid. There's no need to be so somber and so frightened. I'm Officer Bian. As long as you level with me, I won't hurt you."

"Okay, I'll be honest," I said.

At this point, his secretary, a tallish woman in her early forties, stepped in, and he handed her my ID. "Make a copy of this," he told her.

Once the woman was out of earshot, I said to him, "Now, Uncle Bian, you believe I'm a college student studying in America, right? Please let me go."

"I'll be damned. Why did you fool around here? Didn't your studies at Harvard already keep you busy enough?"

"I didn't do anything wrong."

"You showed a banned photo to our students, didn't you?"

"Look, I had no idea this photo was banned." I fished it out and handed it to him. "See, it's a bookmark handed out at a conference about the Tiananmen Square Massacre. The conference was held at Harvard two years ago."

I placed the photo into his open hand. As he was observing it, his straight eyebrows knitted. He sighed and said, "So the Tiananmen turmoil is studied at Harvard?"

"Yes, I took a seminar on this subject. That was why I thought Tsinghua students might already know something about it too."

"Nobody wants to remember that sad, bloody event. Please stop reminding people of it."

I thought of countering him by elaborating on the necessity of fighting against the official effort to make the public into amnesiacs, but I bit my tongue, unwilling to show I was well informed and more sophisticated. I'd better play ignorant and stupid so that they would set me free. Officer Bian didn't look mean or malicious at all.

He seemed to be able to read some English. He was perusing the words printed at the bottom of the photo, which indicated the conference was held in memory of the victims and centered around the role that the People's Liberation Army had played in the tragedy. He rubbed his eyes as if they were irritated. He said, "Amazing, the Americans try to remember our misfortune, our tragedy."

I begged, "Uncle, please let me go. I saw lots of photos and footage in my class. Everyone in the West knows about the Tiananmen Square Massacre. I really had no idea this was banned here."

"Not only here. If you show others this photo outside Tsinghua, you'll be in a big mess."

"Okay, I won't do that. Let me go home, please. My mother will be worried sick if I don't get back before dark."

"Where does your mother work?"

"Here, in the archaeology institute." I thought of withholding her name, but then told him the truth, feeling he might be more lenient since my mother was a kind of colleague.

I guessed right. He asked his secretary to make a copy of the Tank Man photo as well. He turned to me and said, "I've known your mom since she was in her twenties. Tell her Uncle Bian says hi. I remember now, you were the talk for some time a few years ago. We felt happy for your mother. It wasn't easy for her to raise you alone, to do such a great job with you, so for her sake you must stop fooling around."

"Thanks, I will pass on your greetings to her," I said.

When his secretary returned the Tank Man bookmark to him, he fished out a scarlet lighter, flicked it on, and set the bead of flame to the photo. He twirled the blazing strip, and said to me, "You must understand I'm doing this to help you. I can let you go this time, because I know Anmin, your mother, and you're a good kid. Don't ever mess around like this again. If you're caught next time, nobody can protect you and we'll have to hand you over to the city police. Then you'll be handled as a criminal and get a prison term or be shut up in a mental asylum."

I said I had learned my lesson and wouldn't make trouble again. They released me after making me sign the two sheets of their questions and my answers. I wrote out my name with the Sharpie the woman secretary handed me. Then I pressed the scarlet print of my right index finger on my signature too. I thanked Officer Bian and turned to the door.

I guessed I was lucky to run into a man who still remembered the Tiananmen tragedy, and he must have had some sympathy for a "troublemaker" like me. Though set free, I was plunged into a panic, my knees shaky and my heart throbbing fitfully on my way home. I forced myself not to run.

At dinner, I was as uptight as if my stomach had frozen—I was unable to swallow. I was unsure whether I should tell my mother about the brief detainment, but I decided to just mention Officer Bian, who had given her his greetings.

"I'm glad he still remembered me," she muttered. "Where did you meet him?"

"I lost my ID. Somebody came across it and handed it to the police. They called me in to reclaim my ID. Officer Bian said he had known you for many years. Was he your friend?"

"No, he was just a flippant playboy."

"Did you like him?"

"He was merely an acquaintance—he was all right."

I was confused by her petulant tone of voice. I guessed Bian had been one of those men who used to drop by her workplace and flirt with her prior to her divorce, but who then evaded her afterward. So there might be no need for me to disturb my mother with more information about my troubles with the campus police. Neither of us referred to "Uncle Bian" again.

Indeed, my mother seemed unaware of my detention at all. During the following weeks, life continued peacefully.

16

BUT I HAD been cranky during this time. After the high school had let out, I didn't work anymore and was eager to read and study to get myself prepared for graduate school in the fall. But the books I was most eager to read were not available here. I complained to my mother, saying this country would become an immense animal farm if it continued to act like a control freak over its people. This would definitely reduce the whole population's intelligence.

She sighed and agreed that a lot of historical scholarship done in recent years was mere propaganda. She could see that if I wanted to be a historian, I'd have to study in the West, where genuine scholarship was possible. She even said that most fields in the humanities in China were "kind of whitewashing," so it would always be safer to choose a practical profession so that you could make money and live more comfortably. But she also urged me "never to become a slave of anything," neither of money or of power, not even of love. "A woman must be self-sufficient," she said, "to live a good, meaningful life." She often regretted not having continued with graduate studies, believing she'd have become a professor of archaeology if she'd earned a PhD. Deep down, she wasn't really opposed to my interest in doing an impractical graduate degree in the States.

One evening, she placed a small tin that used to hold ginseng in front of me on the table and opened the lid. Inside was a maroon journal in a leatherette binding. She said, "Your dad called this morning and said we shouldn't keep you in the dark about our involvement with the Tiananmen movement anymore. I was in college then and took part in the demonstrations. I kept a diary. Here it is. I thought you might be interested. Hopefully it will help you while away the summertime."

That came as a surprise. I had known she joined the hunger strike in Tiananmen Square but had no idea she'd kept a diary. I said, "I'll read this carefully and let you know what I think. But in retrospect, how do you feel about your participation in the democracy movement?"

"I feel I was used by others."

"Who are the others?"

"I'm not sure, but I feel there were powers beyond the reach of a regular student like me, and most of us, the hot-blooded youths, must have been meant to be sacrificed."

"Does this mean you regret your participation?"

"Not really. I was angry and wanted to join the demonstrators so that we could bring about change and political reform. Like others, I, too, want freedom and democracy. I believe that all people holding a public office must disclose their personal assets."

LOOKING FOR TANK MAN

"Would you do the same today if you were my age?"

"Probably. Look, a lot of things we do in life are not rational at all. No human being can always be coolheaded. I believe that insofar I was motivated by good intentions and genuine passion, I wouldn't have any regrets."

I was amazed that her involvement could have been driven by impulsive emotions, so I pressed further: "Does this also mean you don't regret falling for my dad?"

"Oh, how I loved him at the time!" A reddish sheen crept over her face, which looked younger for a moment.

I was moved and picked up the diary. "Thanks for sharing this, Mom."

"I hope it will be useful for your studies."

"It is," I assured her, though at the moment I wasn't sure how useful it could be to my graduate work.

That night, lying in bed, I began reading her diary. It wasn't long and started two weeks before the hunger strike, right after a notorious editorial in the *People's Daily* that had condemned the student movement as "turmoil," "a conspiracy," and "a serious political struggle" between the government and some "black hands" working behind the students. Her diary ended on June 2, the day before the soldiers fought their way into downtown Beijing and suppressed the protest with gunfire and tanks. So it covered roughly five weeks. Most entries were succinct and some consisted only of four or five sentences. I was a tad disappointed, because the diary was short and some items seemed quite meager.

On April 27, she wrote: *All the students on campus are talking about yesterday's editorial in the* People's Daily:

"We Must Be Clear about Our Position Against the Recent Turmoil." The article obviously voices the view of the hardliners in the politburo and must have been intended to threaten us students and cow us into calling off the protest. But it seems it has backfired, enraging us all the more. Many of us fear that the government will settle accounts with us individually afterward. So on campus there is talk about a larger demonstration.

I knew the contents of the editorial well. It marked a turning point in the student movement, which had actually been on the decline by then, since the students hadn't been able to sustain momentum. But instead of curbing the protest, the editorial simply provoked more anger and fear among young people, who believed there was no way to back down now. I read the other entries of my mother's diary quickly. Her tone of voice was fearful, and I could tell she was deeply involved, both in her emotions and in her protesting activities. During this period she often went to a spot on the campus of Beijing University called the Triangle to listen to speeches given by student leaders and to read big-character posters, most of which were short exposés written in brush. She also listened to Voice of America and the BBC at night, though her English wasn't good enough for her to understand everything yet. For most students, those foreign broadcasts were the only reliable sources of information, because the Chinese media didn't tell the truth and mainly served as the government's mouthpiece.

The April 28 entry of my mother's diary records that the day before, she had joined tens of thousands

LOOKING FOR TANK MAN

of students and marched twelve miles to Tiananmen Square. This was a regular demonstration, though the idea of a hunger strike had already been talked about among the students. Many local residents gathered in the square too, in total about half a million people. They demanded that the government recant the April 26 editorial. Of course they were ignored. The diary entry on April 29 reflected the students' fears: *Yesterday, the* People's Daily *published another article in support of the Shanghai Municipality's decision to fire the editor in chief of the liberal* Monitor of World Economy *and to disband the newspaper, which was viewed by the hardliners as a hotbed of reformists. Such a drastic disciplinary measure indicates that there is severe punishment in store for the demonstrators, so we have no option but to push forward.*

I was more interested in my mother's personal feelings and impressions in the vortex of the historical storm. Among the student leaders, she admired Wang Dan and Chai Ling most. Wang was urbane and looked handsome to her, with soft skin, always wearing a gentle smile. In my mind's eye I could see her girlish eyes brighten at the presence of such a charismatic young man. As for Chai Ling, my mother admired her eloquence and passion. Chai could deliver fiery speeches off the top of her head—like a blazing flame, she could set others on fire. In my mother's view, she was a natural leader and could also be enchanting, though her charm mostly surfaced when she got emotional and fierce. My mother also recorded that food at school was not as good as before, perhaps because the kitchens were severely understaffed now, some of the cooks also having taken part in the demonstration. She worried about suspended classes as well. In one entry, she confessed, *I haven't touched a textbook for more than a week. Awful!*

In early May, Zhao Ziyang, the party's general secretary, returned to Beijing from Pyongyang, to which he had paid a state visit. He and Premier Li Peng clashed in a meeting, and he insisted on a dialogue with the student demonstrators instead of threatening them with punishment. Then, on May 3 and 4, Zhao Ziyang twice spoke about the student movement in his public speeches. My mother liked Zhao, viewing him as a reformer who was sympathetic to the students. He said that all the students' demonstrations throughout the country were patriotic acts. That seemed to negate the views of the April 26 editorial, so my mother's fellow students took heart. At the same time, other party officials spoke publicly about the reactionary nature of the student protests, which they claimed incited turmoil that was more outrageous and more dangerous than bourgeois liberalization, and therefore the government must deal with them with forceful measures.

Still fearful and seeing the government unwilling to change its intransigent position, the student leaders, including Wang Dan and Wuer Kaixi, wanted to apply more pressure on the Li Peng regime and force it to hold a formal dialogue with the students, so they started to organize a hunger strike. There was another thing to consider: Mikhail Gorbachev was coming for the Sino-Soviet summit, which meant there'd be a ceremony held in Tiananmen Square on May 15. So the government would be eager to remove the hunger strikers from it by accepting the students' terms. Initially fewer than nine hundred students participated in the strike. I wasn't sure why my mother volunteered to join them. She must have been quite zealous at the time, eager to contribute to social improvement. But she was just small potatoes. As if always pressed for time, she recorded her personal experiences in the hunger strike succinctly.

MAY 13: *We arrive at Tiananmen Square late in the afternoon, some with blisters on our soles due to the twelve-mile walk. All the hunger strikers are sitting or lounging on the paving stones to save energy, unsure how long the strike will last. It's cold. Without food in our stomachs, some of us can't help shivering. We huddle together, using our bodies to keep each other warm. Not far away stands the immense Monument to the People's Heroes, which has turned bluish in the final rays of sunset. The imposing monument makes me pensive. I am sure there are no bodies interred behind the stones, but thousands of people still come to pay homage to it every day. The monument has preserved the heroic spirit and souls. Such a realization calmed me some. Even if we die in the strike and our bodies perish, our act might be remembered and manifested in something like that colossal monument. We might be held as heroes who sacrificed our young lives for our beloved country. It's quiet, and an aura of solemnity has bathed the entire square. We are told that some student leaders have been in dialogue with the government and that they will keep us updated on any new development, and that we mustn't fall asleep, because the* *cold night can make us ill if we aren't covered. But we have nothing on us except for our thin clothes. Toward midnight, most of us fall asleep nevertheless, our limbs entangled. Some still shiver, even in sleep, but everyone is calm. The fat moon looks pallid, obscured by haze.*

MAY 14: *Thank heaven, some local residents turn up in the morning and give us blankets and quilts. Now we have spread these on the ground so we can sit or lie on them instead of on the hard, cold paving stones. Some of us just swaddle ourselves in blankets. By now hunger pangs have set in, and some of us let out small moans, but everybody refuses to eat. We can drink water. A fellow from the Sport University even brought along dry milk and an extract of malt and sugar. We look down on him, some whispering that he is shameless and might taint our image as genuine hunger strikers. In front of us, a long band of white cloth displayed these words: "Mama, I'm Hungry, but I Can't Eat." Thousands of locals show up to give their support. Around midafternoon, some hunger strikers faint and have to be carried away. A few ambulances stand outside the zone of the hunger strike, but the rescuers can't set foot in our ranks to reach those who have fainted. A very capable student leader, Li Lu, with a square face and speaking with a northern accent, came and helped us make a path through the middle of the crowd—the path is kept clear by security members so that medical personnel can come in. We call this path "the life lane," and without it those who fainted couldn't be sent away for medical treatment at all. Some hotheads have proposed a radical measure. They want us to go occupy Chang'an Avenue to block the traffic; this would create a big problem for the municipality,* *because the wide boulevard, running east and west through the city, is a major artery. But most of us won't go there. We are already exhausted and mustn't move around. Some more radical ones suggest self-immolation and a few even volunteer to light themselves on fire. But we have no gasoline, which some people have left to acquire. The idea of self-immolation seems to possess quite a few students. I don't like it and hope it never happens.*

My mother seemed quite rational. I was reading her diary slowly and carefully. Now and again I paused to think about her mental state. It was good that she was self-reflective and aware of the small changes around her.

MAY 15: *Today the number of hunger strikers reached 3,100! Some have come from colleges in other cities. The ground here is messy and littered. There's an awful smell, since we haven't washed for two days. Still, things are mostly in order. I must praise the security guards, who are students just like us. Three lines of them stand around us to keep others from getting into the ranks of hunger strikers. The guards usually have to work for many hours in a row, and many of them collapse on duty and have to be shipped away. I also passed out this afternoon. I don't know who carried me to an ambulance. When I woke up in the children's hospital, I found myself in a large crib with white lacquered balusters and with an IV in my arm—they were giving me a glucose drip. It was already dark outside, and I wanted to go back and join my comrades. The doctor said they had to keep me for an hour or two to make sure I was all right. I thought that I must stink and wanted to wash up. They led me to the bathroom. How wonderful it was to use a* *regular bathroom and to wash with warm water again! Hurriedly I gave myself a towel bath. In the square, it's too far to go to the public lavatories, especially for women, but it's easier for men to take a leak. Some of them don't go to use the lavatories in the southeast corner of the square. They just pee into empty water bottles. There is also a bus loaded with buckets serving as a stopgap restroom, and it's flooded with urine inside. Fortunately none of us have eaten solid food for more than two days, so few of us are pooping.*

MAY 16: *We have a broadcast station set up, nestled under the Monument to the People's Heroes. It is our main source of information now. The broadcasters are great, speaking elegant and refined Mandarin. They must be students of the Media College. One of them is an older woman in her early thirties who calls herself Bei Ming, which might be a fake name. I am not sure if she is a graduate student. She speaks passionately on the air, her voice crisp and endearing. Before news, she often plays classical music, Beethoven, Bach, Tchaikovsky, and Mozart, which is well chosen. At times, an essay or poem she reads is so well received that we ask her to broadcast it again and again. Early in the afternoon, my name is announced over the loudspeaker. A male voice summons me to the broadcast station, saying a friend of mine has come to see me. So I climb up from the ground and stagger over to the base of the monument. At the sight of me, my boyfriend, Fanlin, rushes over and lifts me up. I'm thrilled to see him. He says, "You're so thin now, Anmin. Why didn't you let me know you were going to join the hunger strike? At least I could have stayed with you for the first two days." I ask, "So you wouldn't have stayed with me here longer than* *that?" "I can't," he says. "We've been making a statue called the Goddess of Democracy and are going put it up here, so I have to work with my fellow artists in the studio." He's an MFA student at the Central Academy of Fine Arts. He's a sculptor and must be a major hand in their project. I tell him not to worry about me; there are so many people here that I will be safe and won't feel lonely.*

MAY 17: *By noon today, over six hundred people have collapsed or fainted. Some are severely dehydrated and have started hallucinating, and some even seem deranged. They are sent to nearby hospitals. By now most of the hunger strikers have reached the limits of their endurance. Nevertheless, we are determined to continue, willing to sacrifice our lives to make a fundamental change in our society. More than seventy buses have parked outside the hunger strike zone. Many of them were sent over by the Beijing Municipality, and the medical personnel can't wait to remove as many of us as possible. This is their task, which ultimately is to remove us all. As a result, many of us are reluctant to leave with them, afraid they might ship us far away so that we can't return to the square again. I am surprised by the amount of supplies that locals have donated. In some of our drinks, they have mixed in sugar and honey. At times even milk powder, which most of us refuse to use. The locals are not allowed to mingle with us, so they just walk around raising bands of white cloth inscribed with supportive words: Children, You Are Brave Heroes! We Are Always with You! You, Stupid Government, Save Our Kids! Down with Dictatorship! We Have No Need for an Emperor!*

We flash the victory sign at them whenever they pass by.

It was already past midnight, so I forced myself to stop reading the diary, which might have made it hard for me to get to sleep. I pulled the string to turn off the light and would resume reading the next day.

My mother wrote on May 18, 1989: *Lightning slashes the sky this morning, and thunderclaps crack gray clouds, some of which are trembling and jumping. The meteorologist says there will be a rainstorm today. This unnerves us, because the fear of infectious disease has already alarmed some student leaders. The ground is dingy and soiled in places. A heavy rain can spawn germs and viruses. If an epidemic breaks out and spreads to the city, we will be blamed, and the hunger strike will be regarded as the cause of a calamity. So after eight, we are led to coach buses parked nearby. First, we put in our blankets and other stuff, and then many hunger strikers get on board. But some of us are not sure about these buses, most of which were sent over by the municipal government. We fear that when we are tired and groggy, they might drive us back to campus. To prevent that from happening, our leaders tell us to do something to the tires. In secret some men puncture the tires of the buses, and some just release the air. So in no time most of the coaches can't move anymore. The drivers are mad at us. The middle-aged driver of our coach blasts, "This is my own bus and I volunteered to come and help you. Now, you ruined my bus. What can I do? I won't be able to work tomorrow. You're such ingrates." One of the culprits explains our reasoning to him. The man says, "In that case, you shouldn't have slashed my tires. You can just disconnect this wire under the steering wheel. Here." He shows them where the wire is. "This way you wouldn't have damaged my bus." Our leaders apologize again and again. Luckily, the man cools down after blowing off steam.*

In the meantime, Wang Dan, Wuer Kaixi, and other student representatives are in the Great Hall of the People, meeting with Premier Li Peng on our behalf. We are clear about our terms, which are basically twofold: the government must acknowledge our activities as patriotic ones and must agree to hold a formal dialogue with the students. Our demands are clear and simple, also reasonable, so we assume there will be a positive outcome. But we hear that the talk has reached a stalemate. At most, Li Peng says, the students are motivated by patriotic sentiments; apparently he intends to avoid clarifying the nature of our movement. Toward evening, the student leaders come back and declare the failure of our effort to reach out to the government, which is responsible for this deadlock.

The rain doesn't fall until it's dark. Fortunately, we can use the bus as shelter and I can write this diary entry on the bus.

I was impressed that my mother was so conscientious in keeping her diary. Her handwriting was delicate, like her frail frame, but the characters were clear and neat. It was a pleasure to read what she wrote.

MAY 19: *Early this morning, about four thirty, Zhao Ziyang, the party's general secretary, shows up with his assistants in the square. The instant we hear of his arrival, we get off the buses and gather around him. It's said that Li Peng also came in the wee hours, but I didn't see him. Zhao holds a red battery-powered loudspeaker and addresses the* *crowd, urging us to stop the hunger strike without waiting for a satisfactory answer from the government, which will take time to come. He looks swarthy and sincere, with a shiny, balding forehead. He says in a tearful voice that he is sorry for coming so late. He sounds doleful, and even claims he is already reaching retirement age, so the country's future rests on our shoulders. Therefore we must preserve our health and not act destructively. He says that as an old man, he no longer cares what will happen to him, but we are still young, with a bright future, so we mustn't hurt ourselves like this. He claims he understands our patriotic feelings and admires our enthusiasm, but we ought to be more patient and more reasonable. If we let such a chaotic situation continue, it might get out of hand and backfire. I can feel his honesty and respect him for speaking from his heart. At times, his voice turns constrained and a bit hoarse. He concludes, "As for the demands you made, let us continue to discuss them carefully. Although adequate solutions will take time to reach, we can solve the problems step by step. I hope all of you on the hunger strike are clearheaded about this. We were all young once and also went on strike, and we know what it was like. Please bring your hunger strike to an end."*

The general secretary's appearance has made many of us euphoric, so the square, washed clean and bright by the night rain, is again full of people in the morning who have come to give donations—banners bearing words formed with banknotes, cartons of pastries, boxes of lunch (for the security guards), rolls of plastic cloth, wood boards, truckloads of mattresses, spring water, popsicles, baskets of flowers. Some of the things we can't use, but we just accept them.

17

MY MOTHER AND the student leaders themselves didn't know that while they were talking with Li Peng in the Great Hall of the People on May 18, more than ten field armies had approached and gathered around Beijing, poised to move into the city. After Zhao Ziyang's visit to the students in Tiananmen Square, the hunger strikers believed a suitable solution could be reached soon, so it seemed like they were having a respite for now. Many of them left the square for a break. My mother also went back to campus toward the evening, feeling smelly and unkempt. She wanted to shower and change first thing when she was back in her dorm. And also have a decent meal—a large bowl of instant noodles.

To her surprise, she found her father waiting for her there, chatting with her roommates. He had arrived the day before but hadn't been able to find her anywhere. (Grandpa remembered it wrong: he hadn't dragged my mother away from the hunger strike. She came back to campus on her own.) He wanted to take her home, but she protested, saying she couldn't leave in the middle of the semester. He said her mother was hospitalized and might not be able to see her again if she didn't go back right away. At that, my mother was speechless and agreed to leave for home. But she was so exhausted that she could hardly walk, and her father had to support her all the way to the bus stop, so that they could get to the railroad station. Once there, she called her boyfriend (my father) on a pay phone in the waiting hall, telling him that she might stay home for a month or two. She was a graduating senior, already done with coursework, and had been assigned a job, which she couldn't start until midsummer.

By now the streets of the city swarmed with local people supporting the students and demanding that the government apologize and that Li Peng step down. There were throngs of new arrivals at the train station, most of them students from the provinces who had come to join the demonstrators. The outbound trains were predictably less crowded, and it was easy for my mother and her father to get tickets.

The train was slow, and it took them sixteen hours to reach Harbin. To her surprise, when she got home, her mother was cooking breakfast in the kitchen and stepped out, wiping her hands on the sunflower apron she was wearing. My mom went berserk and demanded an explanation from her father. With a broad grin he said there hadn't been another way he could bring her back peacefully, so he and my grandmother had decided to lie to her to get her out of danger. Lately there had been demonstrations in Harbin every day as well, college students taking to the streets and shouting slogans. Some even demanded that Deng Xiaoping and Li Peng step down, and some wanted to overthrow the

Communist regime. My grandparents were terribly worried about my mother, knowing she was a firebrand, so they had decided to bring her back by any means. She mustn't go back to Beijing, not until the tumult there blew over. Afraid she might bolt on the sly, her mother took away her student ID. They put her under house arrest. She mustn't join the demonstrations in downtown Harbin and on the promenade along the Songhua River either. She was desperate and claimed that she'd have to start her job at the archaeology institute of Tsinghua University. They countered by saying Beijing was like a battleground now, so she must stay home as long as she could.

Unable to go out, my mother listened to Voice of America and the BBC constantly and also watched TV, which showed the developments in Beijing, mostly from the government's standpoint. The foreign radio stations were far more reliable, so she also made her parents listen to their broadcasts in Mandarin. With more time on her hands now, she could keep her diary more elaborately, though she was no longer at the epicenter.

MAY 22: *I am angry at Dad and Mom, but they don't care about my grumbling and protesting. They just smile at each other, their eyes shiny with happiness. Dad says I ought to appreciate their timely intervention, and that without it I would have been stranded in Beijing, where martial law was declared yesterday. Both Li Peng and the military head Yang Shangkun gave vociferous public speeches. They claimed that the student movement caused turmoil that was destabilizing society and disrupting people's livelihood, so* *it must be stopped. They admonished people not to go out and interfere with the implementation of martial law. Li's and Yang's tone of voice was harsh and menacing, which indicated that the government meant to use force this time. In response to the government's drastic measures, the student headquarters in Tiananmen Square declared that the hunger strike would continue. By now more than twenty thousand students have joined in. On the TV the square is swarmed with people, as if it were a festive country fair.*

Worse yet, over a million local citizens poured into the streets of Beijing to stop the army from proceeding to Tiananmen Square. Many civilians begged the soldiers not to hurt the students, who they say have been demonstrating out of deep love for our country. Voice of America broadcast snippets of their exchanges. Some officers promised that they would never hurt civilians because they are the people's army. They had been ordered to come to protect the central government, without any knowledge of what was happening in Tiananmen Square. In fact, though the army is mostly blocked on the streets, the soldiers and the local citizens were calm and peaceful. People offered them water, sodas, fruits, snacks, thick scallions, large pancakes, hardboiled eggs, cucumbers, and tomatoes, giving them a conventional welcome. Some of these offerings were brought over in wheelbarrows and pushcarts. Many young soldiers seem confused, and some are in shock. Despite the locals' success in blocking the troops, it is reported that some key installations are already occupied by the military without being noticed by the public, such as radio and television stations, the editorial building of the People's Daily, *power plants, airports, and the dispatch centers of the railroad.*

In the square a lot of people urge the students to quit the hunger strike because it is not worth sacrificing themselves for such a brazen government. It is time to rebel and do something more vigorous. It looks like the students can't possibly maintain a hunger strike at such a large scale—there are twenty-two thousand participants, so their declaration of a new one might just be a stunt. The situation in Beijing looks precarious and ominous. Nonetheless, I wish I were there. I am afraid some of my schoolmates might think I am a deserter who fled on the eve of battle.

Because my mother was so far from Beijing, her information tended to be a day or two late, but now she could have a broader picture of what was unfolding in the capital and an international perspective, since the foreign media usually reported with a wider and more comprehensive view. Following the news on Beijing closely, she jotted down a lot.

MAY 23: *As I predicted, the students' hunger strike committee held a news conference yesterday morning and announced that they had decided to call off the strike and that the students would resume eating at four in the afternoon. They had been on hunger strike for seven days, but the government simply ignored them, so there's no point in continuing. More than a million people have shown up at Tiananmen Square to protect the students after they heard that soldiers were heading toward the square. Meanwhile, hundreds of students were biking around together in* *celebration of the victory: for two days in a row they had succeeded in stopping troops from entering downtown.*

As a matter of fact, according to the English-language media, about seven thousand soldiers boarded subway trains and got off at stations along the way so that they could enter the city in small groups. They gathered near Tiananmen Square, inside the Great Hall of the People, the History Museum, and the Forbidden City. But so far, they haven't marched out.

The majority of troops, however, are stranded in the suburbs. On every major road, military vehicles stand in long lines: trucks, tanks, armored personnel carriers, all blocked by tens of thousands of civilians, who beg the soldiers not to enter the city to hurt the students. They try to convince the troops that the capital is in good order and that the students are all genuine patriots willing to sacrifice their lives for the improvement of our society. Most soldiers assure the locals that they won't fire at the students, even though they show the civilians there are real bullets in their guns. Still, many civilians declare that the troops will have to run over them first if they break into the city to hurt the students. Near the Tomb of the Princess, hundreds of local residents are sleeping on the motorway to prevent army vehicles from moving forward. They claim they are not afraid of death. The Beijing Workers' Autonomous Union has declared that many factories will go on strike if the army attacks the students.

I saw a great amount of donations by locals pouring into Tiananmen Square: blankets, quilts, down vests, woolen sweaters, toweling coverlets, tarps, towels, and face masks (probably for tear gas). There is also a lot of food, drinks,

LOOKING FOR TANK MAN

pastries, fruits, snacks, medicine. Many pedestrians drop banknotes into the boxes placed along the street by local volunteers. Amazingly, the donations have been delivered batch by batch to the demonstrators in the square without a hitch. One middle-aged woman told a reporter that her group had sent out thirty-one batches today. The student leaders must be flush with cash now. At times kites were flying over the square. The students have more than a hundred kites and a lot of balloons, and they are ready to fly them up to interfere with military helicopters if they fly over again to drop pamphlets and bark orders.

Yesterday afternoon, a vice mayor of Beijing said on TV that over 170 bus routes in the city had stopped service, that all the subways had stopped running, and that 273 buses had been used as road blockers, so that public transport was out of the question. Consequently, people can't go to work anymore. He declared that all the demonstrators would be held accountable for such a catastrophe.

Evidently all the world is outraged by the Chinese government's deployment of field armies against the students. The day before yesterday, in Hong Kong, nearly one million people took to the streets to demonstrate against martial law in Beijing. There were also a million people in Taipei who went out to show their support for the students. Demonstrations took place before the Chinese embassies in Washington D.C., Paris, Bonn. In China, more than twenty cities have seen large demonstrations, and each of the crowds is tens of thousands strong; some processions stretch for miles. In downtown Harbin, over thirty thousand students gathered to protest the use of military force against the civilians in

Beijing. I can hear their voices rising in the north. I wish I could go out and join them, but my parents are adamant about keeping me cooped up at home.

My mother slackened in keeping her diary, since she no longer had firsthand information on the students' activities in Tiananmen Square. What she could get was a kind of bird's-eye view of the situation in Beijing provided by foreign media and a lot of misinformation and distorted views manufactured by Chinese propaganda. In Loana's seminar I had learned that the kites prepared by the students in the square were never flown to interfere with the helicopters, which came every day now. Heavy rain damaged the kites, and besides, the huge crowds there made it impossible to fly them. There was another major event in the square that my mother didn't know about: on the morning of May 23, three young men from Hunan, Mao's home province, got six or seven eggs from a pancake vendor and mixed them with ink and oil paints. They flung the mixture on the Mao portrait hanging on the front of Tiananmen Tower. Students immediately seized the trio and frog-marched them to the police.

It was said there was intense infighting among the student leaders, and that they issued too many announcements. Some of the announcements were composed in haste, contradicting each other, and were infeasible. For instance, they demanded that the National People's Congress, the highest legislature, but only in name, convene right away to dissolve the current government and put Li Peng on trial. That was like firing at an enemy miles away with a pistol.

LOOKING FOR TANK MAN

My mother must have been aware that what she knew now was available to everyone, so she just recorded some major happenings, as if to refresh her own memory later on.

MAY 24: *Beijing seemed to calm down for a day or two. Many army vehicles have withdrawn from the suburbs and returned to their ersatz barracks in the towns near the city. Despite martial law, which prohibits people from taking to the streets, tens of thousands of local residents are still going out to demonstrate. Many gather at Tiananmen Square, raising banners and scrolls inscribed with their demands. Today most of the crowds consist of media workers: editors, reporters, writers, photographers, technicians, staffers. They march out to show their support for the students and their opposition to martial law. They cry, "Down with Li Peng!" "If Li Peng doesn't go, we shall come every day!" Some are so bold that they shout, "Down with Deng Xiaoping!" This doesn't seem to bode well. The doddering Deng, already in his mid-eighties, could become antagonized and set the army on the demonstrators. In fact, it is rumored that the top circle of old hardliners has reached a consensus that the Communist Party has already yielded too much ground to the students and that there is no way to retreat any further—one more step might trigger a total collapse of the regime, they argue. It is also said that Zhao Ziyang was stripped of his position as the party's general secretary on account of his conciliatory stand toward the students and his insistence on revoking the April 26 editorial that had enraged the multitudes so much.*

Yesterday, more than a million locals gathered in Tiananmen Square to demand that the government revoke

*martial law. They shouted, "Defend the constitution!"
"Save the republic!" "Take Beijing back into our own
hands!" "Smash Li Peng's military dictatorship!" All the
anger is concentrated on Li Peng and Deng Xiaoping now.
Most people believe that Deng, "the emperor in his dotage,"
is working behind the scenes and that Li Peng is just his
front man.*

*In other cities large demonstrations cropped up too, particularly in Shanghai, where many writers took to the streets to
protest. Yesterday, in Hong Kong, twenty thousand students
from middle and high schools gathered in Victoria Park, and
they were joined by local residents there. More than seventy-
five thousand people signed their names to a petition for the
cancellation of martial law and for Li Peng's resignation.
They also donated forty-two thousand Hong Kong dollars for
the students in Tiananmen Square. In Guangzhou half a
million students and local residents demonstrated to protest
the threat posed by the central government against people in
Beijing. The situation is so volatile that the White House
just issued a statement urging U.S. citizens to postpone their
travel to China for three days.*

In fact, there had already been small clashes between
civilians and soldiers in Beijing. Both sides pitched brick
fragments and stones at each other; scores of people got
hurt and sent to the hospital. Some local citizens spread
bamboo mats in front of military vehicles and dozed
away on them. But by and large, the atmosphere was
euphoric, and order seemed to be getting restored. Even
the crime rates had dropped considerably at that time.
More than a third of bus routes had returned to service,

and shops were all open, with a stable supply of goods. Only mail delivery remained a problem, thanks to the congested traffic.

People in Beijing believed that the government would have no choice but to rescind martial law. My mother remained aggravated by her absence from Beijing and wanted to run away from home, but she had no money, and she didn't have her student ID, without which it would be hard for her to travel. She told me that her parents gave her a little pocket money, one yuan a day, which was only enough to buy a snack. She was stir-crazy and often blew her stack. My grandparents just let her be. As long as she stayed home, they didn't care how she felt. They only wanted to keep her out of trouble. They made sure she had no national grain coupons on her, so that she couldn't have bought food on the road even if she had escaped with money in her pocket.

She wrote on May 26: *According to* The South China Morning Post, *Deng Xiaoping is not in Beijing. He has been traveling through the provinces, trying to convince the heads of various military garrisons that they accept his decision to use military forces to control Beijing's situation. He tells them that now is the moment that will determine the fate of the Communist Party. To date, not counting the Beijing Garrison, six major garrisons have expressed their loyalty to him. Amazingly, the Ministry of National Defense has not yet shown its support for Deng's decision, perhaps because most of its officers live in Beijing and are unwilling to see the city occupied by soldiers. The other six garrisons have published their support in* The Liberation Army News. *Deng's trip of persuasion might explain the temporary withdrawal of troops from the City of Beijing, where most people are euphoric, assuming the government has caved.*

Yesterday afternoon, there was a demonstration in the capital. The crowd wasn't large, just hundreds of intellectuals, writers, scholars, artists, and editors. They had formed a union called the Capital's Intellectuals Association. These demonstrators are mostly dignitaries who used to be reticent about the party's policies, but they were all quite bold yesterday. The writer Liu Xinwu, under the banner of the magazine People's Literature, *told a female reporter: "I must express our demand for freedom of thought, freedom of speech, freedom of writing, freedom of press, freedom of scholarship. We are opposed to martial law and want to see Li Peng step down. This is the consensus of our entire editorial department. We hope the whole world supports our struggle for fundamental rights."*

In the procession for China Academy of Social Sciences was Liu Zaifu, a leading literary critic. He told the reporter, "We side with the students because we want freedom of speech and thought and also democracy. Our struggle has nothing to do with the factions within the party." The reporter pressed on, asking about what would happen if he got punished as a counterrevolutionary. Liu replied calmly, "I am ready for that. For truth and democracy one has to pay a price." I admire him for saying that, considering he is a senior official.

Yesterday The Liberation Army News *published a letter from the headquarters of the air force, the navy, and the army. It urged all soldiers to remain firm in their position, clear about their political stance, and dedicated to defending the party and the country. The letter went so far as to claim that a small group of people had been inciting turmoil and fanning evil flames—their goal was to negate the Communist Party's leadership and break the socialist system and to overthrow the government. The letter's tone was quite vehement, and this might herald impending violence. It seems the military might go back to take the city.*

Ever since my mother returned home, she had been anxious to get in touch with her boyfriend, Pei Fanlin. He could be rash and outrageous when he got excited or cornered. She hoped he was safe and confined himself to the studio—to the sculpture that he and his fellow artists had been working on. Her parents had no phone in their home at the time, nor would they give her the money for a long-distance call, which cost a lot, more than a decent meal at a restaurant. Luckily a childhood friend of hers, Leilei, had a phone at home; Leilei's father was a middling official in the provincial trade department and needed to be on call at any hour. When my mother went to see Leilei, her friend allowed her to use the phone to call Fanlin's school. The woman who picked up agreed to go to the studio to fetch my father.

MAY 27: *This afternoon I was able to speak with Fanlin at last. He sounded cheerful, saying that he and his schoolmates had been working hard on the sculpture, which is similar to the Statue of Liberty but isn't an exact copy. They named their work the Goddess of Democracy. It also borrows some elements from the Soviet tradition, Fanlin told me. The artwork will be finished in a day or two, but they have had difficulties transporting it to Tiananmen Square, since* *trucks are not available and the traffic in downtown is impossible. But Fanlin assured me they would figure out a way. I told him not to stay in Tiananmen Square for too long. I said, "According to Western media, the army might clear the square with force at any time. I'm afraid some students might get hurt or even killed." "No big deal," he said. "I know how to take care of myself." I couldn't stay on the line for long. It was a long-distance call and would cost Leilei's dad a lot. I feel somewhat relieved after speaking with Fanlin.*

MAY 28: *It is reported that Deng Xiaoping has finished deploying troops around Beijing, in total about two hundred thousand men from various field armies, and there are the armed police to boot. It's also said that Deng is not certain about the Beijing Garrison, so he has brought over many forces from the provinces to prevent mutiny. There is every indication that the soldiers will break into the city and suppress the demonstrators so as to enforce martial law, even though that would be an extreme scenario. I fear that some people might come to harm.*

Three days ago, Li Peng gave a strident speech, declaring that the government was going to "take resolute measures and a clear-cut stand to stop the turmoil." He demanded that all party members ally themselves with the government and fight against rumors and the dissemination of evil ideas and words. The regime seems to be raising the ante, and there will be another round of confrontation in the offing. On May 25, Li Peng received the new ambassadors from Burma, Mexico, and Nigeria. He told the foreign diplomats that everything was under control in China now and order would be restored soon. He also revealed that Zhao Ziyang had been dismissed from his position as general secretary. Li even implied that he was in command now, taking over Zhao's position. It is said that Zhao's crime is severalfold, including "splitting the party" by revealing to Gorbachev that Deng Xiaoping was still in power to make all the major decisions, even though he was supposedly retired. Zhao's revelation is viewed as a maneuver against Deng, the party's supreme leader, since he disclosed that Deng had been the number one power behind the scenes. Li Peng's appearances on TV and the government's repeated warnings seem to have affected the whole country. Numerous ministries and provinces and some major companies have declared their support for the central government's decisions. People seem to sense the shift in the political wind—that the Li Peng regime is about to "pull in the net" on the rioters. In most provincial cities, fewer demonstrators appear in the streets, and most students have returned to campuses. Many public figures, though they were outspoken against the regime a few days ago, have begun to avoid cameras and refuse to be interviewed. From time to time I can feel a chill of dread running down my back. I wish I knew how the students in Tiananmen Square have responded to the new developments. According to Voice of America, there are now more students from the provinces in the square than there are from colleges in Beijing.

Two days ago the U.S. government urged Americans not to travel to China for now. U.S. citizens in Beijing should stay indoors and exercise increased caution about their personal safety.

MAY 31: *I saw on TV that there are numerous new tents in Tiananmen Square now. They are colorful and* *look lovely; some of the large ones are like Mongolian yurts. The new tents were donated by Hong Kongers. Still, I can see a lot of litter on the ground, and many visitors are mingling with the students. Security seems sloppy. Something might be wrong—the square lacks leadership, and it's mainly swarmed with students from the provinces. It looks like a temple fair bustling with people, and some spots are filled with music, songs, poetry readings, performances.*

Yesterday morning about two thousand workers and students gathered in front of the City Police Station, demanding the return of four arrested men who were members of the Beijing Workers' Autonomous Union. The government fears that workers in the major cities, inspired by the student movement, might go on strike, so it has been very severe in punishing workers. The two thousand people in front of the police station also demanded the release of another eleven men belonging to a motorcycle team, the Flying Tigers. The Tigers consisted of hundreds of workers who rode motorcycles and ran to different places to spread news and deliver messages and orders, and also to encourage people. Occasionally a few of them would do wheelies in unison, as if it were a show. They were smashed by the police, who apprehended eleven of them. Evidently, the police treat workers differently from how they treat students, and they are relentless in suppressing them.

Oddly enough, I was able to catch a few glimpses on TV of the erection of the Goddess of Democracy in Tiananmen Square. The statue stands more than thirty feet tall, and it faces the large Mao portrait on Tiananmen Tower. Indeed, like Fanlin said, it is not an exact copy of the Statue of Liberty. The goddess has a Chinese face and raises her torch with both hands. As the artists were up on the scaffolding, busy installing the sculpture, I saw Fanlin among them, wearing a striped T-shirt, his mane flowing in the breeze. A rope was connected to his belt by a big carabiner. Thousands of spectators were there to see the goddess and take photos with her. At noon, when the opening ceremony started, braids of firecrackers exploded and the crowd cheered, though nobody can tell how long she will stand at that precarious spot. Nevertheless, I am happy, happy for Fanlin and his fellow artists.

JUNE 2: *I heard an ominous interview on the radio given by Fang Lizhi, a liberal-minded astrophysicist. He had once been vice president of the University of Science and Technology of China, but he was fired two years ago. He used to give fiery speeches on various campuses, spreading liberal thoughts and radical opinions, but this time he hasn't seemed involved in the student movement at all. A few months ago he wrote a letter to the party's Central Committee to ask for amnesty for some major political prisoners. Professor Fang is highly respected by college students as a spiritual leader, and we all know that Deng Xiaoping hates his very bone marrow. The interviewer asked him whether he was nervous about the possibility that the party might suppress the democracy movement and punish the student leaders. Fang replied that he had heard about a blacklist compiled by the secret police with 109 people on it—and he was at the top of the list, number one. His wife, Professor Li Shuxian, was also on it. But they were not even attempting to flee. He explained, "There is nowhere to hide*

*in China. Moreover, we must not flee at such a moment."
The interviewer pointed out that some officials in charge
of ideology and propaganda considered Fang and his wife
the ultimate "black hands" behind the student movement.
Fang laughed and said, "They have overestimated us. I wish
we two could be that powerful." It seems to me that he and
his wife haven't been active participants in the demonstrations at all. Fang added, "Clearly those in power compiled
the blacklist with suppression in mind. They have done this
again and again since the Movement of Anti-Rightists in
the late 1950s. The students are too naive in their demands
that the party not seek vengeance afterward. They don't understand that history shows such a demand is futile, like
asking a tiger for its skin." Fang's dark view unnerves me. I
respect him and hope he and his wife will be safe.*

*Another disturbing piece of news is that in some counties
around Beijing thousands of peasants, workers, and clerks
went out demonstrating in support of Li Peng's government
and martial law. They shouted slogans prescribed for them,
such as "Long live the Communist Party!" "Support the pro-
letarian dictatorship!" "Carry out martial law!" "Suppress
counterrevolutionaries!" Obviously, they were paid to take
part in the demonstrations. They made me see that most
common people are spineless and disgusting, and many,
driven by fear, would do an about-face without a second
thought. The central government seems to be mounting an
all-out counterattack and might soon attempt to fall on the
students again.*

18

I WAS PUZZLED by my mother's diary, because it stopped on June 2. I asked her why she hadn't continued.

She said, "After June 3, the police and troops began attacking the civilians on the streets. I was too riveted to the TV and the radio to write anything. Then, when the soldiers actually fired at people, I had a breakdown, I was shocked into hysteria and couldn't stop crying."

"Did you attempt to get back to Beijing?" I asked.

"No, who wanted to head that way? Beijing was under attack and the police were busy rounding up student movement activists."

"Were you afraid of being caught?"

"Not really. I was small fry and far away from ground zero, but I was worried about your dad, who was a hothead."

"Was he in Tiananmen Square when the troops went in to clear it?"

"No, he went there only to put up the Goddess of Democracy. He returned to the arts academy afterward."

"Then he must have been safe."

"No, he was hurt."

"How? By the army?"

"He hurt his hand. You'll have to ask him for details. He and I agreed not to talk to you about this sort of thing. He went berserk, but I can't break my promise to him by telling you more about the Tiananmen Square Massacre. It might have traumatized you. If you want to know more, you should go to Tianjin and ask your dad in person."

"I can't do that this time." In two days I'd be flying back to the States. Right now I was busy apartment-hunting online. Fortunately Columbia's housing office helped some. I went on: "When did you and my dad see each other again?"

"Three days after the massacre, he was wanted by the police due to his role in the creation of the Goddess of Democracy. So he fled Beijing and turned up in my parents' home. He meant to see me and find shelter there."

"How long did he stay there with you?"

"Only a couple days."

"Why didn't he stay longer?"

"He had a falling-out with my parents."

"What happened?"

"My father caught us making out on a sofa. He blew his top and chased your dad away."

For a moment I was flummoxed, then I sensed there must have been more to the story. I pressed on, "I don't think Grandpa would blow his top just because he saw you two smooching. There must be more than that. He must've caught you two in bed, didn't he?"

She sucked her breath, her cheeks turning red and her graying bangs glistening a little in the fluorescent light. She blinked and said, "Why are you interrogating me like this? I'm your mother, no daughter should ask her mother such a question." She was pulling the hems of her cream-colored cardigan.

"Mom, stop hedging! Tell me, did you and my dad have sex during those days when he was with you?"

"What a rude question! Why do you ask me such a thing?"

"I want to know when I was conceived."

"Nobody's entitled to know the time and circumstances of their conception."

"But I have to know in this case. I was born on March 28, 1990, roughly nine months after June 1989. Tell me, when did you see my dad again after he left your parents' home?"

"Not until I went to Beijing to take my job in early September."

"So you two did have sex when he was at my grandparents' home."

"We did it only a couple times. Don't make me sound like a sex maniac. We were so sad, and lovemaking helped us manage emotionally. It was just bad luck that your grandpa caught us in bed."

"Mom, this is not about sex."

"Then about what?"

"This means I am a fucking Tiananmen baby!" Suddenly I got so emotional that I couldn't continue anymore. My nose and eyes were tingling, and I nearly broke into sobs.

My mother pursed her thin lips and nodded without a word. Her round eyes blazed for a split second while she licked the corner of her mouth. She managed a smile, as if she remembered something pleasant or tasty.

My vision misted over, but I got hold of myself and didn't let my tears out. In a way I was pleased about this discovery, because it reassured me that the subject of my future scholarship was an appropriate choice, partly rooted in my own being. This could provide more impetus and make me work on the subject with more devotion. I wished I could go to Tianjin and speak with my father, but I had no time for that this summer. I couldn't call or email him about such a sensitive matter. The official monitor could easily follow such communication, and I didn't want to put my father in danger. I'd talk with him in person next time I came back.

My mother knew I was going to study for a PhD in contemporary Chinese history, and she felt uneasy about it. Well, she had no complaint about my field of study, but she was afraid I might stay away from home forever. She often told me to find a good boyfriend and get married, saying I might be old by the time I finished my doctorate. A girl shouldn't give priority to study, she argued.

I could see she was nervous that I might settle down in America and never come back. That might amount to abandoning her, so such a prospect disquieted me as well. Every year I saw her getting more aged, her steps no longer brisk and firm as before. Her life must be lonesome and cheerless. Fortunately, she was in decent health, except for some tooth and gum problems. I promised her that I'd keep her company no matter

LOOKING FOR TANK MAN

what happened in our lives. I also said that with a PhD from Columbia I should be able to find a decent teaching position in Beijing when I came back. She sighed and confessed, "I'm worried you might have too many difficulties living in America alone." That might be true. But if I found a home in the States, that meant I might not be alone anymore.

"Don't worry about me, Mom," I assured her. "I will be with you. If I need to carry you around on my back, I'll do that."

She nodded, her eyes glistening.

19

THROUGH THE HELP of the university's housing office, I found a small studio apartment in Harlem. It was convenient, close to Central Park North—110th Street Station. On a fine day I could walk to school and it took less than twenty minutes. The stroll was pleasant and leisurely. But I didn't do that when it was dark or windy. I was pleased about such an arrangement, given that it was so hard to find decent lodging in New York, let alone a place just for myself.

Professor Bailey was teaching a graduate seminar, Modern China and Asia, which was popular among my fellow grad students. Since he was going to be my advisor, I took his course and did all his assignments on time. I also tried to be active in class and speak up whenever I had something to say. He welcomed classroom participation, which he announced would form a substantial part of our final grades, 30 percent. As long as students argued and were animated in discussion, it would be easy for him to conduct the seminar. Fourteen of us, all graduate students, sat around a large oblong table. Such a format made the class more engaging and more intimate. When we spoke, we had to face others. I

LOOKING FOR TANK MAN

always forced myself to keep eye contact with someone when I expressed my opinions.

Bailey wore a pepper-and-salt mustache and had the kind of tanned skin that people who work outdoors most of the time have. He had mild manners and could be reserved, but he could also become humorous and even passionate about genuine issues. He disliked abstract ideas and would say, "We must think about this in the historical context before we assess its ramifications." He was more interested in specific and intimate details within a historical event, such as who said what and to whom and in what situation. He could often link small details to bigger pictures and themes. I enjoyed the class, which at times was stimulating and illuminating. We chuckled and laughed a lot.

Besides Bailey's seminar, I was also taking two other history courses. The work was manageable to me. It was understood that during the first three semesters I was to devote my time to coursework. After that, there would be a year or so for reading in my field to prepare for the qualifying exam. Once I passed that, I could go ahead and write my dissertation. But having talked with a few older graduate students, I learned that the sooner I was clear about my area of specialty, the better. If I knew the subject of my dissertation, that would make my study more concentrated, so that I would be able to produce stronger scholarship. I tried to follow the older grads' advice and did my best to keep myself focused. Andy told me, "After my qualifying exam, it took me more than two years to figure out what to write for my dissertation.

That's why my project has been going so slow. Don't repeat my mistake. Start to think about your topic as early as possible."

I was quite sure what I was going to write about for my dissertation. So one afternoon in early October I went to see Professor Bailey and talk about my plan. I told him, "I would like to work on Tank Man. Do you think it's suitable for a dissertation subject?"

He gave it some thought, then said, "Of course, it's a central topic in the study of China's democracy movements. But try to make it as broad as possible."

"Do you think it might be too narrow as a topic?" I asked.

"Not necessarily. It's a powerful point of entry to a vast field, so you shouldn't worry about the scope and gravity of your subject as long as you can branch out and associate your topic with other aspects of contemporary Chinese history. One secret in producing a good dissertation is to make a small topic big, exploring it thoroughly."

Encouraged, I went on, "How big should a dissertation be?"

"You mean how long?"

"Yes, I wonder whether there's a requirement."

"That's flexible. But I usually want my students to aim big. Your dissertation should become a book eventually. So at the very beginning, you should treat it as a book project."

"I'll keep that in mind."

He was going to a departmental meeting, so I took my leave. It was a pleasant and reassuring talk. Professor

LOOKING FOR TANK MAN

Bailey seemed quite understanding and encouraging. A good number of his former students had published their dissertations as their first books and were teaching at fine colleges. In the field of contemporary China studies, he seemed to have a great deal of clout. Some of my fellow graduates said I was lucky to have John Bailey as my mentor. In their words, "A powerful professor can help launch your career after you get your PhD." I sensed that too, as I had looked through the recent job placements of his former graduate students—one of them was teaching at UC Berkeley and another at Cornell, so I tried to build a good rapport with Bailey.

He was warm and friendly to me and even introduced me to his wife and daughter. In late October, he invited me to spend a day with his family at their country house. He said, "Lulu, you should get out of the city every once in a while and see the countryside. It's Indian summer now and it's beautiful out there."

I agreed to go with his family, feeling slightly obligated, since there was no way I could decline his invitation. Besides, I was sort of curious to see what a country house was like. His wife, Hilda, was at least ten years younger than he was, in her late thirties or early forties, with a straw-blond bob, an angular face, and a statuesque build—long limbs and a sturdy bone structure. They had a little girl, Soya, five or six years old, who was lively and needed a lot of attention. Around seven-thirty on Saturday morning, I waited for them to pick me up at the entrance to Columbia. I was wearing a pink long-sleeve sweater, jeans, and sneakers. I also had on a flowered headband that could serve as a bandanna. We left the city in their Volvo SUV, heading northeast along the highway. John was driving, with his wife in the passenger seat. Soya and I were in the back. The girl was excited, saying there was a family of turkeys in their backyard and she was going to check how they were doing. When she'd been there last, the family of birds had been in the woods, with three chicks. Soya hoped they were thriving, and her parents assured her that the turkeys must be safe in nature and that the chicks might be like adult birds now.

The Baileys' country home was a small house up the Hudson Valley, near Newburgh, just beyond West Point. It sat on more than two acres of land, facing the south, with a small water view beyond the undulating forest. Now and again a hulking barge passed by on the broad Hudson in the distance, and small boats darted like white birds. With the leaves turning brown, yellow, and russet, the woods appeared feathery and tiered with colors in the sunlight. The Baileys' homestead was lovely and pretty. The air was fresh, as if it were easier to sink into your lungs here. I liked the tranquil surroundings, where there was no sound of traffic. Only birdcalls throbbed from time to time. As we entered the house, I told them how charming it was. Hilda, who worked at a law firm in Manhattan, told me, "We need a place like this so we can escape from the stuffy city on weekends. I'd feel smothered there and can't breathe properly if I don't often come out to the countryside."

LOOKING FOR TANK MAN

She had a slight foreign accent; she had grown up in Norway and gone to college in London. She still had a lot of family in Northern Europe, where the Baileys took a vacation every year. Soya didn't like Europe that much, saying it rained a lot. She took me into the woods beyond their backyard to look for the turkeys. She held my hand while dragging me along. I enjoyed being with her. She seemed fond of me, treating me like a big sister. As we walked through the thick layer of leaves, a big turkey jumped out. The bird was molting, and small new feathers were growing on its back, which were black and shiny. It had a balding head and a large, red wattle. I could see that it must be pretty when it had its full feathers. We followed the turkey to find the rest of the flock. Another two birds appeared, one adult and the other half grown. The second adult turkey had some white and gray feathers and was smaller in size than the first one.

I asked Soya, "Which one of them is the mother turkey?"

"The biggest one is the dad," she said.

"Are you sure?"

"Of course, I've known them for ages. There're others too, two baby turkeys."

So we continued to look around. But to our dismay, we couldn't find any others. There were only the three birds. Apparently the family had been reduced in size. Soya was heartbroken and kept whining, "Where are the other chicks?"

I thought about their absence and guessed that they had either been eaten by other animals or died of disease, but I didn't tell the girl the bad news. Instead, I pulled her out of the woods, and we headed back toward the house. I told her, "Maybe the other chicks are fully grown now and have left to start their own families elsewhere."

"I don't believe you, Lulu. You don't understand—they can't become adults yet."

Her words shut me up, and I just drew her along to the little white house. Soya seemed to have a premonition that something awful might have happened to the missing young birds.

At the sight of her mother, she broke into tears and wailed, "Mom, we lost two little turkeys!"

I explained to Hilda that the family had only three members now. She gathered Soya into her arms, trying to comfort her, saying "It's normal for chicks to leave their parents when they get big. Like you, when you grow up, you'll go to college and live your own life away from home. You won't stay with me and Daddy forever, will you?"

"But there's still a young turkey in the family," the girl cried.

"It must be the runt chick," Hilda said.

Though their land was sizable and adjacent to a state forest, the front yard was quite small. It was covered with leaves, which John said he must blow away or people might think the house was deserted. He went to the tool shed in a corner of the yard and brought out a blower.

LOOKING FOR TANK MAN

I went out of the house and offered to help, saying I could use a rake and gather the leaves into a trash can and carry them into the woods. He said there was no need to do that. As long as he removed the leaves from the driveway and the front of the house, the property would look all right. He said with a smile, "I can't let a young lady do yardwork for me." He put his hand on the small of my back as if to steer me around toward the house and continued, "Go join Soya and Hilda. We'll have lunch soon." His hazel eyes under his overhanging brows winked at me.

I was a little startled, unsure if that was merely an affectionate gesture or a covert pass. Befuddled, I turned away and went back into the house while I felt my face blushing.

Hilda was making lunch, having brought along pumpernickel bread and canned tuna. On the way here she had picked up vine tomatoes from a roadside farm stand. I was eager to see how she made tuna sandwiches, which I couldn't do. I knew I was supposed to use mayo and vinegar, but every time I tried, I had turned out watery mush that would soak the bread through, making my sandwiches soggy or even pulpy, which my mother had said was too messy. Hilda diced an onion and allowed me to slice the tomatoes. While working at the cutting board, I observed her carefully. She opened a can of tuna but didn't remove the top metal sheet. Instead, she pressed it down to squeeze all the water out. When she emptied the can, I saw that the fish was dry and chunky. So that was the trick. If I got rid of the water in the can, I wouldn't make soggy sandwiches ever again. Next summer I'd make tuna sandwiches Hilda's way for my mother. She would love them, I was sure.

Behind Hilda a dozen or so mugs of different colors hung on a tree attached to the oak-paneled wall. She mixed raisins and sunflower seeds into the tuna. She also put the slices of pumpernickel bread into a toaster before using them. Her sandwiches were delicious, the best I had ever had. I couldn't stop complimenting her on lunch. She was delighted, her green eyes batting. She said if you didn't like sweet things, you could replace raisins with chopped olives. I made a mental note of everything so I could make tuna sandwiches like hers.

By midafternoon, John had cleared the front yard. We had to head south back to the city because Hilda had a business meeting at her law firm the next morning. On the drive back, she said she hated to work on weekends, but this was the nature of her work—there'd be a court hearing on Monday, so they had to get well prepared the day before. John told me that usually they would spend a night at their country house, but today was an exception.

Except for his touch on the lower part of my back, which still puzzled me, the trip was enjoyable. Even Soya seemed to have forgotten the disappearance of her two turkey chicks. I remembered that a month ago, at a conference on Long Island, a Japanese political scientist, on hearing that I was studying toward a PhD at Columbia, told me over lunch: "Work hard. American life is gorgeous," he said. He had been apparently impressed by the white mansions along the shore, which must have belonged to old-money families. All those houses had neatly pruned hedges as well as manicured lawns. At the time I was not sure whether his admiration made sense, but now I could see that even a professor in the humanities or social sciences could live decently here. (Hilda had just started at the law firm and, according to Bailey, she didn't earn a big salary yet.) Perhaps my mother would love living outside a small New England town.

20

I HAD BEEN in touch with Jason, who was doing well at Stanford. He was going to specialize in the relationship between mainland China and Taiwan, specifically their international conflicts and entanglements. In his emails and phone calls he sounded more like a political activist than a graduate student. I was impressed by his development and his savviness in realpolitik. By comparison, I was the same person. I had learned more, but I didn't feel that my graduate work had affected my personality that much.

I had mixed feelings about my friendship with Jason. He seemed to try to get close to me as much as he could. He probably viewed me as his girlfriend and might even have told others that, but I didn't feel comfortable about having a stable relationship with him yet. He was decent and warm, but I was not attracted to him. He seemed too book smart, though he was deeply involved in political activities and even believed that small personal efforts could make a big difference. Unlike a typical graduate student, he traveled a lot, and whenever possible would come to New York. He loved the city, where he hoped he could live in the future. That meant he

LOOKING FOR TANK MAN

was going to look for a job in New York or somewhere nearby after he earned his PhD. Unlike me, he didn't enjoy academia that much and wasn't necessarily going to look for a teaching position, but there were so many research institutes, think tanks, and government offices on the East Coast that he was confident he'd be able to land a suitable job somewhere in or near New York. In our communications, I tried to keep some distance, unwilling to mislead him by giving him the impression that I wanted to date him.

In December, the Overseas Chinese Democratic Coalition was going to hold a conference in Flushing. The event was focused on the great famine in China in the early 1960s. Dozens of scholars from different parts of the world were going to participate in the conference, including some from the mainland, though a few major scholars in this area of study couldn't get official permission, and were unable to leave China as a result. In addition to the academic talks, there'd also be discussions about how to overthrow the Chinese Communist regime. A few preeminent dissidents were going to speak about the future crises the CCP was facing. Loana couldn't come because she had to go to Vancouver to see her uncle, who was hospitalized. She had just started teaching at Wellesley College, outside Boston, and was happy about her new job, which was tenure-track. Better yet, her new book had recently been accepted for publication by Oxford University Press. In both career and life, she was doing quite well, having met her boyfriend, a Korean American, at her college, where he was a physics professor. Loana recommended me to the conference organizers, because they needed help, particularly from those who could speak both Mandarin and English. Wentao also contacted me and asked me to serve as an interpreter. I was happy to hear from him again and agreed to take part.

Jason had submitted a paper to the conference and was invited to give a talk. I was impressed. Just two years back, he had been quite callow, but now he was able to speak like a professional activist and a burgeoning political scientist. The conference was to be held at the Sheraton Hotel in downtown Flushing. That was convenient for the participants, who could also stay there. I heard that the hotel owner from Taiwan was quite supportive and generous, and that he had given a large discount for participants' room and board.

The night before the conference I got a phone call from a Mr. Sheng, who identified himself as a vice-consul at China's consulate in New York. He claimed he knew Professor Bailey well and was curious why I was so involved in the dissidents' activities, specifically the famine conference. I said, "They want me to serve as an interpreter, so I agreed."

"Do you know the nature of their gathering?" Sheng persisted in a rasping voice.

"I don't really know," I confessed, "though I have some vague idea about the conference."

"In that case, you should not be involved."

"I've already promised to serve as the interpreter for one event."

"It's not too late to back out. If you don't want to get entangled with them, you'd better not go tomorrow."

"In America, you can't do that, especially at the eleventh hour. A promise is like a contract. If I broke it, nobody would trust me anymore."

"You're dealing with a bunch of China bashers. What could those losers accomplish anyway? You shouldn't take them seriously. Also, you must think of the consequences if you're embroiled with them. Your involvement will only bring you trouble."

"It's not a matter of whether I like it or not. Like I said, it's too late for me to go back on my commitment. I'm sorry, Mr. Sheng. Thank you for your concern. Bye now." I hung up.

In spite of my calm response, I was incensed by the official's interference. Then I grew apprehensive, wondering how he had come by my phone number. There must be secret informers among the dissidents. I called Wentao and told him about the vice-consul's admonishment. Wentao was not surprised and said, "They have contacted others too. They're doing their best to sabotage our conference. Lulu, if you're too nervous, you don't have to join us tomorrow. The last thing I want to do is compromise you."

"Who do you take me for? A backpedaler?"

"Don't get me wrong. I just don't want you to feel uncomfortable," Wentao said in a soothing voice.

"This isn't a big deal. I'll just be an interpreter. See you tomorrow." I tried to sound insouciant, though deep down I knew the officials did keep records. But I remembered Loana had often said, "Everyone has fear, but brave people just don't let fear dominate them." The last thing I wanted was to live a fearful life.

The conference, in a small auditorium with sloping seats, was well attended. The keynote speaker was Yang Jisheng, a former journalist, whose grand book on the famine, *Tombstone*, was more than a thousand pages long in the original Chinese edition. The recent appearance of its English translation had caused a stir and enraged the Communist Party back in China, but Yang was embraced as a leading historian on the subject and had garnered a number of international awards for his courage and Herculean effort to record the historical truth. Before the conference, Wentao and his colleagues had worried that Yang might not be allowed to come to the States, but fortunately he had been in Western Europe at the time and could fly over directly. Mr. Yang had a lined face and a soft voice, though he spoke passionately, his words gushing out as if unstoppable. He seemed very familiar with the political mechanism in the Communist Party and could quote with ease from many preeminent figures, dead and alive. I was impressed by his extraordinary memory and his full command of his materials. He must have done a great amount of "desk work." He wound up by demanding that the Communist Party face this "horrendous manmade tragedy" and apologize for the loss of more than thirty-six million lives in the famine.

A young graduate from Hunter College served as the interpreter, his English and Mandarin both fluent, but I could tell that he might have grown up in Singapore or somewhere in South Asia, because his Chinese was quite soft, a little "too literary and too gentle." From time to time a bookish expression slipped into his translation. But his soft voice matched Mr. Yang's well.

The second speaker was a middle-aged woman wearing a tight bun at the back of her head, a hairdo for countrywomen. She wrote under the name Eva. I served as her interpreter; she could understand English but didn't speak it well. Recently she had published a book in Chinese, *Looking for the Survivors of the Great Famine*, by the Sunbeam Press, which was based in New York. Just now, in the lobby of the hotel, I had come across a long folding table stacked with books brought out by the press, whose titles, especially the political ones, had been quite popular in Hong Kong, Taiwan, and among the Chinese diaspora. In fact, a lot of mainlanders had smuggled books published by Sunbeam into China as rarities; the more sensitive the topics were, the more valuable the books became as gifts. Eva's historical project was rather intimate and personal. It bordered on what could be called microhistory. In recent years, she had interviewed more than fifty famine survivors in her home region in Shaanxi Province, including some of her relatives. Most people were reluctant to recall the dark times, but little by little Eva had managed to draw them out—they became willing to talk to her. Her accounts of their experiences, recorded in her book, were stark and visceral, at times even macabre. She had come upon forty-nine cases of cannibalism.

Now she was speaking clearly and with amazing calm. That helped facilitate my interpreting. When I was agitated, I tended to be less articulate and less able to render a speaker's sentences into decent English. Eva couldn't cover her topic in depth at the conference, and like Mr. Yang, she mainly gave a survey of her project, which had been daring and at times dangerous. Quite often she had been shadowed by the police, and had even been summoned to their local station twice. They told her to quit her interference with citizens' peaceful lives or they would force her to leave. Due to her U.S. citizenship, they couldn't arrest her, so she managed to evade danger. I had read parts of her book and was impressed. It was plain and straightforward, without any verbal decorations, and it was altogether in the voices of the peasant interviewees. It made the book unique and authentic. It showed a different approach to a great historical subject.

My job as her interpreter was somewhat easy for me, and after that, I stayed around to attend the events in the afternoon. The conference provided a boxed lunch donated by Wine Terrace of Four Seas, which in spite of its fancy name was a small restaurant in north Flushing. The food was excellent, and Jason and I ate together during the lunch break. He introduced me to a few Taiwanese attendees, mostly local businesspeople. Two were newspaper editors.

Jason's event started at one. He spoke in Mandarin and then translated his speech into English. His talk was quite different from the others. He presented

LOOKING FOR TANK MAN

Taiwan's response to the famine on the mainland at the time. He focused on Chiang Kai-shek's personal thoughts and assessments of the situation. The Nationalist supreme leader often didn't sleep well during the early 1960s, because the suffering of the Chinese on the mainland was on his mind day and night. He believed that the famine posed an insurmountable challenge to the Communist regime, and that if the calamity continued, the mainland government might implode. That was why he sent several groups of secret agents across the Taiwan Strait to the mainland to probe the state of the PLA's vigilance and its coastal defense system. But unfortunately, most of his men, who were well trained, got caught when they landed. The mainland government utilized tens of thousands of militia to patrol the coast. There was no way the agents' rubber boats were able to reach shore without being detected. In hindsight, Chiang's effort to regain control of the mainland was futile and mostly driven by nostalgia, according to Jason. He pointed out that many officers in the Nationalist military actually misled Chiang, showing him used train tickets and grain coupons that some agents had brought back from the mainland. Those trifles pleased "Generalissimo" Chiang greatly all the same. The old man's mind was fixated on the mainland, especially on his home province of Zhejiang.

To be honest, I didn't think Jason's presentation was that great, though it was indeed informative and unique in its perspective. He made good use of the firsthand material he had access to in the Hoover Institute at

Stanford, so his talk was engaging enough to hold the audience.

Late in the afternoon, there was a panel on a different topic: China's future. Since most of the audience could understand Mandarin, no interpreter was provided for the panel discussion. Wentao was a key member, seated at the front with three others, two men and one woman. I was amazed to hear Wentao speak in an arresting, resonant voice, which I hadn't noticed before. Evidently the public occasion boosted his self-confidence and even made him appear animated and energetic, with a happy face. The four people on the panel each talked briefly about their views of the current Chinese government. None of them seemed optimistic about the prospect of human rights and liberalization in China. As the discussion went on, the topic shifted to Xi Jinping, the brand-new boss of the CCP. It was reported that three years ago, in February 2009, on his visit to Mexico, when meeting with some representatives of the overseas Chinese there, he had declared, referring to the major Western powers, "A lot of foreigners have eaten too much without a way to digest their food, so they can't stop meddling with our affairs. First, China does not export revolution. Second, we do not export poverty either. Third, we don't go out of our way to make trouble for them. Why bother us without stopping? What can justify their endless grumbles? They'd better shut up!"

The panelists all believed that Xi's blatant statement could herald a troublesome future for China. And for the world. Though at this point it was still too early to see Xi's true colors, we predicted that he might be an orthodox hardliner, or else the Communist Party couldn't possibly have lined up behind him, supporting him as its new boss. On the other hand, as some in the audience believed, Xi might carry on the liberal tradition embodied by his late father and start genuine political reform. I didn't like the drift of the discussion. Why should we pay so much attention to Xi's casual speech three years ago? We had many more significant topics to talk about. Why should we spend time trying to fathom Xi's mind, which might just be a black hole? He was going to show his true colors soon anyway.

My sentiment was voiced by a tall young man who stood up in the audience. He tilted his head to his side and said in a flippant tone of voice, "Why are we giving so much time to Xi Jinping? What he said could just be a fart, and there's no need for us to sniff behind him."

Many laughed out loud. Then Wentao said to the man rather ruefully, "His words might indeed be nothing but a fart. But sometimes by the smell of a fart we can tell if someone is healthy."

More people laughed and some applauded.

A middle-aged woman with permed hair rose and said we shouldn't speculate too much at this point. "Who's to tell what Xi Jinping is going to do? Maybe he'll become another Gorbachev. At least I can see that he has a good-natured face. He can't be as shrewd as Old Mao."

That brought out more laughter. One man laughed so hard it seemed like he was having a hacking, coughing fit. Unlike some of the other attendees, I didn't enjoy the lighthearted atmosphere of the discussion and the vulgarity it had lapsed into—too much casual laughter belied the serious nature of the discussion. Wentao pointed out that Xi had become the party's general secretary not because of his ability and merit but because of the power balance among various factions within the party, so we should not expect major changes. The audience all seemed to accept his conclusion. That wrapped up the conference with an anticlimactic ending.

After all the events were over, Jason, grinning mischievously, asked me to go out for dinner with him, but I had to finish reading a book for the next morning's seminar, so I couldn't. He frowned, his eyes dimmed. I knew he meant to push our relationship a little further. I liked him but didn't want to rush. If I went to dinner and got drunk, I was afraid I might end in bed with him. At this point of my life, I had to concentrate so as to survive my first year of graduate studies. But Jason shouldn't feel frustrated—we were to meet the next day also, for lunch with a Taiwanese official.

21

JASON AND I arrived at Chin Chin, an upscale Taiwanese restaurant on Forty-Ninth Street, in Manhattan. Mr. Lim was an official at the Taipei Economic and Cultural Office in New York, which functioned as a consulate of sorts, since Taiwan no longer had a formal relationship with the United States. All the tables were covered with white cloth and were waited on by slim young men in navy suits and red ties. I was amazed that there wasn't a single waitress on the staff. The waiters greeted Mr. Lim warmly. He must be a regular customer, familiar with the place and its employees.

Lim was about forty, of medium height, and handsome, with large eyes, a square face, and wavy hair. He was wearing a three-piece herringbone suit, a burgundy tie, and a gold ring on his finger. He said he was in charge of cultural affairs at the TEC office and often traveled, mainly going to cities in the Northeast and visiting universities. I gathered that his role was similar to that of a consul in a mainland China consulate here. He had been at the conference the day before and we had met briefly. He said he liked the way I had interpreted for Eva, complimenting me on my English, which he said was "clear and natural." Indeed, after studying for four years at Harvard, I could speak the language with more ease now.

"Lunch is on the office," he told us with a smile. "Order whatever you like."

I opened the menu. The dishes were expensive, the cheapest entrée close to twenty dollars. Jason urged me to try Taiwan beef noodle soup, which he said was "absolutely delicious."

"You've eaten here?" I wondered aloud.

"No, but I can tell this place offers genuine Taiwanese food. And beef noodle soup is a special offering in any fine Taiwanese restaurant."

Mr. Lim laughed and said, "That's true. Jason has fallen in love with Taiwanese things."

I teased, "Bet you one day he'll also fall for a girl from Taiwan."

"Don't poke fun at me like this," Jason said. "I'm already falling for you."

That shut me up, my cheeks and ears turning hot. I lowered my eyes to look more at the menu, which indicated with a star the dishes that were Taiwanese folk fare. There were also rows of tiny chilis printed next to some dishes, showing the degree of spiciness.

For himself, Mr. Lim ordered scallion pancakes and a home-style tofu. "Come," he said, "you two are too modest. Get something extra besides beef noodles."

Seeing us reluctant to have more, he ordered a platter of assorted appetizers, saying we could share them. Lim

LOOKING FOR TANK MAN

was a sophisticated host and must take people out quite often.

A few moments after the appetizers had come, a waiter brought over our entrées. The beef noodle soup was indeed delicious and must have been made from a special stock. Lim seemed well connected in academia, knowing both Loana Hong and John Bailey personally. He said he admired Loana for her work on the history of democratic thought in contemporary China, specifically her scholarship on the Tiananmen Square Massacre. Lim also mentioned that he had lunch with Bailey every once in a while. That was a surprise to me. I'd thought my mentor was a pure academic and had little to do with the official world. On the other hand, Mr. Lim's job must be to get to know influential people, especially prominent academics. Over the years I had noticed that Taiwanese diplomats were a lot more capable and tactful than their mainland counterparts. Taiwanese officials usually had congenial manners and were good at mingling with others, perhaps because they shared Western values and felt more at home here. Almost without exception, they were all educated in the West.

Lim asked us about our graduate studies. I couldn't say much about my coursework except that I was busy, having too much to read and too many papers to write. "History is a hard field," he said. "But I admire your choice. I once attempted to study history too, but after a year I gave up. Most foreign graduate students could hardly survive in the humanities."

215

"Where did you do your graduate work?" I asked.

"The University of Wisconsin–Madison. I switched to international relations after my first year there. I started with labor history, but the amount of reading was overwhelming. That was why I later specialized in international politics."

"So your field was similar to Jason's."

"Indeed, I'm more familiar with what he's been studying."

Jason and he started talking about the Hoover Institute, which Lim happened to know well too, having spent half a year there doing research. Jason said he'd been working on Chiang Kai-shek's diaries, which had changed his views of both China and Taiwan. He'd realized that what he used to know about Chiang Kai-shek was based on lies spread by Communist propaganda. By poring over Chiang's diaries, Jason discovered that he was quite humble and at times even large-hearted. He said, "I was moved by his confessions and his attitude toward Christianity. He admitted that he had converted because he couldn't bear the colossal responsibility for fighting the Japanese alone and that he needed God to help him carry the weight of this enormous task. He also kept saying that the Nationalist Party had indulged the Communists too much, that he had assumed they would reform themselves into true patriots. The indulgence sowed the seed of trouble and helped the Communists grow into a powerful opponent."

Lim nodded appreciatively. He seemed familiar with Jason's research and eager to hear his discoveries. Lim was a good listener and didn't talk much. But he assured us that in the future PhDs in social sciences and the humanities would be in high demand and more valuable than those in sciences. He also encouraged us to visit Taiwan, maybe spending a year there so that we could understand the country and the people better. I was amazed he actually referred to Taiwan as an independent country, given that he belonged to the National Party, which still held the belief in one China that included both Taiwan and the mainland. We went on to talk about the relationship, or the trouble, between the two sides. Already knowing Jason's support for Taiwan's independence, Lim asked me, "What do you think of Taiwan's future, Lulu? Do you believe it should go its own way or be united with the mainland eventually?"

That put me on the spot. I hadn't thought out my position, but managed to reply, "I don't like the idea of Taiwan becoming an independent country, but who am I to say what the Taiwanese people should do? This is a matter that must be decided by the Taiwanese, and no one else has the right to meddle with it. If the majority of the Taiwanese people want to secede from China, we ought to go with their consensus. In short, people's will is the mandate of heaven."

Lim's face lit up. "That shows a true democratic spirit, Lulu," he enthused.

His compliment gave me a slight flutter.

Toward the end of lunch, Mr. Lim said we should let him know whenever we needed his help. He gave us each a business card embossed in gold—he supervised the cultural affairs of the Taipei office in New York and had a PhD in political science. Mr. Lim also mentioned that Taiwan had some foundations that were likely to sponsor young scholars like us, especially if we wanted to study and do research in Taiwan. I was happy to hear that and told him I'd keep it in mind.

On our walk to the subway, Jason mentioned that he might try to go to Taiwan in the future, given that the island state was a major part of his field. But I couldn't see any reason that I would head there. Still, I had enjoyed lunch and liked Mr. Lim. The cold air was nipping our flushed faces, and Jason turned and helped me zip up my Canada Goose parka. I held his arm and together we strolled along the sidewalk.

22

WINTER BREAK CAME. Jason invited me to come to the Bay Area, saying it was lovely and sunny in California. I knew that, but didn't go, because I still had too much schoolwork to do—two term papers to finish and some books to read. I had obtained extensions from my professors, but still had to hand them in before the spring semester started. In addition, I wanted to complete my graduate work as soon as possible. Each of the seminars I'd taken had a long reading list; though we were not required to read all the titles and papers, I could tell what the essential readings were. I borrowed several older graduate students' reading lists for their qualifying exams and compiled my own list, which was approved by Bailey. So the sooner I finished reading the books on my list, the better prepared I'd be. I wanted to spend winter vacation reading as well as working on the papers. I wished I could go back to Beijing, but flights were too expensive, and I needed to save for the summer trip home.

Jason's emails made him sound disappointed by my declining his invitation. He said that if New York weren't so cold and dreary in winter, he would have come to spend his break here. He loved the city but preferred the California climate. I wasn't sure about our relationship and at most considered him a good friend. Above anything else, I wanted to follow my daily rhythm and I enjoyed my solitary life and routine work.

By chance I got reconnected with Rachel. She was working at Bloomberg in midtown Manhattan, but she was an intern there, not a full-time staffer yet. She said it would take a few months for her to become a real employee. The truth was she wasn't sure if she really liked her job, which mainly involved handling data in both Chinese and English. She wished she could work on news at Bloomberg, making better use of her English major. The company had promised to let her report stories eventually, but first she had to complete her internship, which she didn't like. She complained that it was her father who had pushed her onto this "wrong job track." I offered to come and see her, but she sent me a photo of her workplace: a chair and a computer on a desk in a large hall. There were hundreds of desks and chairs around her. The room was vast and bright, but the ambience was disheartening. There was no privacy to speak of, and her own space was smaller than that of a carrel in a university library. So I invited her over for brunch. She said she'd love to come and see me at Columbia, since she missed her student days. I was on winter break, so I told her to come anytime.

She came on a Saturday, the same lovely Rachel, though a little paler than before. She was wearing a blue business suit, fishnet stockings, and brown pumps with medium heels. I joked, "You're the picture of a professional woman." Pointing at herself, she said this was her everyday outfit, and she'd been out for a party last night and had been too tired to put on something else this morning. She said, "I don't want to wear a sweat suit for our meeting."

Unlike the graduate students in my department who had already started teaching, I didn't have an office yet, so I had no space of my own on campus. I showed Rachel the Starr Library and then took her to an Italian diner on Amsterdam Avenue. I was apologetic, saying school life could be dull and weary, and there wasn't much to show her, but she said, "I adore your simple life, Lulu. You have a clear purpose and work hard toward that. This makes life focused, peaceful, and meaningful. I wish I had applied to graduate school last year."

"You can always apply if you want to," I said.

"Maybe I will."

The diner was quiet, as lunchtime hadn't started yet. We took a booth and ordered seafood pasta. Rachel grew more vivacious and said she'd been mad at her parents lately, because of the way they'd pushed her into the business world.

"They're crazy," she said. "When I told them about a job opportunity at Bloomberg, my dad got excited and urged me to grab it. He thought it was a way for me to enter stock trading. My job is ridiculous. I hate it so much that I often zone out at work. I was a Harvard graduate, but now I'm doing data entry. I feel cheated. But to be fair, they did promise to let me work on news once I complete my internship. I told my dad he was an ignoramus and had no clue how the American business world operated. On top of that, I don't have business talent like his."

"How did he respond to your complaint?" I asked.

"He admitted he'd made a mistake."

"Don't be too hard on your parents. They meant well."

"At long last I have figured out what I really need: a desk where I can read and write."

"That wouldn't be hard for you to come by if you go to graduate school."

"I'm seriously considering it."

Her words reminded me of a passage by a dissident writer who wrote about the reason for his self-exile: "Throughout the vast country of China, there was no space for a desk where I could sit down and write. Now I am leaving my motherland to acquire a peaceful desk elsewhere." But that man was in a different boat than Rachel, so I didn't bring his remarks up. Rachel could get into a graduate program without difficulty if she preferred. She was a fine critic, and well-read too.

Our conversation turned to our college days. I was curious whether she was still dating Mark Stone. When I mentioned him, her face dropped with a grimace. "Did you have a crush on Mark, Lulu?" she asked, looking into my eyes.

"I don't know. For a while I liked him. He and I once had dinner, and after eating, he wanted me to go to his place to spend the night. I didn't do it because I didn't know him well enough yet."

LOOKING FOR TANK MAN

"Oh, that was typical of Mark, he can't stop running after girls, several at a time. That was why I broke up with him. He said he wanted a 'polyamorous' relationship. I couldn't stomach that. But he argued that if he didn't spend time with other women, how could he tell who was the best fit? I told him that kind of relationship should apply more to a woman than to a man."

I couldn't help laughing and shaded my mouth with my palm.

"What's so funny?" she said. "Look, a woman should know if a man is good in bed, but I can't say how a man needs that knowledge as long as the woman turns him on. Usually if a man wants to date a woman, that means she's attractive to him, and he doesn't have to sleep with her to see if she can turn him on." Rachel speared a boiled oyster from the pasta and put it into her mouth, chewing without opening her lips. Her eyes blazed, as if she was still hurt.

I didn't know how to comment on that, since I was still a virgin, and I didn't want to tell her that. It was kind of embarrassing to admit that at age twenty-three, I hadn't had real sex yet, though I had made out with a couple of boys. Rachel went on to tell me that Mark had gotten engaged a few months before to a blonde from Poland. He and his fiancée were both living in New York. I was surprised to hear that he had been successful in finding a suitable woman. Even more amazing, he had also landed an assistant professorship at NYU. Evidently he was doing well. There was some wistfulness in Rachel's tone when she talked about Mark's engagement.

I tried to console her, saying "Keep in mind that as women, we can't depend on a man for our happiness and must stand on our own feet."

"I admire you for that, Lulu."

"I'm similar to you, just a beginner in real life."

"But you're so steady and clearheaded. You can help stabilize a man's life like an anchor."

I smiled and said, "I'd rather turn a man's head instead of just being an anchor-provider for him."

"If I were a man, I'd go after you."

"It's good you're fond of men, not women."

We both laughed. "Come on," she said, "I know there're always some guys around you. Have you been seeing someone?"

"Not really."

"I know you have a hero complex. Are you still looking for your Tank Man? Don't confuse an icon with reality."

"I'm just working on Tank Man and know he's more imagined than real. He's beyond my reach. To be honest, I may never get married, perhaps because I saw how awful my parents' marriage was. So many people are unhappy, trapped in marriages. How about you? Have you been dating someone seriously?"

"No way. I've been drifting and can't have a boyfriend now because my life is still uncertain, a mess."

"You mean you might leave New York?"

"That's possible. My parents want me to go to Toronto, where they are thinking of living in the future."

"Do you like it there?"

LOOKING FOR TANK MAN

"Canada is closer to a socialist country."

"Is that good or bad?"

"Bad for young people who want to make big money or have a big career."

I was pleased to see Rachel eating with relish. She said she had developed a weakness for Italian food lately and cooked her meals with only extra-virgin olive oil. She had replaced her rice vinegar with balsamic. I could see that she still had an expensive lifestyle, though her father no longer had a lucrative job. She confessed that he actually enjoyed himself nowadays and spent a lot of time practicing calligraphy, since it was believed that most calligraphers lived long.

Before heading back, Rachel asked if she could add me to her WeChat group. I had no objection but made it clear that I wouldn't respond to messages. It was under the internet police's constant surveillance. If you said something unacceptable, it could jeopardize the whole group and maybe even get the host's account canceled. Worse, there were secret informers in most WeChat groups who could report on you. Rachel was all right with my being a mere recipient and observer. She viewed me as a kind of firebrand. The less I aired my strong thoughts on WeChat, the safer it would be for everyone in her group.

23

THOUGH MY DISSERTATION was still far away, I began to think about how to write it, specifically in what style I should approach my scholarship. I had read a good number of books on historiography and on colonialism and imperialism, but most of them were written in heavy-going prose that was ostentatious and often impenetrable. I had misgivings about that type of writing. Kevin Ernst, a fourth-year PhD student, introduced the French historian Fernand Braudel to me. I read parts of his masterpiece, *The Structures of Everyday Life*, and was impressed by the prose, which was clear and straightforward but also subtle and richly textured.

Over the years I had noticed that many historians, especially the young and up-and-coming ones, tended to write convoluted prose that was theoretical and self-consciously cutting-edge. Loana had that style. When she talked, she radiated charm and intelligence, but her academic prose could be opaque, elaborate, and over-complicated, exhibiting unease and diffidence. Her English was not that great, and the ornate academic prose made it lose energy and power. She seemed unaware of that.

LOOKING FOR TANK MAN

Writing should communicate more than speech, and also be sharper and more transparent. Yet I wasn't sure of my opinion and went to see Professor Bailey to seek his advice. He wrote in a style similar to Jonathan D. Spence's, direct and transparent, perhaps because he had earned his PhD from Yale.

I made an appointment with Bailey to meet him in his office. He looked tired, with red-rimmed eyes; he had been correcting the galleys of his new book and had to meet a hard deadline. "The whole set is a mess," he told me about the proof pages. "There're too many typos and even some misplaced paragraphs."

I explained my concern, which was twofold. First, whether clear, straightforward prose is adequate for academic writing. Second, whether such a plain style might hinder my professional development down the road. I mentioned the great scholar Benedict Anderson as an example. His *Imagined Communities*, regarded as a foundational text on nationalism, was so hard to read, with convoluted sentences that also came entangled with quotations from foreign languages. But *A Life Beyond Boundaries*, a memoir first published in Japanese and composed of several long interviews transcribed by his disciples, was wonderful, fresh and full of life. This small book hadn't published yet, but Loana happened to get a copy of the bound manuscript from one of the transcribers and shared it with me. I loved reading it. Ever since graduating from college, I'd kept asking Loana to recommend me books to read, and whenever she came upon a good one, she'd tell me about it.

Bailey seemed impressed by the extent of my reading. I said, "I don't understand why Anderson wrote like that, I mean in *Imagined Communities*. The style is so labored."

"He was a theoretician and had to speak to the theory people in his field," explained Professor Bailey. "But don't be bothered by this. I don't write that kind of ornate academic prose. Even when I was working on my PhD dissertation, I wanted to write a book that my mother could read."

I couldn't help but chuckle. "That was a wonderful ambition."

"Believe me, Lulu, all historians long to write prose accessible to the public."

"But then why do so many young scholars write such opaque and complicated prose?"

"Because many of them lack confidence and often cover up the absence of substance with a nebulous and ornate discourse—and put an erudite verbal veneer over their superficial thoughts. Their words don't refer to things or concrete ideas anymore."

"I see. I have another question about this. Will other scholars view a plain, straightforward style as an indication of the author's incompetence in his or her field?"

"Not at all. We have so many historians who have produced magnificent scholarship in plain prose. Who doesn't want a bigger audience? You're a smart young woman and must follow your own convictions. You should also bear in mind that genuine scholarship should be useful too. Don't just play with ideas. Every sentence must give information or make a statement and must add something to the whole piece. Theories come and go, and every decade has a new theory, but good books stay."

That was reassuring, and his explanation cleared my mind. I thanked him and took my leave. Indeed, as I recalled, I could see that all Bailey's books were written in the kind of language his mother could read. I wanted to write like that too. If I worked on Tank Man, what was the purpose if the victims of and participants in the Tiananmen movement couldn't understand my writings? Much less other people back in China, who had been fed so much misinformation and so many distortions?

From his office I went to Butler Library to check out some books. At the circulation desk I saw two women, one fiftyish and the other who looked like a fresh college graduate, who were waggling their fingers at each other briskly. They both seemed deaf and were using sign language to communicate. The voyeur in me came out. I stepped closer and picked up a book and opened it as if deciding whether to borrow it. To my amazement, the young woman said clearly to the librarian, "She says she's sorry about returning these so late. She was abroad for a while."

"That's okay. Still, she needs to pay the fine," the middle-aged librarian said cheerfully.

The young woman again signed to the deaf one, who responded back. Then she said, "She'll be happy to pay the fine as long as her borrowing privilege is restored."

The older woman was rail thin and had a gaunt face, which was slightly downy. Judging from her whole bag of books, I could tell she was an ardent reader. I wondered what her reading experience was like if she couldn't pronounce the words. It must be a mystery to everyone but her. She might have a mind's voice understood only by her own mind's ear.

The gray-haired librarian said, "All added up—eleven bucks."

The young woman waggled her fingers to convey the message. The older one pulled a ten and a single out of her purse and handed them to the librarian.

"You're all set," he said and raised his hand, a circle formed by his thumb and forefinger.

The wispy deaf woman beamed and gave him a thumbs-up. Then both women nodded at the librarian and turned around to head to the front door. My curiosity got the better of me, and I caught up with them.

"Excuse me, Miss," I said. They paused, and I went on, "Are you her daughter or a relative?"

The young woman shook her head of tawny hair and smiled. She said, "No, I'm just a social worker, and today I came with Cathy." She jutted her chin out slightly toward the older woman. "She needed someone to help her get her library card back."

"It's so kind of you to do this for her," I said.

"It's my job. By the way, I like your scarf, it's pretty."

"Thanks." I touched my checked woolen shawl.

They sauntered out the front door. I was moved, never having seen a deaf person accompanied by a helper like that. In China I had encountered deaf people signing

LOOKING FOR TANK MAN

with each other, but rarely had I met a hearing person who knew their language, to say nothing of accompanying them around. That dove-eyed social worker, who seemed my age, must have a generous heart, doing good work like that. The world can't have enough amiable souls like her.

24

IN HER EMAIL, Loana advised me to keep in close touch with Wentao as a way to be informed of what was happening in the expat community. That would make my graduate work better grounded and more tangible. In fact, I didn't need to reach out to Wentao. Whenever possible, he tried to get me involved in the dissidents' activities. He was interested in my project as well and often mentioned it to others.

In March he told me that they had recently located a former gunner who had been in one of the tanks that had entered Tiananmen Square in early June 1989. According to the source, the man was present when the column of tanks was stopped by Tank Man. Because the former gunner had left the army, he might be willing to talk now. He was living east of Beijing, in Yanjiao Town. I thought that if I met him in person, I might get some new information on Tank Man. I became excited and told Wentao I was going to find him that summer. But soon I began having second thoughts, wondering whether it would be safe to contact the man. Such an activity might be noticed by the police. If they couldn't get hold of me when I was in America, they could always turn on my parents and make their lives difficult. So I couldn't decide what to do now and would probably just play it by ear when I was back.

Though busy with coursework, I had also kept tabs on the evolution of Tank Man in arts and popular culture in the West. For my dissertation, I was going to write a chapter on this aspect, especially about the Western reception and consumption of the Tank Man icon, so I had been collecting material. There were many posters of him for sale online, and all over the world numerous bands had written and performed songs celebrating Tank Man as a rebellious hero who stood firm in opposition to the powers that be. Four years before, in 2009, an Australian choreographer created a dance, a tango, that imitated Tank Man's defiant movements while facing the tanks. More than a decade before that, Michael Jackson had performed in Europe his famous dance "Tank on Stage," in which the Tank Man of Tiananmen Square forms the emotional and aesthetic basis of the choreography. Toward the end of the dance, an American tank, a gigantic M1 Abrams, rolls onto the stage, and out of it jumps a husky GI who is toting an M-16, threatening to fire at pedestrians around him, including Jackson. Then a little girl appears and presents a sunflower to the GI, who sheds his steel helmet and gets on his knees and tearfully confesses his sins. That leads to the final reconciliation between the dancer and the soldier.

In *Chimerica,* a stage play that recently premiered in London, the protagonist, Joe, a noted photographer, managed to catch Tank Man's brave act on camera and smuggled the photos out of China. But he never saw the hero's face. Two decades later, Joe, with the help of his Chinese friend Zhang Lin, embarks on a search for Tank Man. Eventually, Zhang Lin himself turns out to be Tank Man. Clearly, such a plot twist verged on the melodramatic, but it gave the drama a resounding conclusion.

Recently, Fernando Sanchez Castillo, a Spanish sculptor based in the Netherlands, displayed a life-size sculpture of Tank Man in a large shopping mall in Utrecht. This Tank Man was taller and burlier than the real man, wearing black pants and leather shoes, carrying a navy canvas duffel bag in one hand and a jacket and a white cloth sack in the other. For the first time Tank Man was given a face. As we know, in the original photos and footage, we can see him only from behind and aside. In this sculpture the Chinese man closes his eyes as if ready to receive his destruction, his lean, handsome face revealing a calm intensity. It is a very moving piece of work that gives Tank Man memorable features.

I had noticed that over the years, many Chinese artists had created Tank Man images for memorial gatherings and protest meetings, but none of them had ever given him a face. They had usually presented him from behind or aside, or if they ever showed him from the front, they would put a mask over his face, since none of them knew what he looked like. Evidently Western artists were bolder in their treatment of this historical figure, able to let their imagination flesh out the image

LOOKING FOR TANK MAN

of Tank Man. I would have to think more about this difference in the artistic approaches of Chinese and Western artists. I was sure that eventually artworks featuring Tank Man would have different faces, with multiple forms originating from the absence of his original features. He would appear more handsome, even more strapping, than he had been. Ultimately, it would be unimaginable that Tank Man wouldn't get a face. It's the artist's task to make him memorably human, with concrete features.

At night, when I finished my schoolwork, I turned to my Tank Man project, reading books and gathering information about him online. I had been keeping a file to organize articles and my notes. I enjoyed working in my poky apartment at night, when it was quiet, except for noises or cries made by the couples living above or next to me. I always preferred to work alone and could make progress steadily, as long as I sat at my small Formica desk. So I didn't apply for a carrel in the university library. My tiny studio was both my bedroom and my study. It was so untidy that I never let anyone see it. It had become an inviolate space, just for myself. If I needed to meet someone, I went to the Starbucks nearby or just made an appointment on campus. Among my fellow graduate students, I had a reputation for keeping myself to myself, but that didn't bother me. I didn't want to mix too much with others. I planned to complete my PhD in four years so that I could return to Beijing, where my mother needed me. I looked forward to teaching at a college there.

I loved my tiny apartment—my own nest in spite of the high rent, $1,400 a month. It exuded a faint tobacco smell; the previous tenant had probably been a smoker. The four-story building had twenty-six units, and there was a pungent scent of lilac perfume in the lobby and the hallways. Most of the tenants were blue-collar workers. Some young single mothers lived here too. If it was warm, they'd take their children out to the tiny "tot lot" at the east side of the property. The kids—girls wearing cornrows and boys a crew cut—played on the slides and on the tire swings, which were suspended by rusty chains. They also dangled off the monkey bars and crawled into the plastic playhouse there. From my window I liked watching them frolicking and wobbling about. I often imagined walking in the shoes of the young mothers, who must be quite tough mentally. I wouldn't have been able to raise children alone like them.

On my walk to campus, I often happened on homeless men. They would accost me, holding out their leathery hands and asking for money. I didn't give them any, except to beggars who were frail and old. Every once in a while my disregard for their panhandling made them angry. One of them even called out behind me, "Hey, China girl, don't be a tight pussy!" That flustered me, and for days I took the subway to school instead.

I didn't report such occurrences to my parents, whom I spoke with via WeChat. They each had their own connection with me and didn't mix with each other. Whenever I sent them a message, I tended to be concise and apolitical, wary of the official scrutinizers that monitored

LOOKING FOR TANK MAN

such communications. I wrote my father less than I did my mother, even though once in a while he wired me some money, usually five or six hundred dollars at a time. He was smart enough to send me such relatively small remittances so that he could do it more frequently and thus be able to keep in closer touch with me. Whenever I received the money, I thanked him and said he'd better help Mom instead. But with my mother I texted almost every day. Our messages were brief and at times cryptic, just a few words, such as "I miss you, Lulu"; "I saw a new hot pot joint on Broadway"; "Try it!"; "No, too expensive, $25"; "Eat it for me!"; "If you were here, I would."

Through reading Rachel's WeChat group, I could see that she had a coterie of friends around her. They often dined out and reported to each other their experiences and discoveries: what restaurants offered what new dishes and at what prices and what they tasted like. They talked a lot about how they missed street food in China. This was especially true of the ones from Shanghai, who bragged that within half a mile of their old neighborhoods they used to have every kind of food in the world available. I didn't share their hankering for those snacks and street foods of home. I liked American food, which was at least clean and safe, and generally more nutritious. As usual I just followed their chats and didn't add a word. I could see that I couldn't possibly become one of them. I came from humble roots—nobody in my parents' families was powerful or wealthy. In China people have a strong sense of class and tend to be obsessed with rank and social status; they worship power and money. In recent years I had grown out of tune with that herd mentality. My college education abroad had changed me. Deep down I had become American, but I wasn't sure if I was going to settle down in the States yet. That said, I still disliked American pragmatism. Here, everyone seemed a capable businessperson, and I could never become one.

When the people in Rachel's WeChat group argued, someone, upset or enraged, often snapped at their opponents and challenged them by asking "Are you Chinese or American?" One sharp reply was "I want to be human." I was impressed by that answer, though I never attempted to get in touch with the person who offered it. I liked a line by an old poet: "I wear my nationality like a ring." The same poet also had outraged young and old leftists by saying "Your soul is worth more than your country and your nation." It was the snotty young people who grew up in China, spoiled by their parents and brainwashed by the constant indoctrination, who couldn't exist without turning to the collective to seek their personal identity. Some were content to be their country's slaves and fighting dogs. Their love for their country had to be expressed in their hatred for other countries and for foreigners.

25

I HAD MY mother's diary with me. Even though I was already familiar with it, I often perused through it to find something new that might provide clues for my research. I imagined my dissertation in a unique format—a combination of both macro- and microhistory. The broad historical frame wasn't hard to build, but it wouldn't be that original either, and I sensed that my contribution to the subject might lie in any personal aspects and insights I could bring to it. So I often pored over my mother's diary to look at parts where I could focus and dig up more meaningful personal information.

Her mention of my father's injury caught my attention again. I wanted to look into this in the summer. I wanted to visit him and hear what he could tell me. For such a trip, I asked him what my half brothers Yawei and Yasheng wanted to have from America. He texted back, saying they both wanted a pair of Nike sneakers, size 35 for Yawei and 36 for Yasheng. I was not sure what American shoe sizes matched those. My dad was apparently unaware of the difference. I searched on Baidu and found it giving conflicting figures for the American sizes. After some thought, I decided on 5.5 and 6, hoping they would fit my brothers' feet. Then I ordered two pairs from Amazon, paying about 120 dollars total. I wrote my father that I had just bought the sneakers online. That made him uneasy. He asked, "Are you sure they are genuine?" I replied, "Of course. Amazon is not Alibaba or Taobao."

In the beginning it was not easy for me to sublet my apartment for the summer. I put out flyers on campus in early April, but there were few serious responses the first week. So I lowered the rent by a hundred dollars, and it worked miracles. By the end of the following week a young woman who was going to attend summer school at Columbia's Teachers College rented my apartment. I was pleased with the arrangement.

As soon as I handed in my final paper in early May, I flew back to Beijing. Again, my mother and I spent a lot of time together and often chatted in the evenings. She asked me if I had a boyfriend now. I said I had so much to do at school that I couldn't afford to be distracted by dating someone seriously. "I'll be okay, Mom. Don't worry," I said.

"If you don't hurry now, you might become an older lady in a couple of years."

"Why do I have to get married to live a good life? Many young people are not interested in marriage nowadays."

"I want to see you well-set in life."

I didn't continue arguing, knowing she meant to make me into a model not only of academic success but also of personal life. She wanted me to do well in every way, so that my half brothers couldn't possibly follow in my footsteps, more likely making their mother feel diminished. I was uncomfortable about my mother's motivation, though after all it was only a guess, so I made no reference to it.

A shadow flitted across her face when I mentioned I was going to see my dad. She didn't object, and as usual insisted that I come back on the same day.

Yasheng and Yawei were thrilled at the sight of the Nike sneakers. They both hugged me, but I wanted them each to give me a kiss. That made them hesitate. I said, "Come on now, you have to learn how to kiss a girl." So they each gave me a peck. In return, I kissed them on both cheeks. Our dad was delighted to see us interact like full siblings. I asked them to put on the sneakers to see how comfortable they were on their feet. I was relieved to see that the shoes fit well.

Meichin was happy to see me too, saying I looked healthier than when we had last met. Perhaps she meant I had gained a bit of weight, but it didn't bother me, since I had always been skinny and it was all right for me to have some extra pounds. In high school, my classmates had called me Beansprout. I told Meichin that American food could be fattening—burgers, fries, cheese, cakes. That made her laugh.

My brothers had both enrolled in a ping-pong club for the summer, and that day they had to play in a small tournament, so Meichin was going to drive them to the gym. She must have also meant to leave me and my father alone at home so that we could chat more freely. We both sat at their oval dining table, drinking Dragon Well tea. He had all kinds of teas in the cupboard, given to him by his former students, some of whom had made their names as artists, a few more successful than him and working as independent artists who didn't have to teach.

I said, "Dad, I read Mom's diary she kept during the Tiananmen student movement. She mentioned you fled to Harbin and injured your hand. What happened, exactly?"

"Did she give you her diary?" he said in surprise.

"Yes, the diary could be useful for my dissertation, so I want to know more about your involvement."

"Damn, she and I had agreed not to tell you anything about this. It's the darkest period in our life. Her dad drove me out of their home, treating me like a wild dog." He lifted his yellow, globular mug and sipped his green tea. "All right, you're grown-up now, and I don't mind revealing the truth anymore: I was so outraged that I chopped off my pinkie."

"Why did you do that?" I gasped.

"I saw with my own eyes an armored personnel carrier toppling our Goddess of Democracy. I hated those bloodthirsty soldiers who killed people randomly."

"So you were in Tiananmen Square that night?"

"Yes, after we put up the sculpture, I stayed on, afraid a strong gust of wind might blow it over, so I thought I ought to be around in case they needed me to do repair work. During the following days I biked to the square as often as I could, but I didn't stay there all the time."

"Did you see students get killed in the square?"

LOOKING FOR TANK MAN

"Not in the square. Early that morning the army allowed us to withdraw. Some of us were beaten up by the troops, but they didn't open fire on us directly. I had to leave my bicycle behind and locked it to a young parasol tree. I thought it was an old bike anyway and wasn't worth much. Besides, I thought I could retrieve it later."

"Then where did you go from there?"

"I ran back to the arts academy, angry and shaken, because I had seen locals killed and crushed by tanks. The streets were scattered with burning vehicles, bicycles flattened by tanks, shoes, jackets, bags, puddles of blood. Next to a puddle, I saw some banknotes, fives and tens, and wondered who had placed the money there and why. There was only a sprinkling of people on the streets now. Smoke and fire were rising throughout the city, which was like a deserted battleground. Indeed, the city had been given a bloodbath. Everywhere loudspeakers kept blaring that the PLA had successfully crushed a violent counterrevolutionary insurrection. That was a huge lie, and I felt betrayed by the government. The following day I heard from the BBC that Fang Lizhi and his wife had just sought political asylum at the U.S. embassy in Beijing. I used to worship Professor Fang—we all used to think of him as China's Sakharov, but now I felt doubly betrayed. That night I got drunk and kept belting out songs and wielding a cleaver, slashing at whoever attempted to stop me. Seized by a fit of madness, I chopped off my pinkie to express my outrage and despair."

A sudden pang gripped my heart, and I started sobbing, my face in my arms, which rested on the table. I

243

would never have thought he had guts like that, but now I found a different man seated across from me.

He leaned forward and patted my head. "I'm sorry, Lulu. I didn't want to embarrass you and myself, so I made your mother promise never to disclose the truth to you. Now you must think I was a madman, a crazy drunk."

"No, it was your madness that made you a man," I said in earnest, calming down some. "Do you know about Tank Man?"

"I saw his photo on a billboard in Prague a few years ago. I admire the guy, he had a lot of guts."

"Tell me, if you had happened to be at the same spot, would you have been able to confront those tanks? I know it's an unfair question, but some people say he was just an ordinary guy and that many people would have done the same, given the circumstances."

He bowed his head, then lifted his eyes, which were moist but flashing. He said, "They are right. If I were there, I might have done the same, purely out of madness and outrage. Many people were so crazed they were no longer afraid of death. If you were ready to die, you could face the barrel of a gun or a coming tank. Behind that young guy stood many of my generation—we all might have acted like him."

He sounded so sincere that I had no doubt about his words. I used to take him to be a clown sometimes, but now I felt closer to him.

"I'm going to write a dissertation on Tank Man. Do you think I should do it even though it might get me into trouble?"

"You've got to do what you have to do. To be controlled by fear is not a way to live. You're young, and life is still before you. You should listen only to your heart. Don't let other things intimidate or distract you."

"Thank you, Dad, for the encouragement. It means the world to me." I put my hand on his forearm, and he cupped his palm over my hand. Our hands stayed like that for a long while.

When Yawei and Yasheng came back, Meichin began making dinner. I wondered whether to help her, but decided to spend more time with my brothers. They were speaking English better now; their pronunciation had improved considerably. They said there was a young woman, an English major at Nankai University, who came three times a week to give them lessons, and that had put them ahead of their classmates. It appeared that their mother was determined to send them to a middle school where classes were taught in English as a way to prepare them for studying abroad eventually. This meant my dad would have to work hard for many more years.

26

AFTER SEEING MY father, I wrestled for several days with the thought of whether to look for the former tank gunner in Yanjiao Town. My dad's revelation of his self-inflicted injury and his encouragement strengthened my resolve to work on Tank Man, which had become more important to me. I wanted to gather as much new information as possible, though this iconic figure might remain a mystery until the day when the Communist Party's archives were opened to the public. Nevertheless, I wanted to get hold of the former soldier, the tank gunner, just to see what might come up.

According to the information provided by Wentao, the man was named Feng Ming and worked in a furniture factory in Yanjiao. I phoned him, and to my amazement the call went through and he answered. I explained I was a graduate student living in Beijing and wanted to meet him.

"Well, what's this about?" he asked in a gruff voice.

"I've been doing research on the Tiananmen uprising, so I would like to hear your take on the event, since you were there." I used the term "uprising" to show I was not out of line with the official view.

LOOKING FOR TANK MAN

He seemed hesitant, then asked again, "What's in it for me?"

I said, "Uncle, I'm just a poor student and have no money to pay you, but I can buy you a good lunch, how's that?"

"I can tell that you're a good, well-educated girl, so I don't mind meeting you."

"We can find a place near the Yanjiao bus stop, where we can have lunch and talk."

I told him that I was tallish and rather thin and would wear an orange sun hat and a pair of shades, so it would be easy for him to identify me. We agreed to meet at the Royal Garden stop in Yanjiao Town the next day.

That morning I took a taxi to Sihui Bus Station, where I got on a coach bound for Yanjiao. The suburban town was just ten miles away, so I got there in less than an hour, just past eleven. The noon sun was glaring, and it was a little windy. When I arrived, a small man in his late forties came up. He was wearing an olive tank top and frayed jeans, his shoulders glistening with sweat.

"Pei Lulu?" he asked.

"Yes, that's me," I said.

We shook hands. I could tell he was a manual worker, his grip strong and heavy and his arms ropy. I asked, "Where should we go for lunch, Uncle Feng? Do you prefer some place nearby?"

He pointed at a temple-like house with a portico in front and a roof of red ceramic tiles. "That's a good skewer joint, and it also serves draft beer."

"Let's go there," I said.

We started toward the house. The air was rife with the aroma of roast meats and vibrating with traffic din and hawkers' cries. He walked with bandy legs, his rolling gait bringing to mind a crab. Now and again he greeted someone with a nod of his head or a wave of his hand. Stepping into the shade under the portico, he pulled open the wooden door of the restaurant and let me go in first. A large ceiling fan was revolving lazily with a rasping noise in the center of the dining room, which was rather empty, like a large workshop in the off-hours. We picked a window table. The moment we sat down, a moonfaced waitress came and handed us the menu, which felt greasy to the touch. I knew most blue-collar workers liked roasted meats on sticks, and Yanjiao was known for tasty lamb skewers. I didn't want to appear stingy, so I told the waitress, "We'll have twenty lamb sticks, a plate of sautéed vegetables with dried bean curd, two glasses of draft beer, and a large Coke."

Turning to Feng Ming, I asked, "Will twenty lamb skewers and two beers be enough?"

"I guess so. But why Coke? You don't drink beer?" He smiled, showing his slightly protruding teeth. Apparently he appreciated my big order.

"I don't drink alcohol. If my mother finds out I've been drinking beer, she'll scold me."

"You're a nice girl, I can tell."

As we were eating, I began by placing my phone on the table. "Do you mind if I record our conversation?"

"Go ahead, no problem." He took a gulp of his beer and continued munching on a lamb skewer. Evidently

LOOKING FOR TANK MAN

he enjoyed the meat. Under his fingernails there were thin, purple lines of grime.

"Uncle," I said, "I've heard you used to drive a tank in the army."

His small eyes twitched. "I wasn't a tank driver, I was a gunner, in the First Armored Division."

"So you entered Beijing in June 1989."

"We did. It was a bloody time."

"Did your tank crush people?"

"My tank was Number 017, and our company didn't harm any civilians. We just followed the tanks and personnel carriers of the reconnaissance company ahead of us. It was those vehicles at the front that crushed people."

"Why did they do that? As I understand it, the civilians were unarmed and relatively peaceful."

"Who would hurt people on purpose? We tried to enter Beijing in late May, but hundreds of people lay on the road and we couldn't move ahead. So we turned back to our stopgap barracks in the suburbs. Then, on June 3, the order came again that we had to enter the city at any cost. You know a military order always comes like an avalanche, and all the troops were thrown into motion. Either you executed the order or you'd be executed. That's why we just drove ahead, regardless of any obstacles. Lots of buses were parked across the streets to stop us, some in flames, smashed by the tanks ahead of us."

"So some tanks did run over people?"

"Those ahead of us did. They had to open way for us and for the troops following them."

"Did your tank run over anyone?"

"I don't think so. Dozens of civilians were lying on the street, so we stopped and pitched some cans of tear gas at them. That dispersed the crowds. The street was wrapped in smoke right away, and we seized the moment and charged toward Tiananmen Square. We were told that a large mob of thugs were attacking Xinhua Gate, the front entrance to Zhongnanhai Compound, where the top leaders lived. So we were kind of desperate to carry out the orders to protect the national leaders and their families."

"Let's not rush, Uncle. First, you said you had pitched tear gas bombs at the demonstrators, but according to some victims, those were actually poison gas bombs. Some of the civilians died of inhaling the gas, which destroyed their lungs."

"We were told the canisters were tear gas. There was no way we could've known what they really were." He lowered his eyes and lifted his glass of beer as if to conceal his embarrassment.

"When you reached Xinhua Gate, did you see a large mob?"

"We didn't go there, we just stopped at Tiananmen Square. Or maybe we passed it, but I didn't notice a mob on the way."

"So the story about Xinhua Gate was a lie?"

"I can't say that. We just didn't get there."

"Do you know of the famous Tank Man of Tiananmen Square?"

"Who's that?"

LOOKING FOR TANK MAN

"There was this nameless fellow who confronted a column of tanks by himself and stopped them. Several photographers caught the scene on camera, so the photos appeared in the media all over the world."

"When did that happen?"

"On the morning of June 5."

"Oh, our tank was in that column, but we were at the back of it. It was the company commander's tank that stopped in front of him. We thought he was a madman. I guess everyone was crazed at the time, so it was normal to run into such a fierce guy."

"Why didn't the front tank just go ahead and run him over? Some tanks crushed many people, why spare him?"

"That was different. When we were entering the city, we were under orders to move in at all costs. But on the morning of June 5, that guy stood in our way when we were leaving Tiananmen Square without any urgent task on our hands, so nobody would crush a civilian in peaceful times. He must've known that too. We really thought it was normal for the front tank to avoid a civilian. My crew would have done the same."

"Did you see him?" I was curious to know what Tank Man looked like from the front.

"No, I only heard of him later on."

"Do you think the confrontation was actually staged? In other words, the man might have been assigned to face the tanks so propaganda officials could use his case to prove that the army was lenient and careful about people's lives."

251

"I have no clue. It could've been staged, but for a good purpose, I must say."

"Uncle, in retrospect, what do you think of your participation in the suppression of the student movement?"

He grinned almost innocently. "I was merely an enlisted man, small potatoes, and just followed orders. If I were still in the army now, I'd do the same. The first duty for a soldier is to obey your higher-ups."

"Even if it means to kill innocent people?" I looked him in the face while my anger was rising.

His eyes moved away. He said, "How could we know the meaning and results of what we were doing? We'd been confined in our barracks, no radio, no TV, no newspapers. We were made to study the pamphlets and documents provided by the propaganda officers. They said there was a reactionary insurrection in Beijing, and some hoodlums meant to overthrow the government and the Communist Party, so it was our duty to stop the riot. Of course we were used. But we all have been used, one way or another. I'm working my ass off nowadays, exploited by my boss, a damned capitalist."

"More beer?" I asked, seeing him empty the second glass.

"No, I'm good."

"Some tea?"

"No, I'm full."

"Please take all these lamb skewers with you. I have a long way back and can't carry them."

"All right." He smiled and waved at a waitress for a to-go bag.

LOOKING FOR TANK MAN

I fished out the pack of Double Happiness cigarettes that I'd bought at the bus station in Beijing, and handed it to him. "This is for you, Uncle."

"Oh, thanks." He smiled broadly and pocketed the pack.

We had finished. I didn't want to linger too long, in case the local police noticed me. We stood and headed to the door. I thanked him, said goodbye, and went to the bus stop.

I was a little disappointed, because the interview didn't feel that valuable. Worse, I didn't think Feng Ming's memories were accurate. He might have garbled some details and the sequences of events, but I couldn't question him further. To interview him, I'd already been running a great risk. Besides, personal memories can be unreliable, unless they are put in writing right after what happened. In my dissertation, I might have to reconstruct some of the drama and produce a plausible narrative.

27

AS SOON AS I got off the bus at the Sihui station in downtown Beijing, two men and a woman came up. The older man, the leader of the trio, said to me, "Excuse me, comrade student, can you come with us?"

Startled, I stammered, "What for? Who are you?"

The woman flashed her badge and said, "We're from the State Security Bureau. We'd like to know what you did in Yanjiao today." She pointed at a black Grand Cherokee parked nearby. "You must come with us."

"Can I call home first?" I asked, petrified.

"No need for that now," said their leader. "You can call later."

I realized I had no choice but to leave with them and got into their jeep. The younger man of the three was driving, and we turned into a backstreet. In no time, we pulled up at a gray four-story building. They took me to an office on the second floor, which had a low ceiling and a pair of flat, rectangular windows that faced west. The afternoon sunlight was tempered by the opaque air, still shining and falling into the room. Seated at a laminate-topped table, I closed my eyes, not wanting to let them see my fear. I wondered how they had come to know about my meeting

254

with Feng Ming so soon. Had they shadowed me even before I set out for Yanjiao? Did Feng Ming rat me out right after I had treated him to lunch? Or was our meeting just a trap they had laid for me? Had I been on their watch list all along? What were they going to do to me?

I was terrified, but reminded myself not to appear scared or confrontational. It would be better if I played innocent.

A man and a woman, both middle-aged, stepped in and sat down across from me. Then the same young woman who had arrested me at the bus station also came in, but she didn't join them and instead went to a corner to set up a camcorder. She sat down on a folding chair, next to the chrome tripod, gazing in our direction.

The woman opposite me said, "We know you are Pei Lulu and that you graduated from Harvard. You were a good student, but why did you get into political activities here and make trouble for yourself and for others?"

"What did I do, Auntie?" I asked.

The man added, "We know you met a veteran in Yanjiao today. We have the Net of Heaven and can follow you easily." He was referring to the network of surveillance cams, but I felt there must have been something more than the electronic device that had enabled them to focus on me.

"Tell us," the woman went on, "what do you do in the U.S.? Did you find a job there after Harvard?"

I realized that their information on me was not current. I hesitated to tell them the truth, then changed my mind, believing there was no way I could conceal my identity for long. I said, "I'm a PhD student at Columbia University now."

"Huh?" The man looked amazed, twisting his lips into a smile, and said as if in jest, "Tell me, how many millions of dollars did your parents donate to Harvard and Columbia? It's hard to imagine a girl from a regular family going to those top schools."

"Believe it or not, my parents are not rich at all. I got into Harvard thanks to my academic merit."

"I know, I was just joking," he said. "You're a smart girl, and you mustn't waste your life like this."

The woman jumped in, "You haven't answered our question yet: Why did you go to Yanjiao and interview Feng Ming today?"

"Is he a criminal?" I pretended to be surprised.

"He's just a worker, a regular veteran," she said. "But we suspect you're involved in some criminal activities."

"My field of study at Columbia is contemporary Chinese history," I said plainly. "So I should be able to know what Feng Ming did and how he felt when he came to Beijing to crack down on the local residents in June 1989."

The man smiled again, his wide mouth slightly lopsided. He said, "We can see that your interview might be related to your studies, but it's illegal to do such a thing here."

"I'm a Chinese citizen. Which clause of our constitution have I violated by meeting another innocent citizen?"

They both looked puzzled, as if not knowing how to answer. Then the man went on, "There's no use arguing with us. We were ordered to bring you in and question you. Keep in mind, there're no bad feelings on our part. As a father of two children, I admire you and hope my daughter can go abroad for college. But for a regular state employee like me, that's just a pipe dream."

I didn't know how to respond. His daughter must be a graduating high schooler, cramming for the national entrance exam at the moment, which was just a week away. Any parent with such a child must be as restless as an ant on a hot pan. The woman officer made a face and sucked her teeth. She said, "We're also instructed to get hold of your smart phone."

"Why?" I asked.

She said, "We must check what you have done—we can't let you take the contents of today's interview back to the U.S."

"Feng Ming was honest but also cautious," I told her. "He didn't say anything against the government."

"He'd better not have," she said.

"That's good," the man chimed in. "Still we must check your phone. Please leave it with us for a day or two. Here, put down your address so we can send it back to you through the mail."

I wrote down my mother's address, knowing I had to surrender the phone. I didn't feel too bad about this, since the Samsung phone was quite old and I had been thinking of getting another one. I pulled the phone out of my purse and handed it to them. I said, "You won't have a bug planted in my phone, will you?"

The man laughed. "We don't need to do that to keep an ear on you." He motioned the young woman over to take my phone away. He went on, "We will let you go this time, but you must stop these kinds of activities here. If we catch you again, we'll have no option but to throw you into jail. That means you'll be on a special list and it will make your life difficult in the future. So don't stir up trouble again. You ought to concentrate on your studies abroad and avoid getting embroiled with those dissidents in America."

"Okay, I hear you," I said, looking him in the face.

"All right, due to your good attitude, we won't keep you here tonight." He turned to the woman and asked, "Are we done with her?"

She nodded. "I think so." She looked me in the eye and said, "Take this as a lesson and don't make trouble again."

"I'll stay home for the rest of the summer, Auntie," I told her.

She added, "We might summon you again if we have questions. And you must make yourself available for us."

I was stumped, so I said, "I won't make trouble again, and you can reach me at home."

They both nodded and let me go. The second I stepped out of the building, a car whizzed by, tossing up a plastic grocery bag and a haze of dust. I stopped to wonder how to get home. I asked a girl at a watermelon stand where the subway station was. "Over there," she said, pointing at a blue booth beyond a weeping willow, its branches floating in the breeze.

28

DESPITE MY CALM appearance in the State Security Bureau's office building, the interrogation rattled me. After exiting the subway, as I was walking home, I was gripped by a sudden feeling of panic. And I had to sit down on a bench on the sidewalk for a few moments before continuing home. My stomach was churning a little, and I was afraid I might piss myself, though I was wearing a pad for my expected period. The fat leaves of sycamore trees along the street kept flapping, as if to pooh-pooh my fear. Approaching our apartment, my knees went wobbly, like they were about to buckle.

My mother hurried to open the door. "Why did you come back so late?" she asked, her face pallid. "I was worried sick."

I lied, "I lost my phone and went back to the bus station to look for it."

"Did you find it?"

"No, but I filed a claim there."

"Don't worry. It's an old phone anyway."

She was a nervous wreck already, so I didn't want to tell her about the interrogation. Something like that might make her sleepless for days. I hoped the officers didn't summon me again.

That night I transcribed my interview with Feng Ming from memory. I could remember nearly everything he had told me. After I had finished the transcription, I emailed the five pages to my Columbia account to "archive" it.

My encounter with the police upset my summer plans, especially my plan to see Jason in Beijing. He was already back from America and was staying with his parents in Dalian. Originally I had agreed to let him come and see me here, but after my interrogation by the secret police, I thought it might be unwise to meet him now. I was sure they were keeping an eye on me. If Jason showed up here, they'd mark him down as a target too and summon him to a "tea chat." In my email to him, I described what had happened briefly and told him to avoid me for now. He was alarmed and urged me to be more vigilant, to stop doing my "fieldwork," and not to go out alone. We couldn't be too explicit in our communication. We were both distressed by the fact that even at home we felt like we were living in a tight net, as if there were an invisible wall around us all the time. I had heard that ultimately the government intended to turn the country into a wall-less prison, since most things can be handled electronically, and that we were heading toward a cashless society. If you are identified as an unacceptable citizen, the state can invalidate your ID and close your bank account. And then you will be impounded and even earning a living will be out of the

LOOKING FOR TANK MAN

question, since you can't buy groceries or travel anymore. Whenever you went out, the police would be alerted and then follow you. This electronic imprisonment will become the common condition for most Chinese in the near future. In some netizens' words, "Even if you grew wings, you couldn't fly anywhere. You'll be grounded in this immense pig farm."

Within a week, my phone came back in the mail. My mother was delighted, saying she had never expected to see it again. The days were long gone when lost articles were returned to their original owners. But at the sight of the sender's address—the office of state security, she looked astonished and asked me how come they'd gotten hold of my phone. I explained that someone must have sent it to the police, who managed to track me down.

"State security is not the police," she countered.

"They're secret police," I said.

That seemed to pacify her, and she didn't question me further.

I scrolled through the files in my phone and found the interview with Feng Ming erased. Other than that, everything was still there. Yet I had misgivings about the phone now and worried it might be bugged. On second thought, I felt the middle-aged officer, the man with two teenage children, might be right: they didn't need any additional device to keep me under strict surveillance. They had eyes and ears everywhere. So I decided to keep the phone. A new one would cost more than five hundred dollars, which was a lot of money for my father, though he had never complained about paying bills like that.

These days I spent most of the time at home reading books. I could use my mother's library card and had access to the university library, whose holdings were decent. As an employee, my mother could borrow a hundred titles at a time, and most often I would send the library a request by phone for a book in my mother's name, so when I got there, I could just say I was picking it up for her. It was true that common borrowers were not allowed to go to most book stacks directly, especially those for rare or restricted books. You had to check the general catalog first to locate the titles and then pass the information on to a librarian, who would go to the stacks and find them for you. This also meant that a librarian could always bar your access to some titles if he or she happened to dislike you. They could tell you that a book was already on loan or simply missing from the shelf. There was no way you could find out the truth. So I always tried to smile warmly when speaking with librarians, calling them "Teacher" or "Uncle" or "Auntie" if they were much older than I, so that they might be more willing to help me get what I needed.

I discovered that the Chinese translations of theoretical books by authors like Michel Foucault, Benedict Anderson, and Theodor Adorno were more accessible than they were in English. Apparently, the translators had digested the authors' writings thoroughly and then rendered them into relatively plain language, since academic discourse hadn't fully developed in Chinese yet. The Chinese translations were therefore more readable and enjoyable. I hadn't brought back many books,

LOOKING FOR TANK MAN

because I'd been afraid of confiscation at customs. So taking advantage of my access to the university library here, I checked out a good number of translations of the theoretical books I was supposed to read for my qualifying exam. I wanted to prepare myself well for that, though it would be at least a year away. In truth, I enjoyed staying home alone and reading at my own pace. There was a sense of privileged leisure in poring over those recondite books. I realized that by nature I might be more comfortable with a contemplative life.

My mother was pleased to see me staying home so peacefully, not knowing it was because I felt confined by the police. I dared not go out to meet others in fear of getting them entangled. I regretted having sublet my apartment for three months, which made it impossible for me to return to New York before the summer was over. Yet despite the impasse in my "fieldwork," my days spent with books turned out to be productive and energizing. My mother often said that I should find a job I could do at home in the future and that a flexible schedule would suit my disposition, which is indeed somewhat indolent. She even asked, "How could a lazybones like you be a good wife and a devoted mother?"

"Then I'd better stay single," I said, "and live with you forever."

A worrisome shadow crept up her face. She knew I wasn't really lazy, just a little nerdy and carefree, largely thanks to the love and protection she'd provided when I'd been growing up. Every day I cooked dinner before she came back. I would say I was a fine daughter to her and had rarely made her upset. I'd overheard her praise me to our neighbors, saying I was "a big bookworm."

I had been in touch with Rachel, who was an editorial assistant at Bloomberg News now. She seemed to have calmed down some and liked her new job, though it still didn't allow her to write anything official on her own. She said she was more like a secretary to her boss, an editor in charge of news on global stock markets. She envied my long summer vacation and said she should have stayed in academia, where there was a balance between work and rest. "The summer and winter breaks together mean that at least a quarter of the year is free for you," she said.

I didn't counter her assumption. For me, reading and writing were also work. An academic must have some inner compulsion that drives her or him to learn and investigate, so even when not teaching, one is busy day and night. You have to be preoccupied with your subject continuously. That's how you produce significant scholarship.

Every once in a while, Rachel mentioned Joe Ma, her ex-boyfriend who was at MIT now. She said Joe had gotten into serious trouble. He had plagiarized the work of a biologist in the Netherlands and published it as if it were the results of his own research. MIT had just expelled him, but to everyone's surprise, a military lab in Guangzhou had hired him because his project dovetailed with one of its bioscience projects. Rachel wrote, "See, China is a haven where crooks can thrive."

In my reply, I remained temperate in my wording, knowing there were secret scrutinizers reading our emails. I told Rachel, "Everyone has their own way to survive. Maybe Joe will do better in Guangzhou. I have to admit that a jerk has nine lives."

"Once a monster, always a monster," Rachel replied.

I was surprised by her hate for someone who used to be her lover. She called him a male chauvinist pig, saying he had claimed that most women had "longer hair but shorter views." I never liked Joe, but I don't think I could tear someone I once loved out of my heart as easily as Rachel could. She must have dated a lot of men, so maybe it was easy for her to wash her hands of them. She also said that her parents had succeeded in immigrating to Canada recently. "Through an investment immigration," she explained. "They invested half a million dollars in some Canadian business so they were granted permanent resident cards right away. My dad says he wants to live a peaceful life outside China."

Obviously her family still had substantial wealth, even though her father no longer held a job. I feared she might speak too bluntly and reveal too much in our communication, but I couldn't tell her to stop grousing. Every time I was just succinct in my reply. I would explain to her why when we met again. Having been away from China for so long, she had clearly relaxed her vigilance.

29

TWO WEEKS AFTER the fall semester started, Rachel asked me to go with her to Flushing, where she was going to interview someone and where we could have lunch, a genuine Chinese meal. She was assigned to write a profile on an independent publisher, Niu Jian, whose Sunbeam Press had been flourishing. Rachel was excited about the assignment, her very first, but also felt nervous, so she wanted me to keep her company. I didn't accept her invitation right away because I knew of Niu Jian but was unsure of his background. I remembered hearing Wentao once say that Niu Jian had close connections with the Chinese government. It was also whispered online that Niu Jian was a secret agent in North America working for a faction within the CCP. I had seen him on TV. He struck me as sharp-witted and plainspoken.

I called Loana and asked what she thought of Niu Jian, since he had published a book of hers. She laughed and said, "Lulu, you must be still shaken by your brush with the secret police in Beijing. Rest assured, Niu Jian is harmless. He's a gentleman, honest and humorous, totally different from businessmen from mainland China. You should get to know him."

LOOKING FOR TANK MAN

So I agreed to go with Rachel. The night before the interview, I did a little research on Niu Jian, as if I were the interviewer. He was in his mid-forties and had immigrated to Canada in 1993. Later he had come to the States and started his press and an internet media company. Besides publishing books, he edited seven or eight magazines. No doubt, he was a man of energy and vision and business acuity. It was said that Niu Jian didn't know any English, but he loved traveling independently. If he landed in a strange city and was unable to find his hotel, he'd say "Chinatown" to the taxi driver. That was one of the few English words he knew. Once in Chinatown, he could always find a friend or acquaintance who could help him get to his hotel.

Rachel and I were to meet at ten thirty in front of the Flushing public library, which is just a couple of steps from the subway station. I boarded a 7 train to Queens. There were only eight or nine passengers in the car, and I was sleepy and dozing away, because I'd gone to bed late the previous night, working on a short paper for my political theory seminar. The outbound train jerked to a stop, then lurched forward. I opened my eyes and found a stout pigeon with glossy blue-gray feathers and reddish claws strutting past, picking up crumbs of food from the floor now and again. I was fascinated. The bird must be a frequent visitor here, unafraid of people. It passed by, then in a flash turned back and stopped at my feet, its eye gazing at me. It cooed, as if to see if I would give it something to eat. I thrust my hand into my pocket but fished out only a granola bar, which I broke

267

and crumbled with my fingers. Without hesitation the pigeon went about eating the bits I dropped for it. It cooed nonstop while snacking.

The encounter pleased me, partly because out of all the passengers the bird had picked me to beg from. That meant it must have trusted me and known I wouldn't hurt it. There was something mysterious in this—at least I could say I gave it friendly vibes.

At the sight of me, Rachel rose to her feet at the stone steps in front of the glossy wall of the library building. We hugged and then headed north, I just following her. After three blocks, we turned onto Thirty-Eighth Avenue. She said Niu Jian often met people at Rose House, which was at the end of the short street. He lived on Long Island but came here to meet others. Rose House was an exotic place, a café that served tea in the English style, with a large variety of desserts and light dishes. The tearoom was bright and had roses on the tables, in paintings, printed on the walls, on the menu, on the porcelain tableware. People said that the founder was a passionate lover of roses, so they took central place.

Niu Jian was slightly chubby, thick boned, and wore round glasses. His square face brightened at the sight of us, smiling broadly. Rachel introduced me as her friend.

"I know you," Niu Jian said to me. "I saw you interpreting for Eva at the Great Famine conference last winter. You speak English beautifully."

"Thank you for remembering me," I said, elated.

"I know your name is Pei Lulu, a graduate student of John Bailey's at Columbia."

Rachel stepped in, "My friend was known for her keen mind when we were at Harvard."

"My, I have two young Harvard ladies in front of me."

I told him honestly, "I am here just to accompany Rachel. We planned to have a real Chinese lunch in Flushing today. I can stay outside while she's interviewing you."

"Don't go," he said. "This place offers a decent lunch. Let's eat together after the interview." He turned to Rachel. "We can do the interview quickly, can't we?"

I moved aside to an armchair so that Rachel could sit face-to-face with him. She began by asking a question he was famous for. It was about the "China virus," a term he had coined a few years ago when he had given a speech at Congress, warning U.S. politicians not to be contaminated by the Chinese influence, which could "easily debilitate you and make you sick." He referred to that nefarious power as "China virus." To him, even the Confucius Institute, which had branches in many American universities, could be a poisonous influence, undermining academic integrity and freedom. It should be banned, he believed. After the talk at Capitol Hill, the term "China virus" had gone viral itself, online. Niu Jian was attacked for it by swarms of little red flag wavers. Then the term had been picked up by the Chinese media in the diaspora and become part of the political language.

Rachel asked, "What do you mean by 'China virus' exactly?"

"It refers to the corruptive nature of the Chinese influence, which can little by little dissolve your principles and integrity. This virus can worm its way into your system without your notice, so you must be vigilant against it and fight it from without and from within."

"Does this mean you should avoid having anything to do with China?" Rachel went on.

"Generally speaking, the less you deal with China, the better. We must learn how to quarantine ourselves against the China virus."

"But you're a publisher of books in Chinese. Doesn't your theory of the China virus go against the grain of your business?"

"You nailed me there." He gave a big laugh. "You're so sharp, Rachel. Indeed, that's a deep regret in my life. I was born and grew up in this tongue. I wish I could use English like you, but few of my generation could have had your kind of education. Our parents didn't have enough wherewithal to send us abroad to college. I left China with only three hundred dollars on me and had to struggle to survive."

"My next question is, Have you ever felt homesick?"

"No, I have no home in China, where I always found myself out of place and out of tune with its society. Nostalgia is morbid and useless, puerile. I'm a grown-up and enjoy my civil rights here. Once you have tasted freedom, how can you return to a country that's more or less a large prison? China is a jungle without law, uninhabitable for people like me. I just cannot abide that kind of

LOOKING FOR TANK MAN

supervised life again. I prefer to be a homeless wanderer and find an anchorage wherever I can."

Rachel's face lit up. She went on, "So you're afraid of being called in for tea chats if you go back to China?"

"You all know those tea chats are outright interrogations. I know how the police treat people once they land in their clutches. I'm human and afraid of humiliation and pain."

"What do you think of the economic boom in China?"

"I can see the development, but at what cost? I think Deng Xiaoping did more damage to China than Mao Zedong. He made the whole population more materialistic and helped it regress into barbarism. No ethical values are left in the minds of the Chinese anymore."

"That's harsh."

"I'm just saying the truth. Environmentally, China has been killing the hen to get all its eggs. Look at the Chinese political system. Where is the development? It's still feudalistic and still belongs to the Middle Ages, with an emperor at the top and with all its officials acting like eunuchs. Worse yet, most people's mentality isn't different from those who lived a millennium ago. They're content to be servants and slaves of the state. So don't say China is already a superpower. It's a giant with clay feet and could topple anytime."

"Do you view yourself as an exile?"

"No, I am an immigrant. I'm a Canadian citizen, so my homeland is Canada, a country I love and am proud of."

"What is your vision for your publishing company? Do you hope it will become a Random House in the world of Chinese publishing?"

"Ha ha ha, how can I tell what the future holds? I have no capital and don't even know if we can survive this year. One thing I'm sure of: book culture is dying. That's why we have been branching out to online media, which can easily reach a much bigger audience."

"But you've also been publishing magazines. Why's that?"

"Magazines are profitable. I'm a businessman and have to make money to pay my employees and keep my company afloat."

I was fascinated by his answers, which he offered in a heavily accented Mandarin. From time to time he gave a belly laugh like a young boy. I liked him and could see that all the malicious rumors about him were groundless. He was an honest man with an open mind and a sanguine disposition in addition to his acute intelligence. Unlike most dissidents, he was a man of the world, a survivor. If he had been fluent in English, he might have become a heavyweight statesman in America.

When the interview was over, Niu Jian beckoned me to sit closer so we could have lunch together. He handed us each a menu and said, "My treat. Order anything you want. Their offerings are pretty good, but more Italian than Chinese."

I ordered yang chow rice, and Rachel moo goo gai pan. Niu Jian said he liked Italian food and wanted shrimp scampi linguine. He also ordered a glass of white

LOOKING FOR TANK MAN

wine. I was impressed that he used both a fork and a knife, which indicated he was accustomed to Western dining. I glanced at Rachel to see if she was disappointed in not having a more genuine Chinese meal, as we had planned, but she looked happy about our Americanized Chinese food. She must have been eager to spend more time with the interviewee so that she would have more to write. This was all right with me. We chatted more casually as we were eating. Niu Jian told us to consider his company if we ever looked for jobs. "We can't pay you a lot, but we can make the work exciting. There's no censorship at all, and you can influence others with your opinions. Both of you speak English and Mandarin fluently, and we can let you try out as online hosts or even as news anchors."

"Doesn't a woman need to be a beauty to become an anchor?" Rachel asked. "I don't have those kinds of looks."

"That's the Chinese custom. Here, as long as you are articulate and intelligent, you're qualified. Besides, both of you are quite pretty to me. Keep us in mind in the future."

Though Rachel was unlikely to consider working for his company, I made a mental note of his offer.

30

IN LATE OCTOBER, Jason alerted me to a conference that would be held at Boston University at the beginning of the spring semester. It was about political issues of contemporary China. He was going to submit an abstract of his paper and suggested I send in one too. If our papers were accepted, we both could go to Boston for a few days. He was eager to visit his alma mater, while I'd have been happy to see Loana, who lived in Natick now. I decided to submit a proposal based on a term paper I had written the year before. In it I explored how fear functioned in national leaders' decision to suppress the democracy movement in 1989. I argued that the fear was intensified by misinformation, which also reflected the fear among incompetent officials throughout different echelons of power. Several senior party leaders had insisted that there was no room for retreat anymore, and so from their perspective, one step back from their position against the student movement would have led to a total collapse of the party. I believed that even Deng Xiaoping was driven by fear of being overthrown by the students and other political factions. Clearly such emotions among the national leaders were overwrought and had led to their disastrous decisions.

I wasn't confident about my proposal and just sent it out to see what might come of it. In early November Jason was excited to inform me that his paper had been accepted. Then three days later I received a notice of acceptance as well. I was glad about such an opportunity; this would be my first professional presentation. In contrast, Jason was already good at giving this kind of talk, having done a number of them.

When I mentioned the acceptance of my paper to Bailey, he was delighted, and to my surprise he said he would also be attending the conference. A paper of his had been accepted too. He suggested I talk with Professor Deborah Sundar, the director of graduate studies, because the department had some funds for grad students' participation in this kind of academic activity. He said, "I'll speak to Deborah too, and she might be able to provide some money for you."

I thanked him, grateful for his help.

Later, Professor Sundar told me that the department could offer me five hundred dollars for the conference, and that it was hardly enough. But it pleased me greatly all the same. The hotels near Boston University had agreed to give conference participants a discount, so five hundred dollars would be enough to cover my trip and two nights' hotel there if I took the Chinatown bus. What was left should be enough for the conference's registration fee, which for students was reduced to seventy dollars.

During winter break I worked hard on my paper, treating it as if it were going to be published. I planned to develop it into a chapter of my dissertation eventually, since the topic of Tank Man would need to have a political and emotional backdrop to make sense in context and to reflect the power struggles going on in top circles. I wanted to avoid dissipating my energy and ensure that everything I wrote would be used for my dissertation.

I was amazed by the reasonable hotel rates you could find near Boston University, which is just across the Charles River from Harvard. Both Jason and I booked rooms at the Buckminster for $125 a night. I was pleased that I wouldn't need to spend much for the trip out of my own pocket. The round-trip bus fare was just thirty dollars. Late January was a slow business season in Boston, but the conference was quite lively and well attended. My event was in late morning, and it went well. I was glad it happened earlier in the day, so that I wouldn't feel anxious or unable to enjoy myself while attending other talks and meeting friends. I was delighted to see Loana there. She had been recruited to be on a panel, though she didn't give a talk of her own. We had lunch together. She looked more spirited and more cheerful than before, radiating happiness and looking obviously in love. Her sunny face reminded me of the saying "A woman needs love to bloom."

I asked her about her new job. "I enjoy it," she said, and her eyes sparkled. She told me she had just gotten engaged and was about to leave for San Jose to celebrate the Spring Festival with her in-laws.

LOOKING FOR TANK MAN

I was impressed and asked, "When are you going to walk down the aisle?"

"In a year or two. Alan, my fiancé, is in the middle of a project sponsored by a foundation, so he has been working almost around the clock in his lab, in addition to teaching. When this busy period's over, we'll get married."

"Are you going to have a big wedding?" I asked, nibbling at a piece of cheesecake.

"Not really. Both of us are rather private and don't like crowds. We want to do everything quietly."

I admired her self-assurance. I then told her more about my interview with Feng Ming, the tank gunner, outside Beijing the summer before. She told me to be more careful the next time I was in China, saying she had often gotten into trouble with the police there too. Once she had met with two Tiananmen Mothers—the police cross-examined both of them after first interrogating her. The police removed the women's connections with the outside world—no internet or phone service anymore—and assigned packs of men to stand watch outside their doors for weeks. After that, Loana never again met anyone who was under the authorities' surveillance.

Jason's event was on the next day, so he was a little nervous and spent lots of time going over his paper. Bailey's talk was right after the lunch break. I enjoyed his presentation, which was clear and cogent, a model academic talk. He argued that we must look at the top leaders of the CCP with discriminating eyes, because there were several "different breeds" of them. Some were actually quite liberal and pro-Western, and the United States should therefore cultivate the faction that advocated political reform. Unlike most China scholars in the West, he was optimistic about the country, though changes may come slowly and unexpectedly. We had to be patient and seize every opportunity to help the undogmatic leaders in the CCP.

His argument sounded reasonable and moderate, and was probably even acceptable to some Chinese officials, but I could see that some in the audience didn't buy his views, grumbling under their breath. But Bailey was an authority on his subject, in possession of a vast amount of information and statistics, so few wanted to dispute with him openly, even though they disagreed about his view that we mustn't aspire to quickly change China.

During a coffee break, he asked me whether we could have dinner together. I was surprised and said my boyfriend Jason was here, and that he was going to give his talk tomorrow. Bailey insisted that he'd like to discuss my presentation with me at dinner.

After a moment's hesitation, I said, "Then I can join you for dinner, but I might leave a little early. Jason and I have plans this evening."

He nodded, a shadowy smile flitting across his bulky face.

Around five thirty we left the conference for Eastern Standard, an upscale restaurant on Commonwealth Avenue. Bailey had made a reservation, and a waitress led

LOOKING FOR TANK MAN

us to a small table. I was alarmed when he sat down on the chair next to me, because we were in a corner, which felt like it was closing us in. He ordered a glass of merlot, a shrimp salad, and a rib eye steak. He urged me to also have a glass of wine, but I didn't want to. I ordered an arugula salad and crab cakes.

The food was delicious. I thanked him again for such a treat. He said, "The pleasure is mine too. It's great to spend some private time with you, Lulu."

I asked him what he thought of my presentation. He smiled and said I had done well. Then he added, "Maybe you shouldn't have kept your face quite as close to your paper. You should have appeared more at ease, a bit more casual. That would help to make your talk even more engaging and charming."

I nodded, but the truth was that I'd felt tense and nervous. If I had let my eyes go away from my paper, I might have forgotten what I was going to say. I didn't say this to Bailey and just thanked him.

Something touched my knee. I looked down and saw Bailey's hand. He was stroking me, his fingers moving up my thigh as they caressed my skin. He tilted his head and looked me in the eye, smiling suggestively. He said, "You know I'm very fond of you, Lulu."

I grasped his wrist and pushed it away. "Please don't do this," I said.

"Let's go to my hotel room after dinner, and I can talk about your paper in more detail."

"I'm sorry, Professor Bailey. Like I said, Jason and I have plans tonight."

"What fucking plans do you have, going to bed together?" he snapped, his cheeks red and a little puffy. "You'd better level with me. What's your true relationship with Jason Wang?"

"I can't tell you that."

By now, I was too angry to enjoy dinner. I pulled two twenties out of my purse and put them on the table. I stood, saying "Sorry, I have to leave. Good night."

"You can forget about what I just said. Keep in mind, I'm still your advisor." He waved at me almost dismissively.

I hurried out of the door, my heart thumping, while my lungs were straining against my rib cage. A gust of cold wind threw up a wisp of my hair and sent an icy shiver down into my gut. I shuddered a little as I plodded up the street. I was in such fright that I felt my skin crawling.

31

I DIDN'T MEET Jason that night. He had many friends at his alma mater, and he went out with them instead. I felt miserable and humiliated and buried my face in a pillow, sobbing from time to time. I didn't want to talk to anyone about the episode at the restaurant, not even to Loana. Bailey was a distinguished scholar and had just been promoted to a chair professor. Without concrete evidence, few people would be likely to take my words seriously. If I reported him, the whole thing might end up as just my words against his. What's more, he was my mentor, and I was in his clutches academically. I had to be careful to navigate the situation. I slept fitfully that night and felt somewhat woozy the next morning. Before leaving my room, I looked at myself in the mirror and found dark circles around my eyes. I rubbed my face with a warm towel again. I had to hurry, since there'd be some talks I mustn't miss.

Jason's talk was unusual. He spoke about the prospective relationship between mainland China and Taiwan. He argued that both sides had different agendas and goals. The Chinese government was pursuing so-called peaceful national unification as its long-term objective, while the Taiwanese government was seeking peaceful secession and independence. This division in their purposes decided the inherent conflict between the two sides. Taiwan must be patient and avoid any military confrontation and must wait for opportunities delivered by heaven, such as a famine or a pandemic that could weaken Communist rule on the mainland. Whenever the regime in China was in serious trouble, Taiwan would be able to make progress in pushing its agenda of secession. But this should be done methodically. He also suggested practical approaches, such as insinuating Taiwan into as many world organizations as possible and working on the populations of major Western countries, turning them into supporters of Taiwan's independence. If a public petition in support of Taiwan was initiated, it might snowball into an avalanche. By law, once enough people signed such a petition, their parliament or congress would have no choice but to deliberate it openly. If one major Western power recognized Taiwan as a country, many others would follow suit. No matter how powerful mainland China was, there was no way it could fight the whole world.

I felt uneasy about Jason's talk, which seemed to mostly be an array of political strategies—an exemplar of realpolitik. He seemed too deeply involved in Taiwan's politics. After his talk, there was a brief Q and A. People raised questions about the possibility of a war in the Taiwan Strait and how to make the young Taiwanese more willing to identify themselves as Chinese.

John Bailey then stood up and criticized Jason's talk. He said, "What you offered is nothing but a medley of political ruses. You're being trained to become a political scientist, a scholar, not an official aide or a lackey in a government's office. I'm not opposed to pragmatism in our research, but your presentation falls below professional standards. Actually, it debases our profession. Keep in mind that you're supposed to be a scholar, with your own independent views and spirit. You must learn to be impartial and disinterested." Bailey continued trashing Jason's paper. The audience looked muddled, and some were shocked too.

Jason was too flustered to respond coherently. He just said he welcomed Professor Bailey's critique of his talk and would make efforts to fully digest his suggestions. I felt awful, and even ashamed, but there was no way I could explain to Jason why Bailey had launched his outburst like that.

As planned, Jason and I had dinner nearby at Sichuan Gourmet on Beacon Street, which served genuine Sichuan dishes. I ordered water-boiled fish, roast beef and tendon, double-cooked pork, stir-fried bean sprouts, and a seafood soup. I meant to let him enjoy a good meal so as to lift his spirits a little, but he hadn't recovered from Bailey's attack and still felt wounded. He wanted to have some *baijiu*, which after a moment's hesitation I ordered for him. The liquor came in a silver flask placed in a jar of warm water, in the traditional Chinese style. He poured a full shot cup and downed it in one swallow.

He asked me to share the *baijiu* with him, but I refused, saying I couldn't hold my alcohol.

The dinner was depressing. At one point he even cried and said he couldn't understand why John Bailey, a scholar he had always admired and whose vigorous prose style he had even tried to imitate, had attacked him so viciously. All he could think of was that Bailey might have some deep connections with the mainland government and had trashed his paper to defend the interests of the Communist regime. I said Bailey was just a malicious asshole.

"But he's your advisor," Jason said. "Why was he so angry at me?"

I sighed, unable to answer.

We didn't eat much and left most of the dishes behind. Jason was drunk and started reeling when he walked, so I helped him get back to the hotel, which was just a quarter of a mile away. He kept murmuring, "I love you, Lulu. I don't know what I'd do without you."

His room was on the second floor and mine was on the third. After I had taken him back to his place, he held my arm and begged, "Please don't go, Lulu. Stay with me." His other hand began touching my breast.

I kissed him, and we started making out on the sofa. I slipped my hand beneath his shirt and touched his chest. I liked his smooth skin and handsome face. Putting my palm on his crotch, I felt him getting hard.

We went to bed together and had sex. I wanted to please him to make him feel better. He fell asleep afterward, still tipsy and giving a grunt now and again. His

LOOKING FOR TANK MAN

breathing was deep, bordering on snoring. I can't say I enjoyed the sex that night. It hurt some, in spite of the palpitating sensation. He wasn't good at it either, being too drunk to make the right moves to please me, but I was glad I'd done it with him.

The next morning, he was surprised to see two stains of blood on the sheet. "What are these?" he asked me.

"My blood."

"You're having your period?"

"No, I lost my virginity last night."

"You were a virgin?" He almost gasped.

"Yes, you're my first," I said, trying to smile, but my face was going rigid, and I might have blushed too.

"Why didn't you tell me?" he sounded grave.

"Why do you look so sad? Don't you feel lucky I gave you my first night? Didn't you have a good time?"

He turned to hug me tightly and mumbled, "I'll be responsible. Believe me, I'm not a frivolous man."

"Don't be so serious. I just wanted to make you happy."

"You gave me your first time, so I must be responsible for you."

"You have an old-fashioned mindset, Jason. I'm glad I'm no longer a virgin. You know it can be embarrassing to be a twenty-three-year-old virgin nowadays."

"You're a good woman, and I'm a lucky man."

"Don't be such a prude, treating sex as a matter of honor and responsibility. That can make life more of a burden, and it's already heavy enough."

"So losing your virginity wasn't a big deal to you?"

285

"Was it to you?"

"No, I didn't think much about it after my first time."

"It just happened last night. Something natural. Like you were hungry, and I happened to have food, so I was willing to share. That's all. Don't think of me as obsessed with chastity. If you fucked other girls, I'm just another one of them, as long as you enjoyed going to bed with me."

"Please, you're different. You're the only virgin I've slept with, and I won't treat you like the others."

"Okay, you think I'm special?"

"Yes, different from everyone else."

"So it's all right if I tell others you're my boyfriend."

"Of course I am."

He seemed to have recovered some from the previous day's despondency. He left Boston in a buoyant mood.

32

JASON WAS GOING to Taipei for a semester, having received a research grant from the Chiang Ching-kuo Foundation. He was excited about this and asked me to go there and spend some time with him, but I had to do my graduate work at Columbia and couldn't go. I liked him but couldn't say I loved him. From time to time, I mentioned him as my boyfriend, mainly to preempt some other man's attempt to approach me, if I didn't like him. Another reason I didn't want to go to Taipei was that I needed the library here to prepare for my qualifying exam.

Many graduate students, once they were done with coursework, would teach to earn their stipends. But I didn't teach in the spring, because Bailey had helped me secure a fellowship from the department after I'd told him that I wanted to complete my PhD as soon as possible so that I could join my mother back in Beijing. I was grateful to him for the fellowship. But I still felt uneasy about his special attention and avoided meeting him in private.

When the spring semester started, he emailed me and asked me to come to his office to report on my progress in my reading. I was obligated to go, since I was supposed to read books for the qualifying exam, scheduled in the early fall. I had roughly eight months to prepare. Because I had read a good number of the books the summer before, I thought I'd be able to finish the remaining titles.

I went to Bailey's office the next afternoon. He looked happy to see me, calm as usual. I sat across from his desk and said I had been busy reading Edward Said's *Orientalism* and enjoying it immensely. The prose is clear, elegant, sharp, and erudite. And compared to most other scholars, Said wore his erudition lightly. I knew Said used to teach at Columbia, and wished he were still around so that I could have sat in his class. Bailey said he had once audited Said's seminar on imperial culture. "He was brilliant," Bailey said. "What a mind!"

"He's a fabulous stylist," I said.

"I totally agree. That's a model for a public intellectual."

"You mean he wrote for the general public?"

"Yes, he did."

We then talked about my plan for this semester. Bailey demanded that from now on I meet with him every week, because he wanted to ensure I was making enough progress. I agreed to come to his office once a week in spite of feeling uneasy about it.

Before I left, he said, "Lulu, please forget about what happened in Boston. I had a drop too much and lost it. It won't happen again."

"Thank you. See you next Tuesday," I said and stepped out the door, my heart drumming.

Later I talked to some older graduate students about Bailey's demand to meet with me weekly. They all said

LOOKING FOR TANK MAN

I should count that as a blessing, because few professors were so involved in their students' work. Kevin and Andy said they hadn't met their advisors since the previous summer. In general, once you completed your coursework, you were left alone. Many PhD candidates couldn't finish their dissertations in part because their advisors hadn't made them work hard enough. So I ought to feel fortunate to have Bailey pushing me hard, acting like a "slave driver." With such a demanding mentor, I should be able to complete my dissertation soon.

Due to Bailey's demands, I forced myself to read at least three books a week so that I would have something new to report to him. He was pleased about the progress I was making, and said he was impressed by my perseverance. I guessed he had thought I might break down or give up under the kind of pressure he had put on me. To a degree, I enjoyed the reading and cramming. Whenever I finished a good book, I felt enriched. This turned out to be a rewarding period for me.

Besides reading voraciously, I had also been in close touch with Wentao. Whenever there was a gathering in the expat community, he alerted me. Sometimes, before or after an event, he and I would go out for lunch or dinner in Flushing, where I especially liked the small Taiwanese restaurants, where the offerings were clean and tasty, not too spicy or greasy. In recent months he'd been dejected, because his ex-wife had moved away. This meant he wouldn't be able to see his son as often as before, even though he had visitation rights. She had left for Las Vegas to join her current husband, who had accepted a job offer there.

289

I felt awful for Wentao, knowing how much he loved the child. But I also believed he had made a mistake in becoming a full-time democracy activist. As a married man, his first responsibility should have been toward his family. At his age now, already pushing fifty, he must have felt like it was too late to restart his life here. So the promise he'd made to his college friends who had died in Beijing two and a half decades ago might have just been his excuse for remaining within his comfort zone. But I kept reminding myself not to feel smug. I could tell that his pain and suffering were deep and intense. In most aspects, he was a fine man, and I respected him. Who was I to judge a selfless man like him? So whenever he asked me to help him, I made myself available.

In mid-March he called and invited me to a book event. A group of local writers who wrote only in Chinese had just published a book together and were going to hold a gathering in the Flushing public library. On the phone Wentao mentioned a few of the authors, none of whom was that accomplished, but some of them were still fine writers and just unable to publish books individually in America. They had therefore banded together to bring out an annual anthology that contained fiction, poetry, essays, and literary criticism. Wentao said the book included an essay of his. There was also a poet, Wan Fei, who was a fascinating woman I was curious to meet. It was said that she was so absent-minded that once she had gone to the post office to send a pair of kneepads to her son in Dallas, but somehow she had also put into the parcel the hamburger she had been eating. Wentao also mentioned an essayist in his nineties who too had contributed to this annual anthology, even though he could publish his books in both Taiwan and mainland China now. The old man wrote only in Chinese, but had over the decades managed to build a reputation as a major essayist among those in the diaspora. In China there had been several master's theses written on his works. I wanted to meet the old writer too, so I agreed to come.

The event was attended by some thirty people, many of them local artists, but the editor of the book, a plump woman who was a literary critic, had flown in from the Bay Area. Seven or eight authors were also present, most of them middle-aged women, their faces heavily made-up. Wentao seemed to be an oddity among them—he was the youngest author. The nonagenarian essayist was well preserved—he looked like he was still in his early seventies, with a long white beard and overhanging brows and vivid eyes.

The writers sat at a table in the front and began to speak by turns; each said a few words about how meaningful the book was to them. Wan Fei, thin and frail, told us that she had been nervous about its publication, but when the book came out, she was relieved to see everything in her two poems printed right, including the punctuation marks. I could see that she was a knot of nerves, but at times she grew vivacious and even cracked jokes, saying "We need more young faces among us. In a couple of years we'll become fossils, like dinosaurs."

"I'm already a dinosaur," said the old essayist.

"None of the rest of us here may even reach your age, Uncle Tung," replied the poet. "You should feel lucky twice over. I'll be blessed if I can make it to seventy. These days I feel like a cabbage that has gone spongy."

That cracked up the audience again. These amateur authors seemed to belong to another era. Yet they must be living a comfortable life here to have enough leisure for dabbling in writing and other arts. Two or three of them also painted flowers and animals and ancient gods.

The meeting felt like a reunion for the older people. I bought a book and asked Wan Fei and the old essayist to sign it for me. The poet wrote her name in a flourish. Mr. Tung, the old essayist, carefully inscribed his name and then pressed his big scarlet seal beneath his signature. Wentao looked uneasy, a little out of place here. So when Wan Fei invited him to join them for dinner, he said he had other plans and couldn't go with them. As he and I stepped out of the library, the traffic was surging on Main Street, while the last rays of sunset fell like a shimmering haze. It was almost the tail end of the rush hour. Wentao asked, "Can we go to Red Chopsticks for a bite?"

"Okay, I'm famished," I said.

"If you're really hungry, we can go to another place that serves working-class meals."

"All right, let's go there."

He led me to Golden Mall, across the street. In its basement there were a number of regional eateries. We went into the one in the center, where the dining room was larger than the other stalls and where they offered a dish called Spicy and Hot. It was served in a porcelain pot one foot across and about one foot tall, and it contained meat stock, shredded pork, thawed tofu, mung-bean noodles, squid, enoki mushrooms, napa cabbage, and slivers of seaweed. The steaming dish was huge, weighing at least two pounds, and there were so many diners, men and women, hunched in booths, each of them over their own pot and eating. I was fascinated. Though it would be impossible for me to finish a pot of Spicy and Hot, I said, "Let's have that."

"All right," Wentao said and took a seat opposite me. He turned to a scrawny waitress. "Two pots of Spicy and Hot."

"Do you often eat here?" I asked him.

"When I'm starving. The dish is cheap and filling, so it's a good deal. See, a lot of young people are eating it. It only costs ten bucks. I don't like dining out with those older ladies, the local writers. They often go to a fancy restaurant where I have to be careful about my table manners. I try to avoid attending their dinners unless it's a buffet."

"When they go out, who picks up the tab?" I asked.

"Two of the women are wealthy and always take care of the bills. Even outside of book events, they eat together regularly."

Our order came, two pots placed in front of us. Wentao broke his chopsticks and picked up a spoon, while I just used a spork. We began digging in. The dish was quite tasty, the warm soup soothing too. I enjoyed it very much, though as predicted I couldn't possibly eat the whole thing.

Halfway through the dish, I stopped. "I'm full," I said and put down my spork.

He kept eating with relish, sucking in the noodles. I waited, looking around to observe the other diners and the other food stalls, each of which offered a particular provincial food: stuffed pancakes, fried dough sticks served with hot soy milk, tofu jelly, meat skewers, wontons, chive calzones, congees, hot pots, and various types of dumplings. In an adjoining stall, a chef wearing an apron and a tall hat was pulling noodles with his hands. Beyond him two teenage girls, also wearing white hats, were stuffing and wrapping wontons. This small dining mall must be popular with new immigrants.

Wentao finished his dish. I left three singles on the table for a tip. "Why give so much?" he asked.

"Fifteen percent is the minimum," I said.

"Most people just leave one dollar."

"I don't mind giving her three." I was referring to the anemic girl who had brought over our orders.

After we stepped out of the mall, Wentao invited me to his place for tea. I was curious to see how an exile like him lived, so I agreed. We walked east for a few blocks and stopped at a brick building. On its ground floor two or three windows were boarded up with plywood. His place was on the fourth floor. It was not bigger than mine, and its furnishings were even shabbier. There was no kitchen to speak of, and he cooked on a double hot plate. Next to it, on the wooden top of a metal rack, sat a rice cooker. His bedroom was also his office—in the corner spread a full-size mattress on a box. "Sit down and relax," he said, and pointed at a Naugahyde loveseat.

LOOKING FOR TANK MAN

He turned to put the kettle on for tea. I saw a few photos on top of his small bookcase and asked, "Is that your family?" I pointed at the one that featured a young woman and a boy.

"Yes, my ex-wife and my son." He grimaced.

"She's beautiful, and so is your son."

"We could have had an excellent family. I remember when we walked on the streets, people would turn to look at us. I often saw young American women observing us with envious eyes. But that's all gone now. It was all my fault. I don't blame my ex for leaving me for a man who could give her a stable life."

My curiosity aroused, I asked, "If you could rewind the past, what would you do differently?"

"I'd go to graduate school as soon as I landed in the States. But at the time I was so naive that I thought the Chinese government would admit the blunder of the Tiananmen Square Massacre and we'd go back home soon. Everybody could see plainly that the accusations against us, the student leaders, were groundless, so we all assumed that the Communist Party would at least correct their mistake in the near future. I was stupid to wait for that monstrous country to change its course—I couldn't come to terms with exile as my condition. The long wait turned out to be a terrible waste of life, a nightmare. Now I'm too old to restart. Democracy activism has become my profession and sucked me into it, body and soul. For most people this is a loser's business." His eyes were brimming with tears, while a grimace crept over his face.

I was touched and said, "But you've still held on to your original ideals, haven't you? You should feel proud of that."

"Do you like music?" he asked, changing the subject. He put a cup of oolong tea next to me.

"What do you have?"

"I like Brahms," he told me.

"That's Borges's favorite composer."

"I didn't know that. Do you like his stories?"

"Not really, but I like his poetry. Brahms might be too serious for us. We don't need him now."

In fact, I hadn't read many poems by Borges. It was Rachel who sent me poems whenever she came across a good one. The previous fall she'd emailed me Borges's "In Praise of Darkness," which is such an ambitious and gorgeous poem. According to Rachel, it echoes Milton's "When I Consider How My Light Is Spent." I didn't say more to Wentao about how I had come to Borges's poetry, since he didn't know Rachel and I hadn't read much of Borges.

He sat down next to me and said, "You're a smart girl, honest and kind." He put his slim hand on my arm. "Lulu, would you stay with me tonight?" He sounded like he was begging, his eyes gentle, also shy.

A wash of pity swelled in my heart. Overwhelmed by the emotion swirling in my chest, I nodded. Then his hand went up to caressing my face and neck. I could hear his breathing—he was panting slightly.

He was actually a handsome, kindhearted man. If he had been twenty years younger, I might have fallen for him. But tonight I was glad to oblige him and to warm his bed. Before I took off my clothes, I said, "You should know I already have a boyfriend, who is in Taipei this semester."

"Really, you don't mind staying with me for a night behind his back?"

"I like you, as a friend."

He hooked his arm around me and kissed me on the mouth, and I reciprocated. We fell into each other's arms on the mattress. He said he hadn't touched a woman for more than four years and might be clumsy. He *was* clumsy, but he tried his best to please me with his fingers and mouth, caressing and kissing me gently. He went on touching me between my legs until I began moaning. Then he got up and turned to the closet and took out a condom. "I hope this won't break," he said. "It's already five years old." He didn't need to worry about that. Soon after he had entered me, he came. He sealed his ejaculate in the rubber by tying a knot at its mouth, folded it carefully, and placed it next to his slipper. Embarrassed, he said, "I'm sorry. I will need to practice with a woman to get my sexual stamina back."

"Don't feel that way. You're a kind man. If only I were twenty years older."

I had no idea why I had said that. Those words had just come out, like a sigh. Then he cried, almost wretchedly, lay down beside me, and buried his face in the pillow. I began combing his thick hair with my fingers. He must have realized there wouldn't be a real relationship between us and he'd have to let me go when it was light.

33

FOR DAYS, I was agitated. I was half-expecting Wentao to call me, but he didn't. His silence eventually made me feel relieved. If he had persisted in reaching out to me, that might have complicated things, and I wouldn't have been able to act without hurting him. He had a keen mind and understood it would be better for both of us if he kept me out of his life. By nature he was a good-hearted man.

I felt lazy in the spring, but my life was simple and orderly. I stayed indoors most of the time, reading and writing notes on index cards. I preferred the traditional way of research and kept a box of cards that were filed by topics related to Tank Man. Gradually my dissertation began to take shape in my mind. In addition to an intimate narration of the unfolding of the student movement, I was going to analyze the abnormal fear that was in the top echelons of the CCP. I wanted to explain how this fear made the hardliners misjudge the situation and motivated them to bring in the field armies and ultimately unleash their forces on peaceful civilians. Besides discussing the possible origins of Tank Man, I would

LOOKING FOR TANK MAN

also describe the dissemination of the iconic image in the West and throughout the Chinese diaspora—how it was consumed and evolved in artistic presentations. More essential, in the last part of my dissertation I would meditate on my personal investment in this academic project since I was a Tiananmen baby.

That was just a rough outline I had in mind. As I continued with my research, I could see that my project had been growing more substantial by the month. That meant I should be able to complete the dissertation quickly. But for now, I had to finish reading the books, about fifty titles total, for the qualifying exam. Only after that could I begin writing.

Recently I had realized I had neglected some of the deeper implications of my project, which I must unconsciously have pushed aside in order to proceed with full steam: if my topic of Tank Man remained taboo to Chinese authorities, it would be difficult for me to find a teaching position in China after I earned my PhD. I thought of discussing this problem with Bailey, but was unsure of him. He might try to use my vulnerability to pressure me to cave in to his advances. I called Loana one night and talked with her about my concern over the consequences of my dissertation topic.

"I can see that it might become a serious problem," she said, her nose blocked due to the flu she had just caught. "But we can't always adapt ourselves to the world. It would be better to stick to our own position and make the world adapt to us."

"That's right." I was so impressed that my shadowy room seemed to brighten for a few seconds. "Any more suggestions?" I asked.

"You ought to follow your heart," she said. "You should first consider how well your project will meet the academic requirements here. That is the first step."

"So forget about job opportunities in China? My mother would be mad at me if she knew this. I promised to go back and take care of her."

"With a PhD and a good dissertation in your hands, you should be able to find a teaching position in the States. As a matter of fact, you shouldn't rush back right away. You can teach here for a few years and then find a more suitable job in China or Hong Kong. That way you won't have to please your superiors in any department, because they might decide to hire you as an associate professor, as if you already had tenure."

"That makes a lot of sense."

"You must be careful about going back. There's no academic freedom in China, so in the long run your scholarship might suffer there. If you go back, you should make sure you have a way to come back to America for research and professional exchanges."

"I'll keep in mind what you said, Loana."

We turned to other topics. By chance Rachel came up in our conversation, and I told Loana that she was an editorial assistant to a news editor at Bloomberg now. Loana remembered her fondly and said Rachel shouldn't be wasting her mind like that. I wondered how I could pass her opinion on to my friend, but didn't know if I should. Maybe Rachel liked her new work now, since it allowed her to do some journalism.

On Tuesday afternoon, I went to see Bailey again. I reported my recent readings to him and also talked about the schedule for my qualifying exam. I would need the whole summer to get fully prepared, so I suggested taking it in early September. He gave it some thought, then said, "That will work. I'll tell the department to schedule for it."

"In a couple of weeks, I am heading home. My mother misses me and wants me back as soon as I can."

"So we should meet at least twice before you leave, shouldn't we?"

"That's true."

"I want to be updated on your progress. Don't think of me as a slave driver. It's my responsibility to make sure my students complete their work on time."

"I appreciate your efforts, Professor Bailey."

"You don't have to keep calling me professor. Please just call me John."

"Okay, see you next Tuesday, John."

I stood to take my leave while he smiled without opening his lips. There had been a rave review of his new book, *The Politburo of the Chinese Communist Party*, in *The Times* last Sunday, so that was probably why he appeared cheerful.

Over the next two weeks, I tried to figure out which books to take back with me for the summer. In other words, which books could pass customs in Beijing? I decided on a dozen or so titles that didn't contain graphics or bear any reference to China on their covers or in their front matter. Tsinghua University's libraries didn't show their online catalogs to outsiders, so there was no way for me to tell from here what would be available there. I had to guess what books I might be able to find at Tsinghua so that I didn't have to bring those along. I also set up some Gmail and Hotmail accounts, because I couldn't take my index cards back with me. Even if I could have, I might not have been able to bring them out of China when I returned. I meant to use the email accounts as safe-deposit boxes: whenever I accumulated some notes and materials, I emailed them to those accounts so that I could access them when I was back in the States.

Meanwhile, I applied for a dissertation grant from the Chiang Ching-kuo Foundation. I described the Tank Man topic pretty elaborately to give the impression that it was well researched and that I was ready to embark on writing. I called Mr. Lim in the Taipei Economic and Cultural Office and talked to him about my project. He was delighted to hear from me and asked me to send him my application as well so that he could have some idea of it. He also said that he would put in a good word for me if he could. According to the requirement, I needed to get two letters of recommendation for my application and have them submitted by the end of April.

At my next meeting with Bailey, I mentioned my application for the fellowship. He was pleased to hear that, saying it would help speed up my research and writing if

I was granted one, and he'd be happy to write on my behalf. I was relieved. Bailey could be sly and mean, but he wouldn't break a promise. He often used the phrase "the word of a gentleman," which meant one must keep one's promise after it was made. He had once explained that if you went back on your word, people around you would consider you a liar, and in America, that was a serious character problem and people would shun you. Today he mentioned that his wife's law firm had just taken a Chinese company's case, and because it involved millions of dollars, Hilda was going to have to go to Shanghai and Guangzhou frequently with her colleagues. He would probably also go to keep her company on one or two of those trips if he could take a break from teaching and writing.

As for the other recommendation, I asked Loana if she would do it. She had received a grant from the same foundation before, so her letter would carry plenty of weight. She was always ready to help, saying she was familiar with my project. A letter for me was in her file, and she just needed to update it.

In late April, I heard from Jason again. He said he would be returning to Dalian in late May and would be staying with his parents for the rest of the summer. He wanted to go to Beijing to see me, and I was pleased but made clear that I wouldn't be able to take him around, given the more than forty books I had to read. That was fine with him. I was still unsure if I wanted to develop a long-term relationship with him, but I thought my mother might like him, so it wouldn't hurt to keep her pacified with his presence in my life. She always feared I might end up as a *sheng nü*, a leftover woman. That didn't bother me, though. I could imagine a good life without having a man with me. America had taught me solitude, and I could accept it as a normal condition for me.

Jason invited me to Dalian, saying it was a wonderful city for a summer vacation. A cool breeze blew over from the ocean at night, and it was never too sultry during the day. It was similar to Boston in climate, only less humid. I guessed he would want his parents to see me, but I felt uneasy about meeting them so soon. Nevertheless, I was tempted, having heard so much about that elegant city. I had to curb my urge to go so I could finish reading my books. I said I couldn't join him there this time, though I might in the future.

34

IN EARLY MAY I was back with my mother again. I promised her that I wouldn't go anywhere during the summer, and my life began to involve only three points: home, the university library, and the market, where I went to buy stuff for dinner that I cooked for both of us. I even told my father that I wouldn't be able to come to Tianjin this summer because I had to cram for the forthcoming exam, which for a PhD candidate was like a matter of life and death.

In mid-May he came to Beijing to see an expert herbalist for his arthritis. He stopped by while my mother was at work and we had lunch together—rice noodles sautéed with bean sprouts and slivers of chicken. He enjoyed the meal I'd made. Over lunch, we talked about my plan. He was happy to hear about the progress I had been making. He was well-read and had a lot of common sense, so in general I trusted his judgment. I told him about my dissertation topic and my worries about potential trouble with the Ministry of Education when I came back.

He lowered his head of graying hair and took a sip of the tea I had poured for him after lunch. He said, "You shouldn't worry ahead of time. Who's to tell what will happen in a couple of years? Maybe Tank Man will become a significant public topic one of these days."

"What if the government makes my life difficult? If the Ministry of Education interferes, I won't be able to find a decent job here."

"Who knows what will happen? Maybe you won't need a teaching position when you come back. Didn't you used to say you wanted to work at home, as a freelance translator?"

"You're right. How come I forgot I could do different things? I promised Mom I'd take care of her in the future. If I can't find a job here, I might not be able to do that."

"Keep in mind, your mom wants what's best for you. She must hate to let herself become an obstacle to your development."

"I haven't talked to her about this yet."

"There's no need to make her worry in advance. You must first complete your PhD. I'm sure that's what your mom wants you to do, since you've already come such a long way."

Before he left, I made four big tuna sandwiches for him to take back. I told him my brothers might enjoy this typical American food. I wrapped each sandwich in cellophane and then put them into a small blue cooler for him to carry back. The conversation with him put my mind at ease, so I never brought up my concern to my mother. As planned, I proceeded with my graduate work in earnest.

LOOKING FOR TANK MAN

In early June, I still hadn't heard from Jason, though I had emailed him a few times. I was certain he had finished his research in Taipei and was back in Dalian now, but why didn't he respond to my messages? This was unlike him. He was supposed to be with his parents now. My mother was excited about his imminent visit and kept asking me what food he liked and whether I wanted him to stay with us. I had no idea about his plan or his preferences and couldn't answer her.

By mid-June, I still hadn't heard from him. Something must be wrong. I had the phone number of his parents' home, so I called the Wangs one night. His mother picked up, and I introduced myself as Lulu, a friend of Jason's.

She said, "I hope you're not his girlfriend, are you?"

"Not really. We went to college in Boston at the same time." I was somewhat relieved that Jason hadn't told his parents that I was his girlfriend.

Mrs. Wang said, "So you went to college in America too?"

"Yes, he and I have known each other for some years."

"His dad and I think we made a terrible mistake in letting him go to the U.S. for college. The American education has warped his mind."

"Why do you say that, Auntie?"

"In recent years he won't stop talking about Taiwan's independence. He said we must respect the will of the Taiwanese people. We argued with him a lot, but there was no way to bring him around. Originally, we didn't object when he began to look into the Tiananmen

307

insurrection, but we didn't expect he would adopt all the Western biases against China. He kept saying our country had betrayed him and the Chinese people, and that our government is the world's number one liar."

"But I remember Jason once said that Mr. Wang had participated in the Tiananmen movement."

"Yes, but now my husband regrets getting entangled in that."

"Why does he feel differently now?"

"What was the good of the whole thing? Look at those former student leaders. Where are they? They've all settled down in the West and enjoy themselves, eating bread soaked with the blood shed in the Tiananmen suppression. Do you think they would become better leaders if they toppled the government and seized the power? Do you think they'd be better than the Communists?"

"I've no clue, Auntie. But where's Jason now? Is he staying with you at this moment?"

"No, the police have detained him."

I was shocked by her words. After a moment, I went on. "How did he land in the police's hands?"

"We didn't know what to do with him, so we let the police handle him. Maybe they can straighten him out."

"You mean they arrested him?"

"His father is here. Let him talk with you."

A smoky voice turned up and said, "If you're Jason's friend, you should persuade him to give up his reactionary views and irreverent behavior. None of you youngsters should become a separatist in support of Taiwan's secession from China."

"I'm not a separatist, Uncle. Just now Auntie said the police apprehended Jason. What's his crime?"

"The police kept an eye on him for a long time. I'm sure they have some evidence against him. It's good to let them stop him before he falls too deep into the swamp of crimes. What's your full name? I will let him know you called when I go and see him again."

I was alarmed. If they could turn in their own son, they could easily sell me to the police without thinking twice, so I lied, "My name is Mei Ru. Just tell Jason I wish him a quick release and smooth return to Stanford."

"No problem, I'll do that."

My heart kept kicking. I sensed that Jason must have done something more than express aberrant views to prompt the police to take him into custody. Probably he had done something unacceptable to the government. Still, even for that, they shouldn't have arrested him like a criminal. It seemed like something terrible had happened.

Jason's trouble made me restless. What's worse, I didn't know how to break the bad news to my mother, who was still expecting to see my "boyfriend." In her mind, he might have already become a prospective son-in-law. I got online to search for any news about Jason, but there wasn't any mention of his detainment by the Chinese media. This made me more apprehensive. I realized someone could vanish in China without any trace or noise, like a leaf that falls in a dark night and is swept into a valley or river—nobody notices its disappearance or cares to know its whereabouts.

I also tried to scale the Great Firewall to access Google, but to no avail. I emailed Loana to see if she had heard anything about Jason, whom I wasn't even sure she remembered. Luckily, she got my message and responded within a day: "It's big news here. Jason Wang was arrested for spying for the Taiwanese military. It's said that he went to Port Arthur and shot photos of a nuclear submarine. The coastal sentries seized him and handed him over to the police. He is in serious trouble now. Don't attempt to contact him from within China or you'll endanger yourself. Try to keep a low profile and come back safely soon."

I was flabbergasted, and dared not communicate more with Loana about this, since emails were monitored by the internet police. I had known that Jason was active in advocating for the Taiwanese cause, but I never thought he'd be willing to serve as a spy. They must have paid him for that. Of course, the so-called crime might have just been something pinned on him, as the police can always trump up a charge. I hoped Jason hadn't revealed anything about me. But again, I had done nothing against the Chinese government and shouldn't be afraid of any charges. But as far as politics was concerned, there was no rationality in China, and anything could happen. What I feared most was a long detention that would disrupt my graduate work at Columbia. Just by keeping my passport, the police would have been able to ground me here permanently. Ideally, I should have headed back without delay, but my

LOOKING FOR TANK MAN

apartment was already sublet and wouldn't be available until the end of August.

But following my intuition, I stayed put and continued my daily routine. My mother was amazed that I could be as peaceful as a Persian cat. She even said that at my age, she had been boy-crazy, sneaking out of the house to meet someone whenever she could. She couldn't possibly have discerned the turmoil and grief in me. I simply couldn't afford to attract any attention while I was here. This was the way to survive, but I was reluctant to explain it to her. She'd have been scared out of her wits if she'd heard about Jason's detention.

35

IN LATE JULY I heard from the Chiang Ching-kuo Foundation that they had offered me a fellowship for a full year. I was overjoyed. With a grant like that I'd be able to work on my dissertation dedicatedly and should be able to complete it within a year, since I had done most of the research. On the other hand, I felt more apprehensive than before. If the Chinese officials knew about my receiving this fellowship, they might scrutinize me more hostilely and connect me with Jason's case. If they found anything suspicious, they could stop me from leaving China.

So I only told my mother about the grant and made her promise not to breathe a word to others. I didn't even let my father know, afraid he might get too excited and not be able to stop talking about it. Once I was back in New York, I would notify him of my grant and tell him to stop wiring me money every month, since the fellowship was quite generous, $24,000 for the year, perhaps because living expenses in New York were much higher than elsewhere. My award seemed to be an exception. In general, a doctoral fellowship from the foundation only brought in $20,000 a year. I wrote to Loana and

LOOKING FOR TANK MAN

Bailey to thank them. They were both thrilled to hear the good news. Bailey replied that with this fellowship, I wouldn't need to teach in the next academic year, so that I could complete my dissertation sooner. That was what I planned to do.

Except for worrying about Jason, my summer was peaceful and productive overall, and I finished reading the books as planned. I managed to keep a low profile, staying under the radar of the Chinese police, so they didn't attempt to deter me from coming out. When I got back to New York, I told John Bailey, Deborah Sundar, and Joe Davison, the trio on my dissertation committee, that I was ready for the qualifying exam. Joe was an assistant professor in East Asian history who had come to Columbia just two years before. Bailey had said it would be better to have a junior faculty member on my committee, because usually young professors' scholarship was more up-to-date. In retrospect, I see that Bailey might have been trying to keep firm control of the committee by having the other two faculty be very junior to him. I had taken his advice and asked Sundar and Davidson, both of whom were willing to supervise me as well. The date for the exam was scheduled on the second Wednesday of September.

On Monday evening I got disturbing news: Wentao was ill and hospitalized. I called him, but his phone was off. I contacted another expat in Flushing and was told that he had suffered a heavy stroke and been rushed to the hospital. The man said Wentao was still in a coma. I couldn't go to the Queens Hospital to see him, since I had to prepare for the exam, which was just a day away. I had to do a final review of my notes.

The exam was oral. In a classroom I was seated at a large folding table across from the three professors. One after another, they asked me questions that covered three areas: East Asian history, modern and contemporary China, and political theories. I was well prepared and answered their questions fully. Following an older graduate student's advice, I kept talking and gave the examiners the impression that I could speak endlessly, being thoroughly informed of the areas I was supposed to know. Toward the end of the three-hour exam, Bailey said, "Tell us something about your plan for your dissertation."

I said I was going to write about the creation and evolution of Tank Man, exploring its origin and dissemination, its iconic evolution, artistic consumption, and its suppression in China. They all nodded their approval. I went on, "I would like to examine the historical event in a manner that is both macro and micro, combining the national and the personal. My parents were involved in Tiananmen Square. In fact, my father was one of the sculptors who created the Goddess of Democracy. I hope to make the dissertation into an intimate piece of writing as well as an academic treatise."

They approved of my approach. Then Bailey asked me to step out of the room and wait in the hallway for a while. I went out and sat on a long windowsill, feeling I'd done pretty well. Four or five minutes later they called me in. They all said, "Congratulations!"

They then shook hands with me—I had passed the exam.

Now I was officially an advanced PhD candidate, an ABD—all but dissertation. I felt excited and was looking forward to sharing the good news with my parents without delay.

But my euphoria was short-lived. That evening word came that Wentao had just died. I hurried to the hospital the next morning, but was told that his body had already been shipped to Peaceful Passing Funeral Home in downtown Flushing. I called them, saying I was a friend of the deceased and would be available if they needed me to help. The woman on the phone said that his body would be cremated after the wake, which would be held the following day.

Early the next morning, I went to the funeral home. I meant to help with the arrangements as a way to make up for not paying a visit to him when he had been hospitalized. In the lobby of the house I ran into two men I knew by sight. They were both expats and said they had been Wentao's friends and accompanied him during his last hours.

"Does his ex-wife know about his passing?" I asked the shorter one of them, who had a kind face with a balding head and large ears.

"She can't come today. There'll be a memorial service this weekend, which she and their son will attend."

That was understandable, since she must be busy with her life and work in Las Vegas. I went into the main hall; at its far end lay a brown casket, surrounded by flowers, with four wreathes standing at its front. I regretted not having brought along some flowers or a wreath. But who was I to Wentao? We had had a one-night stand but we were not lovers, and I would have felt uneasy letting my name appear in his service. People would imagine things and gossip about me.

A withered old man was busy working on Wentao, powdering his pallid face to make him appear more presentable. His hair was combed back, neat and shiny now, but the corner of his mouth slightly turned down, as if still showing traces of pain and misery. In fact, it was an expression I had known well when he showed his misgivings. His right hand rested on his stomach, as casually as if he were dozing. I went over and bent down a bit. The two expats came up too. I stifled the urge to kiss Wentao on the cheek; instead, I put my fingertips on my lips and then placed them on his lips, which to my amazement were quite dry. Then my tears flowed, but I kept quiet. The old man was startled and looked up at me. I forced a smile and said, "I was his friend and knew him well."

"It's very kind of you to come to see him off," he said, in Mandarin with a Cantonese accent.

Then, to my horror, I noticed that the casket containing Wentao's body was made of thick cardboard. The glossy color was mere paint on the outside, but the inside of the casket was still the naked surface of pasteboard. Seized by a gust of grief and anger, I asked the old man, "Why didn't you use a wood casket for my friend? This looks so cheap." I slapped the side of the cardboard.

LOOKING FOR TANK MAN

"We offered that, but they couldn't afford it. They said they had to collect money for his cremation and memorial service, so they couldn't rent a standard casket for him."

I turned to the two expats and demanded, "Was that true?"

They didn't reply, both fixing their eyes on the floor of ceramic tiles. I asked the old man again, "How much does a wood casket cost, Uncle?"

"One hundred forty dollars a day."

"Then let me pay for him. Please change the casket this minute so that people won't see him lying in this trash can!" I was possessed by a sudden fit of anger and had to force down my tears.

"Of course we'll do it at once. It's so generous of you, Miss. Please come with me."

He led me into an office at the side of the hall, in which a woman in her thirties was typing at a computer. He told her that I'd pay for a standard pinewood casket to replace the one the deceased was occupying. I handed the woman my Mastercard.

She started processing the payment and said, "Don't worry. It's easy for us to switch it. The wake doesn't start until nine thirty."

"Please change it quickly. I don't want people to see him humiliated, lying in that shabby box."

Her eyes lit up. "Of course, we'll do it right away." She lowered her voice to a whisper. "I can see you must have loved him dearly."

"I don't know about that. We were just friends, but I know he was a kindhearted man, very dedicated to the cause of China's democracy. He was a full-time human-rights watchdog besides."

"An idealist, huh?" said the old man.

"Yes, he was too idealistic to live a good life in America." I didn't want to talk to them more about Wentao, as grief kept stirring in my chest and made me heady, with a stuffy nose.

I stayed in the main hall for about an hour, during which a dozen or so people came in. A few of them I knew in passing, but most of them were strangers to me. After seeing Wentao lying in a decent casket, I slipped out of the funeral home before the wake started, unwilling to meet more people. I was sure that the two expats would tell others that I had paid for Wentao's temporary casket, which might make it seem like there was an unusual relationship between him and me. They might even say I had been his girlfriend. That was why I didn't want to stay at his wake to mingle with others.

As expected, rumors about Wentao's death appeared online. One woman even mentioned me, saying I had paid for the expenses of his wake and evidently I had been his lover or something. The woman even said Wentao used to tell others that I was his girlfriend. There might have been a grain of truth in this rumor—I could see that he might have brought up my name as a salve to soothe his wounded ego and damaged manhood. In spite of my bitterness about the gossip online, I didn't feel like I'd mind being used by him that way.

LOOKING FOR TANK MAN

Still, the association of my name with him could cause other kinds of trouble for me. He had been known as a top democracy activist against the Communist regime. My intimate connection with him might make the officials view me as a potential enemy, or at least a hostile element. If so, they might take measures to frustrate or even ruin me. But I couldn't possibly step out and deny my relationship with him, and all I could do was remain silent.

One night Rachel called and asked me, "What's this rumor about? It says you were a married man's girlfriend, basically a home-wrecker."

"You mean Meng Wentao?"

"Who else?"

"I came to know him long after he and his wife had been divorced. He had lived like a bachelor for years."

"Were you really his girlfriend?"

"Not at all, we were just friends."

"Are you telling me the truth, Lulu?"

"Why should I lie to you?"

"Then tell me, did you sleep with him?"

"Well, only once, a one-night stand. He was miserable because his ex-wife had left New York with their son. He wanted me to stay the night with him, so I agreed. Why are you so nosy?"

"I want to see if you're really a chaste lady like you are in appearance."

"Of course I'm not. I can be crazy too, crazy about a good man if I meet one."

"So Wentao wasn't the man you loved?"

"He was my dad's age. He and I were not compatible, but I respected him."

"Why?"

"I can't say for sure. He was attractive in his sad, tragic way."

"I know you have a hero complex. I wish I had known him. You have better taste in men than I."

"Come on, you're much more experienced with men. I didn't lose my virginity until last year."

"To whom?"

"That I can't divulge."

"I know you're a slut at heart too."

"All right, say that if you want."

She laughed and said we were two peas in a pod. She relished the analogy as if it brought us closer.

Wentao's passing made me think a lot about the dissidents in North America. There were different ways of looking at his life in exile. One way was to compare it with the image of Tank Man. Like that defiant hero, Wentao had year after year faced the overwhelming power embodied by the Chinese government. His defiance might have demanded more courage and tenacity, and also more sacrifice. His ex-wife might have been justified in calling him "a loser" and "a feckless man" here, but in some respects he must have been crazed and traumatized and couldn't help standing up to that crushing authoritarian power. You might even call him another type of Tank Man, crazed into a prolonged confrontation with the Communist regime. Who can deny that Wentao was a brave man and a hero? On the other

LOOKING FOR TANK MAN

hand, he couldn't see that those in power didn't fear a pipsqueak like him.

What does upset their complacency is the truly independent and fulfilled life that a dissident should live, without constantly resorting to fighting the evil power for meaning. He was right that he should have gone to graduate or professional school and learned to put his feet down in America. He ought to have lived his own life fully first. He should have looked down on their nefarious power as garbage, as not worth his effort.

I kept thinking about how to include his tragedy in my dissertation, as a comparison to the outraged Tank Man. I was positive there must be some emotional connection between the two men. Evidently because Wentao had never stood in the limelight, we tended to neglect him, and at most to regard him only as a run-of-the-mill dissident. But in spirit, he must have been similar to Tank Man, willing to be driven by a kind of madness and ready to make sacrifices for the ideas he had believed in.

36

ONCE THE WRITING of my dissertation started, I proceeded rapidly. With the reading and research already done, I was in full command of the topic. I had divided the dissertation into five chapters plus a prologue. The prologue gave a broad backdrop of the Tiananmen democracy movement. Since there was no way this part could have much originality, I tried to enliven the narration with detailed descriptions. In addition, I presented the intense fear that had possessed the top national leaders and affected their decision-making. The first chapter focused on the implementation of martial law in Beijing and how the field armies were prepared by brainwashing the soldiers insulated within their barracks. I also tried to answer the question of why fourteen field armies, and even paratroopers, were deployed. I argued that Deng Xiaoping feared some armies would disobey him, so he needed more forces to come to Beijing to check and offset one another. In spite of his iron hand, he planned the crackdown with trepidation and actually prepared to flee China lest the suppression fail and he fall from the treacherous pinnacle of power. He even had an evacuation plan—having tens of millions of dollars transferred to a Swiss bank and an airliner at his disposal.

My second chapter was devoted to the confrontation between the civilians and the military, which culminated in the violent bloodshed and the unnamed man confronting a column of tanks on the morning of June 5, 1989. The third chapter analyzed who Tank Man might be, described how his image was caught by four foreign cameramen separately, and how the footage of the confrontation galvanized the world. The fourth chapter traced the evolution of Tank Man as an icon in the Western media and in its artistic works, and in contrast, it also reported how Chinese censorship suppressed the image after promoting it briefly. The final chapter was mainly my meditation on Tank Man as a political, cultural, and psychological phenomenon. Though the last part was less academic, to me it was essential for the dissertation and also helped explain why I took up this topic for my dissertation. So it was rather intimate, discussing my personal involvement in the investigation. I valued this chapter the most and considered it more original than the other parts.

I analyzed two episodes as precursors to Tank Man's confrontation on June 5. These happenings were recorded by numerous eyewitnesses. In the early morning of June 4, a group of civilians gathered on Chang'an Avenue to stop the army. Both sides got into a tug-of-war. The soldiers opened fire and some people were shot down. But after being dispersed, the civilians came back to face the army again. Most of them sat down on the street, about seventy yards away from the troops. Neither side budged. Then suddenly a girl in a white dress ran out toward the soldiers, as if to fight them barehanded, by herself. People gasped, and some men followed her, running toward the army too. The troops fired and shot down a few men and forced them all to lie down in their tracks, but the girl in white continued charging toward the soldiers. When she almost reached their ranks, the troops fired at her directly. She fell. A bunch of men, with their hands raised above their heads, went over to retrieve her body. Her thighs were shattered, but she wasn't dead yet. They rushed her to an emergency clinic.

A few hours later, around six a.m., another crowd at Liubukou, near Xinhua Gate, was still lingering to welcome and protect the students who had just retreated from Tiananmen Square. Residents had been blaming the soldiers to their faces for killing civilians. For hours the troops had not advanced, as though they, too, had been stunned by such an eruption of violence. Then their ranks opened and a group of tanks emerged. It looked like they wanted to use the tanks to push forward. A few middle-aged women went over and lay down on the street, and about a hundred people followed them, all lying face up on the asphalt. The tanks roared and moved toward those brave souls. The tanks were coming closer and closer. When the first vehicle was just fifteen feet away from the women, it stopped so abruptly that its rear lifted from the ground. All the tanks stopped, their engines idling. Then their hatches opened and the soldiers began tossing gas bombs at the crowd on the asphalt. The yellow poison gas enveloped and choked the people, who coughed and gasped for breath, their throats and lungs burning. They had to climb up to breathe and look for water. The tanks seized the moment and charged at them. The attack scattered the crowd. One tank crushed a few people, who yelled and shrieked, and then it did a 360 in place. This maneuver crushed some of the injured ones who couldn't get away. According to eyewitnesses, this tank was Number 106. It belonged to the First Armored Division and carried the title of Heroic Vehicle, which meant that its predecessor had performed valiant deeds in the civil war and the Korean War. Altogether eleven people were killed on the spot and two were injured, having limbs cut off, including Fang Zheng. Their names and brief bios are clearly listed by various sources. (The historian Wu Renhua recently just identified a former crew member of the Number 106 tank, Wu Yanhui. Some people phoned the veteran, who acknowledged that he had been in the tank that day, but he refused to name the commander of the tank. Then so many calls came in that he stopped picking up.)

In such a mental state, people, outraged and desperate, might do anything to confront the violent soldiers. The episode of Tank Man took place the next morning. By then the army seemed to have cooled down some, although people's anger was still mounting. Clearly the restraint the tanks manifested in the footage indicated that the whole scene might have been staged to show how rational the army was and how it respected human lives, since this episode was broadcast that very evening by the Central China Television. If an official camera hadn't been on the scene, there would have been no way the state media could have used the footage so quickly— they'd have had to get permission first from foreign media companies. Plainly the scene had been set up. But no sooner did the footage appear in Western media than it was removed from Chinese media—apparently the propaganda effort had backfired. Nevertheless, four days later Deng Xiaoping praised the soldiers in the front tank for not running over the civilian, saying that if the tank hadn't shown restraint, "that could have caused more confusion." Clearly, to the officials, the episode displayed how lenient the army had been. According to Professor Josephs, an anthropologist at UC Berkeley, the body language of the three men who dragged Tank Man away to safety indicated that the three were definitely not civilians—they were trained security personnel. I hazard a wild guess: the propaganda people might also have intended, though covertly, to display the civilians' defiant spirit. In other words, the propaganda skit could have been a subversive gesture from within the regime.

I continued to analyze other experiences of the massacre. My father's came first. On the same afternoon that Tank Man performed his rebellious deed, my father got drunk, and picking up a hefty cleaver, shouted he'd go and "hack down some fascists," who had killed so many civilians and whose tanks and armored personnel carriers had toppled the Goddess of Democracy. But there were no soldiers around, so he had just slashed the air

LOOKING FOR TANK MAN

with his cleaver. He was so enraged that he called himself a coward and chopped off his own pinkie. I was certain that if there had been a tank in sight, he'd have charged at it with his cleaver raised, shouting "Kill!" So in spirit, he was similar to Tank Man, mad enough to stare death in the eye.

I then mentioned Liu Lan, the solitary protester from Hong Kong, who had over the decades never missed an opportunity to keep the memory of the massacre alive. In recent years her protest had taken such a heavy toll on her that every time she gave a speech, she'd have to lie down afterward to rest for half an hour before she could get back on her feet again. She had also kept publishing articles and books on the Tiananmen movement. Undoubtedly she, too, was similar to Tank Man in spirit, fixated on the idea of justice and truth, willing to sacrifice for it. It might even take more courage and stamina to keep doing what she had done for two and a half decades, confronting an overwhelming power that could destroy her.

Finally I brought forth the exiled dissidents. In spite of defects in their characters, some of them still carried on the cause of the Tiananmen democracy movement. I used Meng Wentao as an example. He was so dedicated to the cause that he didn't take care to put his own life in order. His life in America was still driven by a kind of madness and courage that had originated from the same source as Tank Man's. Wentao sacrificed so much to the improvement of human rights back in China that he had lost everything, including his family and his life.

I concluded by turning self-reflective, saying that I was antagonizing the Communist regime by taking up this project, and as a result I might jeopardize my future if I intended to go back to take care of my mother, but something deep within me compelled me to do this work regardless of my personal loss. The last paragraph of my dissertation was "Despite the ambiguity in the original creation of Tank Man, he embodies the indominable spirit of many people and serves as a blazing beacon that gathers the light of hope for freedom and human dignity. He symbolizes what we can do and who we might become. I venture to say that in essence he also bespeaks many others, including myself."

I pondered over the last sentence and wondered if I'd gone astray from the academic discourse and lapsed into a merely personal assertion. Then I decided to keep it, assuming that some subjectivity would give the writing an edge. If the three professors on my dissertation committee turned out against it, I could revise the last statement. At this point I shouldn't feel diffident about rendering the national into the personal, or vice versa.

37

HOWEVER, I DID worry about the length of the dissertation—only 126 pages—but I didn't know how to make it longer without inflating it with filler. So I didn't show it to the committee members right away. Instead, I shared it with Loana and Rachel and wanted to get their feedback first.

Loana's response was enthusiastic. She urged me to translate it into Chinese and was sure that an overseas press would publish such a small book—*A Terrible Beauty Is Born: In Search of Tank Man*. But as a PhD dissertation, it might be too short. On the other hand, she had seen a doctoral dissertation at Harvard that was a lot shorter than 120 pages. The quality of the work should count more than the quantity. But it wouldn't be too difficult to expand my dissertation to 150 pages. Loana told me to show it to the members of my committee, who should be able to help me figure out how to expand it. But these pages should remain the core of the dissertation and should also stand alone as a book for a general audience, specifically for Chinese readers. Of course, there could be consequences from publishing such a book, because the Communist authorities might consider me a troublemaker, even an enemy, and make my life difficult. I needed to take this liability into account when deciding what to do with the manuscript.

I didn't really give a damn about how the Chinese government would respond, I told Loana. I guessed I carried my father's genes, somewhat touched and impulsive. If I hadn't meant to tell the truth and share it with others, why did I write such a thing in the first place?

Rachel also liked what I'd written, but she couldn't judge its academic value. She only praised the fluidity and clarity of the prose and the insights I brought to the topic. She also shared it with her father, who could read English. He was touched by my writing and urged Rachel to do something as meaningful. She confessed to me that she had decided to apply for graduate school, since her job as an editorial assistant bored her. She said she had just taken the GRE and scored decently. Ideally she'd wanted to go to SUNY at Buffalo, which was excellent in poetry studies. I teased her, saying "Didn't you used to say you'd get bored if you sat at a desk day in and day out?"

"Well," she admitted, "the business world is a lot more depressing."

I was glad to see her figure out a way for herself, or in her own words, "I've found my bearings at long last."

"Academia can be hard and boring too, if you don't do it for the love of it," I told her.

"At least I'll have a flexible schedule," she said. "I can't keep a nine-to-five job anymore."

LOOKING FOR TANK MAN

Following Loana's suggestion, I spent two weeks rendering my dissertation into Chinese. The translation process was rewarding and helped me catch some slips in the wording of the original and a few inaccurate facts. When the translation was done and I'd made all the edits and corrections, the dissertation was a lot more polished. I sent it to Bailey, Sundar, and Davidson, and hoped they would accept it.

Loana suggested I send the translation to Niu Jian at the Sunbeam Press; she said she would put in a word for my manuscript. She didn't know I was still in touch with Niu Jian. Nevertheless, I needed her endorsement. I received the publication catalogs from the Sunbeam Press regularly and had noticed they just published a book on the Tiananmen Square Massacre by Liu Lan. I was amazed to see that Niu Jian was brave enough to bring out so many politically sensitive titles.

I phoned Niu Jian, who sounded cheerful and friendly. He invited me to send him my manuscript, and he promised to read it the moment he got it. I mailed it out the same day.

Sundar and Davidson both gave me their feedback. They liked the dissertation but said it might be too short, since it seemed more like a big master's thesis. But Davison said it shouldn't be hard to expand it some. My angst proved right, and I was eager to hear from Bailey. But for two weeks he remained silent; this agitated me. I was afraid he might not accept the dissertation.

Fortunately, Niu Jian responded quickly, as he had promised. He was willing to publish the book, but he

331

also warned me about the party officials, who might get furious at me. I told him that I wouldn't mind that, as long as my work was valuable and could be appreciated by readers. Of that he assured me. He said, "Truth to tell, Lulu, I was glued to your manuscript while I was reading it. At times, it touched me and made me tearful. When I finished it, I was in awe."

"Please, Mr. Niu, I'm just a regular graduate student. We met, and you know how ordinary I am."

"I mean I was in awe of the brave spirit and the intelligence in the writing, especially the last chapter. We will be happy and honored to bring it out."

"I can't thank you enough."

"I must thank you. You make me feel that my publishing business is worthwhile."

"I'm so lucky to know you." I was blown away, unable to speak appropriately.

"Please send me the electronic version."

I agreed to email it along that same day. Niu Jian promised to send me a standard contract through snail mail. After I signed the two copies, I was to save one for myself and mail the other one back to him.

Then I heard from Bailey. He wanted me to come to his office on the third Wednesday of March. I went as agreed. He appeared warm and friendly and motioned me to sit down opposite him. He said, "I like what you wrote, but at moments you lapsed into 'personalia,' and the writing became less academic. Also, the dissertation is too short. For a PhD, you need to write at least two hundred pages. I mean substantial pages, nothing

LOOKING FOR TANK MAN

padded. Ultimately it should be a book manuscript for an academic press."

"Can you suggest how I can expand it?" I asked in earnest.

He gave a suave smile, then said, "I'm going to print out a hard copy and mark the problematic spots. We will discuss how to enlarge the whole thing. Can you come with me to my house in Newburgh this weekend? We'll need many hours to work on this together."

"Will Hilda and Soya come with us?" I asked in alarm, but managed to feign calm.

"No, they have left for Norway to see Hilda's parents."

"I'm not sure of my weekend schedule, but I will check and let you know."

"Of course, take your time," he said emotionlessly.

I rose to leave. I was so flustered that I almost rushed out of his office. My mind was in a whirl, knowing he had devious plans. Once we were up in Newburgh, alone in the woods, anything could happen. He might do everything he could to make me join him in bed. By no means would I go with him if his family was not there. So that evening I emailed him, saying I was obligated to serve as an interpreter at a public event in Brooklyn, so I couldn't join him on the weekend. "Can we make another appointment for next week?" I asked.

But I got no answer from him. His silence unnerved me. He probably didn't want to leave any trace in writing for fear of accusations I might bring against him. Thus far, I didn't have any concrete evidence at all. But I knew that to some extent, he held me in his clutches now. If I didn't cooperate, he wouldn't approve my dissertation. Both Sundar and Davidson were very junior to him in the department and would have to defer to his authority. To date, they hadn't given me any practical advice as to how to expand the dissertation and both seemed to leave the matter to Bailey. I felt cornered and had no clue how to deal with my mentor appropriately.

In early April, there was a conference on contemporary Chinese culture at NYU. In the poster of the event I saw that Mark Stone was a speaker. He was going to talk about the global dissemination of Jin Yong's fiction. He seemed to be thriving in academia now. His topic intrigued me, so I went to the conference for his talk. In the back of my mind lingered the vague desire to find out what he was like now and whether he was still the same playboy.

He was good at presenting his discoveries and talked with ease in a large classroom. Now and then a titter of approval rang out in the audience of more than sixty people. Aside from his mastery of his material, the fact that he spoke at his home school might have contributed to his ease and seeming casualness. He claimed that Jin Yong's greatest achievement was that he had invented a kind of universal fiction language, accessible to all Chinese readers no matter what dialects they spoke. That explained why his fiction was so widely read and embraced by the multitudes as well as the elite. Mark made a valid point, and I was amazed to see that he had become an authority on kung fu fiction. I used to think of him as a bit of a joke, his graduate project too lightweight, maybe even frivolous. He had seemed to have been just wasting his time while reading those novels in the library, and his dissertation hadn't been going anywhere. Who could have seen that he could blaze a trail for himself? I had heard that he had been invited to speak at many international conferences, especially in East Asia. It can be so hard to tell willfulness from perseverance.

After Mark's talk, I went over and greeted him. He must have noticed me in the audience, but his eyes still lit up at my greetings. He said, "Lulu, I'm so happy to see you here. Thanks for coming."

I congratulated him on his talk, which had made me see Jin Yong in a different light. "It's truly enlightening," I said in earnest.

He asked, "How's your work going? Still struggling with Tank Man?" He gave a fruity laugh.

"Yes, I just wrote a draft of my dissertation. Believe it or not, I have found him."

"Really, that's such great news. You know, I still hold him as my hero. That poster you disliked is hanging in my office now. Tell me where or how you found him."

"I've found him in me."

He looked astonished. "You mean you're a tank girl or tank woman now?"

I giggled and said, "You might say that. By the way, would you mind taking a look at my dissertation? Your opinion would mean a lot to me, since both of us have been emotionally involved with the topic. Trust me, it might be worth your time. I just translated it into Chinese and the Sunbeam Press is going to bring it out as a book."

"That's admirable. Please email it. I will read it and let you know what I think."

I was delighted he would look at it and thanked him with an exaggerated curtsy, lifting the side of my dress a little, which made him laugh again.

38

I HEARD FROM Mark a week later. He had read my dissertation and asked me if we could meet so that he could talk to me about it in detail. I was eager to hear his opinion and agreed to come and see him the next afternoon.

His office was easy to find. It was on the fifth floor of a brownstone on University Place. At the sight of me, he stood and held out his hand. He was in a navy tracksuit with white stripes along his legs and arms, as if he had just left the gym. He said, "Let's go out for coffee."

"Sure." I shook his hand, then saw the same Tank Man poster on the wall. "I know him," I said.

He laughed. His honest face, though a little heavier now, still had boyish features and bright, intelligent eyes. His simple manner reminded me of the same insouciant Mark at Harvard. "You must know her too," he said and pointed at a framed photo propped on a bookshelf. "She's my wife."

I recognized the woman's round face and smiling eyes and the little mole on her chin. "Of course, that's Yuko!" I said, amazed to be seeing the Japanese woman who used to be a master's student in East Asian studies at

Harvard. It had been whispered that Yuko was easy with dates and would go out with anyone who offered to take her out. Who could have imagined she would become Mark's wife? I couldn't help but feel a twinge of envy. That woman must be good at keeping hold of a man.

"Yes, Yuko and I got married last year," Mark said with some pride.

"Really, I heard you were engaged to a Polish woman."

"Oh, Zofia didn't want to live in the States. She loves Paris, so we split."

"Are these your kids?" I pointed at two babies, whose gender I couldn't tell.

"Yes, Sean and Naomi, twins. They're the center of my life now."

"I can see you're a happy man."

"Yep, a happy family man. Let's go."

We went to the Dunkin' Donuts on the street in front for coffee. After we had sat down at a table deep in the back, he said, "I have to say I was impressed by your dissertation. The prose is so limpid and passionate and honest. It was a pleasure to read. You should continue to write like that."

"Even for academic papers?" I asked.

"Absolutely. Believe me, most academics are eager to produce prose accessible to a general audience."

"Do you think my last sentence was too personal?"

"No, I can see the logic in your saying you are a tank girl, having found him in yourself. Your writing persuaded me."

LOOKING FOR TANK MAN

I smiled, feeling a pleasant embarrassment. Encouraged, I revealed to him my trouble with John Bailey, who might reject my dissertation. I also mentioned he wanted me to go to his country house on a weekend, but that I had declined for fear of his intentions.

Mark sighed, his thick eyebrows joined together. He told me, "I've heard stories about Bailey from his former students. He does have a reputation as a lech. If you feel unable to continue to work under his supervision, you might consider changing your advisor."

"But I don't have any evidence for his harassment. Without sound reasons, how can I persuade the department to assign me another mentor?"

"I see. You must be careful. Bailey is powerful in the field. Without any concrete evidence, the department might not take your side. If you bring an accusation against him, it might end as your words against his. It won't stick that way."

"What should I do? I might be able to expand the dissertation some, but Bailey can always find more faults with it if I don't cave to him."

"How about going to another school? You might ask your department to give you an MA, then apply to another program."

That was an interesting thought, which I would consider seriously. Before leaving, I asked him whether he could provide a letter of recommendation for me if I applied elsewhere. He said he'd be happy to write a strong letter on my behalf.

HA JIN

In late April I heard from the Sunbeam Press that they were working hard to bring out my book as soon as possible for the summer book fair in Hong Kong. So the proofs would be ready in a few days. Once I got them, I needed to finish correcting them within a week so that they could stay on their publication schedule. I was amazed by the rapid development.

Two days later I received the proofs. Having put aside everything else, I began working on them day and night. I was excited about this process and eager to see my first book in print. In four days, I went over the pages twice, then mailed them back after xeroxing a copy for my records.

Meanwhile, I informed Bailey that I was going to enlarge my dissertation during the summer and make it more acceptable to him. He replied that he wished me luck. He didn't give any specific instructions. This might imply that he wanted to see me lose my bearings in my effort. I had been thinking whether to leave for another program, but I mustn't reveal my intention too early in case he tried to thwart my plan.

Unlike other years, I didn't leave for Beijing in early May. I waited for my book to come out so I could bring a copy for my parents. My father would be impressed and even proud of me, I hoped.

39

IN MID-MAY, I finally got early copies of my book. It was well made, with glowing blurbs, one of which was from Simon Pond, a well-known scholar at UCLA barred from entering China by the mainland government because of his helping Chinese dissidents. Professor Pond spoke such impeccable Mandarin that when he had traveled alone on the mainland in the old days, people had often taken him for a Uighur with sandy hair and green eyes who had grown up in inland China. But he could no longer enter the country he loved so much and had spent decades studying. I was ecstatic at the sight of the two copies that the Sunbeam Press had rushed to me. I packed them into my baggage in hopes I could bring them into China without incident.

At customs in the Beijing airport, a policewoman wearing a peaked cap looked at my passport and pinned her wide-set eyes on me. She stood up and said, "Can you come with me for a moment?"

"What for?" I was startled.

"There's some problem with your passport and we have to straighten it out."

I followed her into an office at the end of the customs hall. In there, a group of police were drinking tea, cracking sunflower seeds, and watching a soccer game on TV. The woman went up to an older officer and whispered to him. He nodded and rose to his feet and motioned me and another man to follow him. We went into an inner room, and they seated me at a rectangular table. This didn't bode well, and my heart started fluttering.

"Miss," the older officer said to me, "we received instructions not to let you pass, so you might have to head back to America."

"Why? I am a citizen of the People's Republic of China. To return to my country is my right."

"I understand, but we were ordered to stop you."

At that moment a tall young woman brought over the two copies of my book that I had hidden in the pockets of a windbreaker I had bought for my mother. The man took up a copy and flipped through it. "Impressive," he said. "Did you write this book?"

Before I could answer, the tall woman said, "This picture is not allowed to get into China." She pointed at the Tank Man photo on the front cover and glared at me.

I had to admit my authorship, but challenged them by asking "Is it a crime to write such a book? It's my doctoral dissertation, purely academic work."

"We can see that, but we have to carry out orders from the Ministry of State Security."

"If you don't let me pass, where can I go?"

"Back to America," another woman officer cut in.

LOOKING FOR TANK MAN

"I have no place there for the summer." Indeed, I had sublet my apartment.

"That's your problem. Nobody can vilify our country with impunity," the woman spit back.

"So you bar me from entry because you found my book?"

"Don't blame us, Miss," the man said. "The order came in long before we found the books. We can't say the exact reason for rejecting your entry. We're just doing what we were told to do."

The urge to start sobbing was surging in my throat but I forced it down. I reminded myself not to let them see my weakness and suffering. The man said, "The flight to New York is in the evening. You can take it back."

At this point two middle-aged men came in. At the sight of them, all the police rose, turning to the door. Before leaving, one of the women officers ordered me to let them have my phone for a while. I realized I had no choice but to surrender it to her, so I pulled out my Samsung phone and handed it over.

The two new arrivals sat down across from me and said they were from the Ministry of State Security and would like to ask me a few questions. One with a mop of gray hair opened a suede briefcase and took out an envelope. He pulled out some photos and placed one in front of me. "Do you know this man?" he asked.

I looked at it. It was Jason, who smiled with a corner of his mouth tilting up a bit. "Yes, Jason Wang and I went to college in Boston. I was at Harvard and he was at Boston University."

HA JIN

"Were you his girlfriend?" the same man went on.

"We were just friends, not that close."

"Did he introduce some people to you?"

"Who are you referring to by 'some people'?"

"Taiwanese officials and dissidents from mainland China."

"I can't remember anyone he introduced to me. Like I said, we were not that close. After college we went to graduate school in different places. I was in New York and he was in California, so our paths didn't cross very often."

The two men looked at each other, as if unsure how to continue. The other man, who had a bald spot and a long, rugged face, picked up another photo and handed it to me. "How about this person? Do you know him?"

In the photo Wentao was still a young man, with muscular arms and an angular face and prominent eyes. He looked confident and spirited, as if gazing at something faraway. I said, "Meng Wentao is already dead. Why dig up dirt on a dead man?"

"We still need to collect information on him," he said.

"I knew him briefly when I acted as an interpreter at some conferences in New York."

"Did he introduce you to other expats?"

"He introduced me to a few Taiwanese writers who lived in Queens and Brooklyn."

"Who were they?"

"I don't remember their names. They were just amateur writers, mostly housewives. I met them in passing and at a book event."

LOOKING FOR TANK MAN

The gray-haired man butted in, "We know you bought a casket for Meng Wentao, why?"

"I didn't buy a casket, which would have cost close to a thousand dollars. I just rented a casket to hold his body for the wake."

"How much did you pay for that?"

"One hundred forty dollars."

"Why did you do that?" the long-faced man persisted.

"Wentao's friends couldn't collect enough funds to cover all the funeral expenses, so I helped to make the wake appear decent."

"Were you his girlfriend or mistress?" he asked, his fierce eyes fixed on me.

I felt my cheeks heating up, but managed to reply, "No, I was just his friend. I wanted his last appearance to have some dignity. I didn't want to have him humiliated for his last appearance."

They looked at each other, as if impressed by my answer. The gray-haired man nodded, then handed me another photo. "You know her, right?"

It was Loana. I was surprised, but got hold of myself. I said, "Professor Hong was my teacher at Harvard. She has studied the Tiananmen Square Massacre and is an authority on the subject. She's an excellent teacher, a great woman, kind and generous, loved by her students and well respected in academic circles."

"Did she introduce you to any Taiwanese officials or scholars?" the same man pressed.

I shook my head. "No, she never did."

"Then how did you get a scholarship from the Chiang Ching-kuo Foundation?"

"I applied for the dissertation fellowship with letters of recommendation from my PhD advisor, John Bailey, and from Loana Hong, who was my teacher too. I got it through the normal procedure."

"All right, how about this person?" He placed another photo in front of me.

It was a thirtyish man with smiling, hooded eyes and a lean face. He was someone I'd never met. I told them, "I don't know him. Who is he? He doesn't look Chinese."

They didn't bother answering my question. The long-faced man smiled and said, "I have another little question for you. You went to Harvard, didn't you?"

"I did." I wondered what was new now.

"Chairman Xi Jinping's daughter was at Harvard when you were there. Did you know her?"

"Yes, Mingze was just an ordinary girl, modest and easygoing. She studied hard. At the time she had a different name, Muzi. She applied for Professor Hong's seminar on the Tiananmen Square Massacre, but the class was already full and Loana didn't take her. I believe that was a mistake. Loana should have let Mingze take the seminar so that she could have seen the bloody truth and maybe eventually influenced her dad."

"Were you a friend of hers?"

I thought about lying, just to scare them a bit so that they would be lenient with me. But I confessed, "No. At the time we had no clue her dad would be the boss of the

LOOKING FOR TANK MAN

Communist Party, so I only had a nodding acquaintance with her."

"Thank you for clarifying that. You know, you can have a bright future if you're willing to serve our country."

"I've kept that in mind all the time, of course. That's why I plan to return to our homeland after I get my PhD. But it's hard for me to become a little red flag waver—serving the country like a civilian soldier or a brainless slave. It's just not in my nature. Even though I am a citizen, I can serve our country only on my own terms."

They both looked astonished, then smiled, looking at each other.

Before leaving, they said they were sorry I'd have to fly back to the States on the same day. But it was not they who had made the decision, which came from their superiors. They rose and shook hands with me before walking out. I wished I had been gutsy enough to repulse them, but I held out my hand anyway. It made me feel disgusted.

A young man stepped over and gave me my phone. "You're all set," he said, grinning.

"I hope you didn't put some device into it," I half joked.

"We just checked your communication history and your photos. No bad feelings. That's our job."

Two women officers, one stout and the other bony, escorted me to the gate, which was deserted. The departure flight to New York was still five hours away, and the gate wasn't manned yet. They told me just to show my passport to the staff when the gate opened.

"What about my baggage?" I asked.

The skinny woman officer said, "It will be put on the plane and you can collect it at your destination."

They warned me not to attempt to sneak out of the airport, or I would never be able to get out of China. I said I understood and then turned my face to the wall of windows, not wanting them to see my tears.

Once left alone, I couldn't hold back my sobs anymore. As if a dam had burst in me, tears flooded down my cheeks and wet the front of my shirt. "This is a ruthless country, a monster," I told myself. "You mustn't show that you've been crushed by the state's power. You must be brave."

Calming down some, I called my mother and told her that I wouldn't be coming home for the summer anymore. She asked, "What happened? Haven't you already arrived?"

"I'm at the Beijing airport now, but they won't let me through customs and they have forced me to take the flight back to New York this evening."

"How come you got into such trouble? What did you do?"

"I guess because I published my dissertation."

"What's it about?"

"The Tank Man of Tiananmen Square. I mentioned that to you long ago."

"I told you not to dabble in politics. See, now you've gotten more than you can carry."

LOOKING FOR TANK MAN

"Don't worry about me, Mom. I'll be all right."

"I am worried. I'll be worried sick. When will I see you again, Lulu?"

"I'll figure out a way. Now my head is too full to think clearly. I have to contact my friend in New York to find a place to stay for the summer."

"Lulu, my baby, I'll miss you." She suddenly turned whiny, as if she had broken down.

"Take care of yourself, Mom. I'll be all right and will figure out how to care for you in the future. We'll be together, no matter what."

"Okay, be careful and don't get into more trouble."

"I hear you, Mom."

I thought what to do about my mother. If I couldn't go back to join her, I might be able to get her out of China once I settled down in America. Eventually we both might immigrate, or we could go to another country in Asia. I was not sure if she'd be willing to uproot herself from China, but at the moment I had more urgent matters to attend to. I texted Rachel: "I cannot get through customs in Beijing and have to fly back now. Can you put me up for a couple days? My place is already sublet."

I thought of emailing Loana, who didn't handle text messages on her phone, but decided to wait. I shouldn't spread word of my plight now. Once I was back in the States, I would explain the situation to Loana in detail. Clearly some officials had seen my book and decided to turn me back on arrival. But my book hadn't hit the market yet, so how could they have known about it

349

beforehand? There must be spies in New York who had access to the Sunbeam Press and who had gotten hold of an early copy. This realization sent a chill down my spine. I'd have to be very careful in the future when mixing with the dissidents in North America.

About an hour later, Rachel texted back: "Oh, girl, you're in deep shit. But no problem. You are welcome to stay with me, my sofa bed is ready for you. We'll have a great time together."

I felt relieved and tried to doze away while waiting for the flight. Still, grief kept rising in my chest. Even with my eyes closed, tears seeped out of my lids from time to time. From now on I might have to live in exile.

40

I ARRIVED AT Rachel's place with my pair of suitcases in tow. She was happy to take me in, saying her parents had told her she must do her best to help me. My trouble at the Beijing airport had become news. The local Chinese media reported that the mainland had barred my entry to my own country because I had published a scholarly book on Tank Man. Such an occurrence caused some stir among the expat and immigrant communities in North America.

Rachel placed a glass of iced tea in front of me. "Well, you're famous now," she said in a giggly tone of voice.

"Nobody wants this kind of fame," I muttered.

"I know. I'd go bananas if they stopped me from entering China. Those in power are monsters and you can't reason with them. In fact, you should just ignore them and live your own life."

I took a sip of the sweet tea. "My mom is in Beijing. She's worried sick, but I can do nothing for now." I forced myself to continue, "I'll have to find a way to get her out of that animal farm."

"China definitely feels like an immense aviary," agreed Rachel. "It's impossible for wild birds like us."

"It's more like a vast madhouse," I said.

My mind was still in turmoil. There were so many things I had to sort out that I often felt at a loss. I contacted Loana to see if I could go and see her in Boston. I had to talk with her at length in person to figure out how to overcome my impasse. She invited me to come and stay with her, saying she and her fiancé had just bought a townhouse near Wellesley College so that they could walk to work. I was impressed, knowing that it was a charming town, peaceful and affluent. She and Alan, her fiancé, were going to get married near the end of the year, during the winter break, though they had lived together like a couple for more than two years.

I hopped on the Chinatown bus the next morning and headed for Boston. The ride was pleasant, though the bus didn't run along the shoreline in Connecticut and took the northern route, I-91 and then I-84 instead, so this time I missed the ocean views, which had always thrilled me so much so that I'd feel my chest expand with a leaping heart. I dozed most of the way.

I arrived at South Station in the afternoon and took the Red Line, then the D train of the Green Line to Riverside. From there I took a cab to Loana's home. She was so happy to see me that she couldn't stop beaming. At times her smiles made her look like a young girl radiating health. Obviously her fiancé was a fine man whose love had been nourishing her and making her glow with happiness.

LOOKING FOR TANK MAN

She said she was going to cook some chive dumplings and a couple of small dishes for dinner. I was glad she didn't treat me as a special guest, more like a friend. By now I took her not only as a staunch friend but also as an older sister of sorts. To her I could unburden myself and from her I could seek sound advice. I joined her in the kitchen and began slicing lotus root, which she was going to use to make a salad.

When the table was almost set, Alan came in with two bottles of wine sheathed in paper bags. He was tall, with wavy hair and a small, pointed beard. I was astonished to recognize him. He was the man in the last photo that the interrogators had shown me at the Beijing airport. I couldn't help tittering.

"What's so funny?" Loana asked.

"I'll tell you later," I said.

When we had started eating, I told Alan, "Believe it or not, we have met before."

"Really?" He tried to recall, but still looked perplexed. "Where did we meet?"

"At the Beijing airport."

They both looked puzzled. I went on to explain that an officer from the Ministry of State Security had shown me his photo at customs and asked me if I knew him. I had had no idea he was Loana's fiancé, so instead I asked them who he was. They didn't tell me.

Loana and Alan were surprised. She said, "They may have shown you my photo as well." She cut a dumpling in half with the side of her fork.

"They already knew you. Right before Alan's photo they asked me about you. They wanted to know if you had introduced me to any Taiwanese officials and scholars. You had never done that, so I told them the truth."

"What else did they ask you?"

"They wanted to know under what circumstances I had come to know you. I told them that you were my teacher at Harvard, a great woman, well respected as a scholar. They were impressed."

Alan said to Loana, "My goodness, I got tied together with you by the Chinese government."

Loana grinned while eating a shrimp. "Didn't I tell you at the very beginning that I could be a liability to you?"

"I'm just a physics professor. What can they do to me? As long as you're safe, I don't give a damn about their investigations."

I told them that the police hadn't seemed to have anything concrete against them, but that they still must be careful if they stepped foot in China. They both raised their glasses while Loana said, "Cheers, for all of us on their blacklist." I touched my glass with theirs and took a swallow.

That night Loana and I had a long talk over aster tea. I described Bailey's advances, which had often unsettled me. I was scared of him. Loana said I had been wise not to go with him alone to his country house. She could also see that it would be hard for me to continue working under his tutelage. To my surprise, she said Bailey had just sold his new book on the CCP's politburo to Fudan University Press in Shanghai, so he might force me to modify my dissertation to make it less offensive to the Communist Party. I told Loana, "It's true Bailey complained that my dissertation at times got too personal. He said it lapsed into 'personalia.'"

"See, that's what worries me. He might have his own agenda, which overlaps with the CCP's. In my opinion, without the personal part, your dissertation would be just an accumulation of the historical materials with few insights."

"That's what Mark Stone said too. But do you think Bailey can be swayed by the Chinese government that easily?" I asked, still in disbelief.

"Of course," Loana said. "Even though he might not make much money from the publication of his new book in China, he can get a lot of perks and advantages, like being able to give lectures there and serving as a visiting professor at top universities. His family could go on vacation with him in China for free. He can gain a lot."

I was so astounded, I said, "His wife's law firm has some lucrative business in China too. Hilda often goes to Guangzhou nowadays. It looks like I might have to leave Bailey."

"Yes, you should seriously consider going to another PhD program."

We both saw the necessity now. She said that if I wanted to change schools, I'd have to plan carefully and proceed without disturbing my dissertation committee.

I said, "Mark Stone suggested using what I've done at Columbia to get a master's and then apply to other PhD programs."

Loana gave it some thought, then said, "How will you support yourself before you go to another program? It will take time to make that leap."

"Maybe I can work for Niu Jian. He said his company was going to expand the online media part of the business and would need bilingual people."

"Don't do that. I respect Niu Jian, but his business is shaky and might be sabotaged by the Chinese government. Your life might become precarious if you work for him. Now that you've become an exile of sorts, first and foremost you must secure your livelihood. You're just a step away from getting your PhD. Why abandon what you have already accomplished?"

Seeing me puzzled, she smiled and added, "It just flashed across my mind that you must not apply for an MA from Columbia."

"Why? That way at least I can make some use of the work I've done there."

"In academia, once you have used your credits, you can't use them again. You should save everything you have earned for your future PhD. I am positive that some programs will be eager to admit you because if you're an ABD, they can support you just for a year or two for you to complete your degree. So with the accumulated credits you can become a more advanced PhD candidate. Besides, if you applied for a master's from your department, your dissertation committee might get upset, and Bailey might come up with other maneuvers. That's why you'd better not show your intentions for the time being."

LOOKING FOR TANK MAN

"That's smart." I was impressed.

"Another thing you should do—get some teaching experience and be ready to support yourself for the next academic year. That will also help you a lot in your career."

"How should I handle that? I mean to get a teaching assignment."

"Tell your dissertation committee that you need financial support so that you can complete your dissertation quickly. They have already seen what you have written and will be eager to help you. That's the normal way in most PhD programs—professors do everything they can to help their students complete their dissertations. Otherwise, their investment in you over the years would be wasted."

Again, I saw the clear logic in her reasoning and I agreed to follow her advice and write a request to my committee without delay. I was sure they had heard I had been rejected entry at the Beijing airport and they might be more willing to help me. I ought to seize this opportunity to get a teaching assignment. Some teaching experience could help improve my CV.

I asked Loana if she could write a recommendation for me when it was time to apply to other PhD programs. "Sure thing," she said. "I will also figure out who might be willing to take you over from Bailey. There are a good number of fine China scholars, like Diana Costello at Hunter College, Perry Link at Princeton, Naomi Loughry at Rutgers, Gordan Zhao at Georgetown. But don't ask Sundar or Davison to write for you.

Both of them are junior to Bailey, so to write on your behalf might make them anxious. Most likely nobody in your department is going to volunteer to offend Bailey, who is powerful and well connected. You must be cautious."

"If I can't ask anyone in my department to write for me, I'll have to get another letter of recommendation. Do you think Mark Stone is a legitimate option to write on my behalf?"

"He has known you ever since your Harvard days and he has read and admires your dissertation, so he should be qualified. You can ask him. If a place wants three letters, we can look for another person. Most of the time professors judge your application mainly by the quality of your writing sample. You're a superb writer. Don't worry about your qualifications."

"To your mind, what are my chances of getting into another PhD program?"

"Without any interference from Bailey, I would say more than 90 percent. It's a pity Wellesley doesn't have a PhD program, or I'd do everything to admit you. Any professor in China studies who has read the pages you wrote can see your potential and intelligence and will be happy to accept you. What's more, you have already published an important book, albeit in Chinese. Most professors would be impressed. Cheer up. I'm sure this will work out. I have great confidence in you, Lulu, and want you to accomplish significant work and live a good life."

She stopped as if having hit on a new thought. "Let me call Simon Pond. He loved your book and raved about it."

LOOKING FOR TANK MAN

Professor Pond was a close friend of hers, and he had also gotten his PhD from the University of Toronto.

She moved to her desk and called Pond. He was delighted to hear of my interest in his program, and he told Loana to let me apply to UCLA toward the end of the year. He even said that his department might be the right place for me because they had just started a project on dictatorships and public amnesia, which might dovetail with my work.

Loana said to me, "See, practically any professor would be willing to take you on."

I stood and hugged her. "I can't thank you enough, Loana."

We said goodnight.

I slept peacefully in a comfortable bed for eight hours straight. When I woke up, birds were warbling and twittering beyond the window, bustling in the branches. Their feathers were flickering in the sunshine. I felt refreshed and finally able to continue the journey I had started long ago.

ACKNOWLEDGMENTS

My heartfelt thanks to my agent, Lane Zachary, and to the people at Other Press who helped me refine the novel: Judith Gurewich, Yvonne Cárdenas, Janice Goldklang, Gage Desser, and John Rambow.

AUTHOR'S NOTE

Except for some subordinate characters, all the main characters in the novel are fictional. But most of the historical details are factual, and for this I am indebted to the following authors and their works:

Chen Xiaoya, *The History of the 1989 Democracy Movement,* Vols. 1 and 2 (Washington, D.C.: Citizen Press, 2019).

Wang Dan, *6.4 Memoir* (Taipei: Qucheng Culture, 2016).

Daily Reports on the Movement for Democracy in China from April 15 to June 24, 1989, Vols. 1 and 2, compiled by Wu Muren and others (n.p., 2009).

Zhang Boli, *Escape from China*, trans. Kwee Kian Low (New York: Washington Square Press, 2002).

Zhang Liang, *The Tiananmen Papers*, compiled and ed. by Andrew J. Nathan and Perry Link (New York: Public Affairs, 2001).